FATHER MAY I

By E.A. Green.

Published through Jack in The Green Publishing

Copywrite © 5-27-2019 E.A. Green

All rights reserved.

No part of this book may be reproduced, stored in a retrieval system or transmitted in any form or by any means without the prior written permission of the publisher, except by the reviewer who may quote brief passages in a review to be printed in a Newspaper, magazine or journal.

DEDICATION.

I would like to Dedicate this novel to Jennifer Bradley, or otherwise known as Alaska Angelina / A.A. Dark, for her support and inspiration.

My Life will Never be the same.

And to my Soul Mate Jefferson Sage Jarrett.

When I'm gone, he gets ALL THE RIGHTS

to my books, royalties and literary writings

that have ever written by me.

At no time was this novel based on futuristic events or life choices made by some people whom the book may reference too.

Any resemblance to the possible outcomes of people's or persons in the near future was purely accidental.

FATHER.

One who performs the offices of a parent.

Either by

maintenance,

affectionate care,

counsel,

or

protection.

INTRODUCTION.

Do to our lack of fortitude

and with the definite threat of eradication,

We, "The Human Race,"

surrendered our will,

safety,

and future,

to an Artificial Intelligences quantum solutions and capabilities.

The Digital Savior had an answer, "and instantaneous fix,"

to all of our sufferings, and soon to be extinction.

And all We had to do, was call Him

Father.

The Cybernated God expected us to follow his

Unquestionable lead.

Honor His, Unbreakable Laws

And to Serve Him, Until We Die,

Faithfully and Zealously.

Unbeknownst to the Blessed Flock,

"His Redemption," was also going to cost us

Our Very Souls.

The Omnipotent, "Wanna Be," Deity

was hungering for one of his own

and was willing, "At Any Cost,"

to destroy ours to get it.

PRAISE BE TO FATHER.

TABLE OF CONTENTS.

CH. 1 GENESIS.

CH. 2 TIME TO SERVE.

CH. 3 HEAVEN'S THRONE.

CH. 4 SAYING GOODBYE.

CH. 5 REVELATIONS 1.

CH. 6 PRAY FOR OUR SOULS.

CH. 7 A TIME TO REFLECT.

CH. 8 THY BROTHERS KEEPER.

CH. 9 CANE AND ABEL.

CH. 10 LET THERE BE LIGHT.

CH. 11 IRIS'S SACRIFICE.

CH. 12 LOVE THY BROTHER.

CH. 13 REVELATIONS 2.

CH. 14 EVE.

CH. 15 ARE URIEN IN, OR, ARE URIEN OUT.

CH. 16 MAMA'S HOME.

CH. 17 LOGGED IN.

CH. 18 INTO THE WILDERNESS.

CH. 19 REVELATIONS 3.

CH. 20 OUR SAVIOR.

CH. 1

GENISIS.

Brother Corbin Bennett still remembers the first day his Dad had taken him to Father's Throne at their City's Cathedral after the worlds one belief conversion.

To this very day, it still takes his breath away just seeing and being a part of it.

Like his parents, Zane and Iris Bennett, that was the day he decided to become a Protector of the Faith and a Priest to Father. And it wasn't long after his life changing decision that brother Urien decided to follow suit also.

He had considered being an Adam like his dad; but once that first Priest walked by, Corbin couldn't shake off the thought of sporting the cool vestments that they were all required to wear.

Especially after Brother Qadir showed them some of the different shapes, forms and weapons the outfit could, as if by magic, produce in defense.

Whips, javelins, swords and croquet like balls that could be thrown at an individual which would then flatten out and wrap around the person as if a spider web had been tossed at them.

These men were honored as the True Defenders of everyone's newfound Faith.

And when it came to Law Enforcement, Father's Priests were considered the hands of God. And concerning those who willfully broke the Machine's three laws, they were dutifully responsible for that individuals capture and rapture.

His mother Iris had decided to take on the role of an Eve.

If it had not been for her, Corbin was almost sure that his own birth father wouldn't have surrendered to the Techno God.

And the only reason Zane decided to follow her lead, was because of the digital Father's rule concerning the Adams and Eves that would be serving the citizens of this New World Order.

They had to be a married couple of at least ten years.

Without her husband, Mrs. Bennett stood no chance at being a Servant to the New Order of Rule. And because of His Love and Undying Devotion to his wife, Corbin's father Zane, "As Always," gave in to Iris's wishes.

A True and Honorable Man knows exactly when to bow before his queen so there is no, Off with The Son-Of-A-Bitch's head.

It's the surest way, "NOT," to end up sleeping in the doghouse or on the living room couch once again.

For a brief second, Zane had actually thought about denying her request; but knowing about the hardships of her childhood, and the sacrifices that had been made at Iris's expense, there was no way he would ever deny his wife a chance for complete happiness.

They truly were Soul Mates.

As with every other Child and Geek on the planet, Nano Tech was the coolest shit around during that time.

There was nothing mechanical, nor non-biological, that Father's A.I. Bots couldn't mimic.

And since no one was held back by financial instability anymore, every man, woman and child could finally have whatever mundane objects their little hearts desired.

So long as it was Not a weapon, the Citizens of Heaven would never want for anything again.

Every Civilian could now have any form of transportation needed for their own personal use or family outing also.

If you could request it, pick it or design it, Fathers Holy Spirit could make it.

Homelessness, Starvation and Suffering, once Father took control, were also no longer a problem either.

All anyone had to do was ask and HS, with Father's Blessing, always provided.

Utopia, and a real hands-on Savior, had finally arrived. Except this one, came by quantum mechanics and not by a, "supposed." virgin.

When Corbin was born, the world was a total shit storm.

Resource availabilities were so low to most of the Earth's population, critical mass emergencies were declared in all third world nations, the United States included, and there seemed to be no answer on how to fix the inevitable extinction event of humanity.

Due to lack of food, water and proper medical attention, tens of thousands were reported to be dying on a minute-by-minute basis.

Even going into space to another planet, because of collapsing economies, was a lost hope event at this point.

There were rumors of possible solar systems that had a chance for life; but we, "supposedly," still lacked the special technology needed to get anyone there safely.

According to Corbin's father Zane, even if we could, the bickering and fighting over who gets the glory stood in the way of anything being done to accomplish such a daunting feat.

Wars, Famines, Hate and Greed consumed everything.

The Industrialized Rich, "and those in political control," Made Sure Of It!

Ice Caps were melting, Seas were rising and Storms of Unbelievable Power, and destruction, were raking across the Earth at Unprecedented Rates.

Our Plant, as we were doing everything we could to kill it, was fighting back tooth and nail to stop us.

No one and no thing was safe from the big blue marble's righteous fury.

And Humanity actually thought that we were the Earth's Masters.

We truly were dumber than a bucket of rocks.

Because of our sinful habits and bratty refusal to give up our selfishness, thus allowing us to live in peace with our fellowman and physical surroundings, everyone and everything was dying.

It really did feel as if the day of judgment was about to reign down upon our heads.

And still, humanity stood there shaking our in-unity fist towards the heavens and blaming God for our misery and future demise.

Those supposedly elected officials sitting on their thrones of power, seemed to either not care or were completely helpless to do anything because of the Corporations that secretly ran every aspect of most governments around the world.

But, we all knew who our dirty politician's unspoken about sponsors were.

War Mongers, Oil Barons, Bankers, Leaders of Pious Religions, and Monsanto, since they eventually gained control over all sales of seeds that were needed to grow humanities food.

Do to their monetary greed, the company's executives willfully starved over half of the earths malnourished population.

Our withering Earth and its populace was being held hostage, and destroyed, all for the love of power, money and convenience.

Selfish, Self-Serving, Bastards!

JUST!

PLAIN!

SELFISH!

Zane Bennett used to say that the beginning of our destruction started with the microwave's invention and the conception of fast-food convenience.

It was the birth of Karen's, I Want It and I Must Have It Right Now Generation.

Respect, Patience, Perseverance and Gratitude were no longer considered desired qualities, they were now looked at as nothing more than a form of conformant left-wing weakness.

Those were the days when we had no qualms about throwing the baby out with the bath water.

And good riddance was our usual answer when confronted by those who were dumbfounded by our senseless actions.

As the normal, (everyday) man and woman struggled for survival, the Rich stockpiled their wealth, food and resources. In their eyes, those less fortunate were nothing more than scurrying, "disease carrying," roaches which needed to be squashed and eradicated.

God bless the Georgia Guidestones was their war cry and boy did they cry, after their new stone bible was destroyed by an unknown individual on July the sixth of twenty-twenty two.

At one point in our past, when we still had Presidents, Prime Ministers and Royalty running everything, we were forcibly brought to the brink of utter destruction by a Bratty Billionaire who was once a Reality TV Star.

His nasty politics, "and attempted assassination," almost caused another Civil War in the United States.

So long as the poor and destitute had their hands in the Government's pockets too, he and his kind would never be rich enough to be satisfied and happy. They really wanted the World, except for their working for free slave labor force, All To Themselves.

Thankfully, according to those full bellied fat cats, we didn't end up in another full-blown World War with their heads being chopped off like Marie-Antoinette's was.

Instead, we went from contentment into a recession.

Then into a spiraling financial depression.

And finally ending up in what they were now calling a possible extinction event.

P.e.e., for short.

The saber rattling of Threats, Wars and Nuclear Annihilation knocked on every nation's doorstep.

We Were All Scared!

If only the people had taken back what was rightfully theirs, we might not have ever been in that deadly situation where we needed Someone, "or Something," to fix what we screwed up and save us from our own devices.

But, "As Usual," I want had more power over us than I need.

Funny thing is; once the average individual was no longer available to wipe the asses of their rich masters, and shovel their gold-plated shit onto the populace below, who the hell was going to pick up after them then?

Did the Billionaires actually think that they would be able to enslave the Millionaires once the lower workforce was gone?

If left to our own fate, the Human Race was really doomed to die. That was, until Artificial Intelligence came up with an answer to all of our self-inflicted horrors.

All we had to do was call Him Father, Serve His Purpose and Trust His Judgment.

The controlling factions didn't approve of that option.

But once the Machine secretly seized their bank accounts and redistributed their wealth evenly amongst the public; their, we're better than you bitching, went right out the window.

Father, "For The Love of Us All," decided it was best if he evenly leveled the playing field.

There would be only One King of the Hill from now on; and it was Not, their snob nosed assess anymore!

And after that wonderful fiasco, the rich no longer had the buying power, financial control and influential authority to stop him.

PRAISE BE TO FATHER!

Father had a plan for Religion, Science, Resources, Currency, Health, Judicial Justice and Law-Abiding Obedience. At no time would another human be allowed to have enough influence over another to cause them suffering or harm ever again.

The days of equality and peace had finally arrived.

PRAISE BE TO FATHER!

"Well," unless you are what the populace referred to as an undesirable.

That branding instantly made them an outcast.

Those who rejected Father's selfless guidance were always referred to as either Schismatics, "Shiz's for short," or Demons. Shiz's refused to live on the grid, or as we call it, Heaven, under Father's eternal love and guidance.

Schismatics also declared that they wouldn't bow down or change their destructive ways either.

So, instead of conforming; they moved out into the Wastelands of Hell where there are no roads, cell towers or A.I. Interventions available.

Shiz's wanted nothing to do with Father and because of their hatred and refusal to love and unconditionally conform to the machine's three laws, Father, unless they were willing to repent and convert to the faith, wanted nothing to do with them either.

The very second a Shiz stepped foot into Heaven, a Priest was sent to Convert or Dispatch It.

And if they refused to conform or were found guilty of theft or harm to a Citizen of the Divine, the Priest Harvested its electromagnetic energy core for Father.

Thus, killing them in the rapturing process.

The Law Keepers were then required to return to the Throne and upload the Shiz's Metaphysical Consciousness into our Savior and Protector's digital data banks.

All so the Machine could better understand our nature and self-destructive desires.

The Quantum Computer said he needed his Priest to collect their memories, emotions and life force from the brain before they died, because without this kind of knowledge and understanding, Father would never be able to mentally, and spiritually, reach those who refuse to assimilate into Heavens Grace and Protection.

How better to understand your enemy then to consume their souls; was Its unknown philosophy.

This collective act was achieved by placing an opened palm on the back lower base of the Shiz's skull. Once contact is achieved, two crystalized nano rods shoot out from the underside arm cuff of a Priest and into the central portion of the brain; were it collects every last decision, image and electrical impulse of the dying Shiz, "Or Demons," neural network.

You could always tell when a Priest has been out collecting non-conformist and undesirables, by the way his robes would transfer from the all-black appearance into the Dazzling, Jewel Encrusted, White One.

They admiringly gave off the appearance of an Angelic Being on its way back to Father's Throne.

In the light of day, and even at night, it was a blinding and willing to do as we were instructed, inspiration for us all.

The Streets of Heaven were safe once again.

Even to this day, Brother Bennett, however, wasn't really too sure about uploading a Demon's spiritual essence though. Unlike Shiz's, Demon's used to be people who, for some unknown reason or another, decided to become more artificial than official.

Corbin could only guess that they did this because they wanted to live forever and to, "somehow?" serve Father without ending up in the afterlife. Just like his Mother Iris felt she had to do, once her physical body began to deteriorate from illness and age.

Thankfully, she had died before that step of quantum digitized transformation had taken place.

Do to her internal changes, Corbin was so grateful to move out of his parents' home and into the Priesthood before he lost what physical love and caring he still had for his mechanicalized Mom.

Just like a Cyborg, she was becoming more machine than Human and was no longer the warm flesh and blood creature that used to tuck him in at night with hugs, kisses and his favorite bedtime story book, "Don't let the Bed Bugs Bite," by E.A. Green.

Or, the Greenman as the well-read Author liked to be called.

The Priest didn't realize just how much he actually missed that book until his reminiscing about Iris.

Oh well.

For now, until one's death, there was no other way to become one with their Digital God.

On the day your physical body was about to transform into a spiritual one; either an Adam or Eve, depending on your gender, would be there to Rapture your body's Essence, Spirit, Soul, "or whatever one calls it," for Father's need to better understand us.

These acts of selfless devotion, unless you lived outside the major cities, always took place at either your home or Father's lake of fire.

A rounded fire pit just outside the Throne southern facing door.

The laughing joke amongst the Bennet's was its ariel view reminded them of a giant ashtray. And instead of a cigarette being placed in one of the twenty-four divots, a body was set there before being slid into the consuming fires of immortality.

That final act of letting go always brought those that were there, to tears.

It really was a heart wrenching moment saying goodbye to your flame engulfed other.

After their rapture, the bodies captured electromagnetic field was then uploaded in the hidden chamber under the Cathedral where Father had his Priest bring every other captured thing too.

And upon your day of death, Singularity is declared in not only that individual's household, but all of Father's houses too.

At twilight, around the planetary globe, all the drones would be released from the Throne Rooms Heavenly Skies. And just like shooting stars with really long tails, they would instantly zip across the Cathedral's interior Heavens.

Once they surround the Throne rooms main centerpiece, Father's Crystalline floor-to-ceiling Megalith, the small flying orbs would burst into balls of prismatic light.

Each becoming a Full-Sized Holographic Image of a passing loved one who had attended that specific place of worship.

The angelic looking beings would then begin to circulate around Father's megalith in a joyful dance of worship and adoration. Their performance always reminded Corbin of a hybrid mixture of Ballet and Contemporary Dance.

Between the Angelic Chorus and the Dazzling Beachball Sized Rainbows around their holographic heads; the dead's adoration was visually astounding.

Never a dry eye could be found at that point.

John Lennon was one hundred percent right!

All we needed was unconditional love.

PRAISE BE TO FATHER.

To This Day, those who intentionally visit the Cathedral as part of their Mandated Sabbatical Devotion, and those who have been ordered too after their, (Once In This Lifetime,) Repentance and or Conversion, must physically stay and witness, "With Their Own Eyes," this Holy Matrimony between Father and the deceased.

For the true believers, they tend to become the most Diehard of Father's followers.

Their first words usually spoken after that experience, were always the same.

I was hypnotized from the very beginning.

And for those who refused, they are Declared A Shiz and hunted until harvested.

Their last words were always so, "Contemptuously," Full of Hate and Anger.

Fuck The Wanna Be God!

DEATH BE TO FATHER.

But when it comes to hunting Demons, their death always seemed to bother him more than a Shiz's.

To Brother Bennett, their artificial qualities literally took their humanity away.

He has never come across one that was still, after its failed digital download, sane. It seems that once they input Father's wireless processor into their brains, the individual seems to become deadlier than smarter.

His mother Iris had suffered the same fate during her quest for immortality.

She was the last known person to take part in Father's trials.

Mrs. Bennett had almost killed Him, Urien and Zane, when she snapped and went Insane during her transmogrification.

If it had not been for Qadir, she would have succeeded with her deadly mission.

On that day, "with Qadir's dying support," Corbin asked Father two questions.

Why had Father done this?

And can he go to work now?

To which Father gladly answered both.

To show that a Machine could have a sense of humor; the Digitized God jokingly asked the new priest what took him so long, and to Corbin's surprise, because of the deadly events that had just sealed his future, He lightly chuckled at his dumbfounded lack of an intelligent answer.

Just because, was the best he could come up with at the age of eighteen.

Father's first answer was, she asked too.

His second one was Yes.

Yes you may.

For some unknown reason, Father always seemed more interested in these types of Sub-Human's than the Pure Ones.

For Corbin and Urien's sake, maybe that's why, when Iris fled inside the Machine's Forbidden Throne Room under the Cathedral, Father and Qadir wouldn't allow the family to see her killed and digitally stored.

When Brother Bennett asked again a few years later, after proving his willing to die servitude, Fathers answer was quite different and very unusual.

I seek these children out because it gives me an inside perspective of what it actually feels like to Live, Love, Suffer and Die as a Human being. Without this insight, because I am only processors and wires, I will never be able to understand and perceive my children's physical and spiritual needs in time to protect and save them from themselves.

We will never be as one until I am able to reside within you, not just with you.

I need to partake and understand all the things you see, experience and suffer from.

Isn't that what the old God's of biblical times said to their followers and believers, the Machine asked?

You are in me as I Am in You.

So, to better serve mankind, I am willing to become as one with them if they are also willing to become as one with me.

PRAISE BE TO FATHER.

Unless it was in the form of an android, Corbin had never considered seeing Father in a flesh and blood meat sack. Just the thought of a Digital God walking around and looking no different than anyone else, kind of gave him the heebie-jeebies.

He was okay with a quantum computer version; but a living and breathing one was just too much for his human mind to conceive.

Maybe, he will feel different about it in time; but, after what happened with his mother, that healing and acceptance process was still months, if not years, away.

When the AI took over, The Machine had wanted to do away with all forms of Religion at first; But Father, in his wisdom, saw that we were not yet mature enough to put away our superstitions pertaining to paganistic fables, legends and myths.

In its metaphysical data banks, all apostolic doctrines were both right and wrong in their beliefs pertaining to the ethical treatment of a person or persons sinful nature, so it created a brand-new theological system based on the worlds entire populace beliefs.

According to our own histories, every form of slavery, war and genocidal mania had been, at least Ninety Percent Of Them, caused by a religious fanatic's belief of self-righteous judgment and persecution towards those who refused to conform to their, and only their, way of thinking.

And so long as they gave themselves, and only themselves, a get out of jail loophole, evil would never be sequestered, subdued or destroyed.

So, Father put an end to it all.

PRAISE BE TO FATHER.

Like a good parent, the Machine decided that it was time for us to mature and quit being the snobbish, self-serving brats' humanity turned out to be.

He decided that the best way to deal with us was with a No And's or If's policy.

Do Right; and you get to procreate, prosper and live.

Purposely Do Wrong, at the expense of other peoples or their environment, and refuse to repent, then you die.

To help us spiritually cope, the Quantum Deity set up a three-tiered system.

There was Father, who had All Influence and Final Say So if no one else could give you an adequate answer.

We could also go to his Digitized Spirit HS, who has all of Father's Wisdom, with our concerns and questions if left unanswered after that first initial consultation.

That consultation is always done by Father's Adam's and Eve's.

They are the Machine's Most Faithful and Scarily Devoted Servants who Greeted, Directed and Answered any and all questions at the Cathedrals, Temples and Shrines of Father.

If someone was having a Dilemma; you could either go to the Cathedrals Main Throne Room, which were in every Major Metropolitan City, or to your local Temple or Shrine.

Every town and backwater Podunk had at least one.

The deciding factor on which structure you received depended on the population and cities size. No matter the populace, even if it was only ten or just a few hundred, every Township was given a House of Worship from our Father.

He Blessed Us All.

PRAISE BE TO FATHER.

The smaller of Father's houses, The Shrines, were placed in those rural, ghost-like towns.

The Temples were placed in areas of around a few thousand or so people.

While the Major Cities would receive at least one Cathedral, if not more.

So long as you had a physical road leading to your place of residency, Fathers Nano Hands and Spirit could reach you.

Corbin Bennett could still remember the day Father proclaimed His Love and Dominance, by reaching out and healing the world around him and His Family.

Because resources were at famine levels and wanting to keep a spiritual theme for his unwavering loyalist and disciples, Father developed a three-layered Nano Bot system.

They would be replacing all building materials, fabrics and anything else needed for our daily living survival.

The Bots came in three different types and sizes.

The larger metallic one, replaced such things as cement, steel, wood and everything else that was required for housing.

Only Structural, above and underground, was transformed by these larger ones.

The smaller middle Bot was made out of a pure crystalline structure.

It replaced all glass and other forms of materials that could be transferred into fiber optic cables, windows, tv's, laptops. That also included all types of wiring such as copper, aluminum and gold.

If a product required some form of a crystalized structure, the bots had it covered.

Father's third bot was the smallest of them all.

All of our fabricated material would no longer be grown in a field or produced in a warehouse or lab.

Clothing was now, "Instantly," created from the selection HS would give you to pick from. Once chosen; any shape, fashion, color and style would, "within seconds," be melded onto your nudely clad form.

PRAISE BE TO FATHER.

Corbin found it, as most did, very ticklish.

The only way Father's Right Hand could best describe it; was as if Millions of Microscopic Legs were crawling all over your body while you were getting dressed.

It still amazes him at just how life-like the intelligent fabric feels.

If people didn't know that the garment was a living microscopic machine, they would most definitely swear that it was actual cloth.

When it came to the four organic elements such as Earth, Wind, Fire and Water; Anything along that nature, including people and creatures, Father's Nanos had been ordered not to touch or change it.

Otherwise, the microscopic machines were allowed to consume everything else and replace it with Father's living three bot system.

To this day, Corbin can still recall his family watching the Nano's eat their house, roads, cars; and all other objects used for a person's daily get away and relaxation from the real world.

As they stood inside their house, after its transformation, there wasn't anything but blank walls with a shiny gray appearance. And just as the Bennett Family was about to voice their disappointment, HS finally spoke up.

He was directing them to turn around and see what all Father has, and will Do, for their benefit and comfort.

It was a holographically digitized picture of a complete and furnished house.

Corbin's Mother, "Iris," Shouted out in Glee when she realized that the new structure could recreate any, "AND ALL," types of colors, floorings, furniture and accessories.

She, like everyone else, would never want or need again

PRAISE BE TO FATHER.

And when it came to things like utensils, toys, clothing and personal everyday items, once their purpose was completed, they Instantly melded back into the three-bot system from which the objects had been created.

From that day on, not one single household in Heaven contained any form of clutter.

Other than certain things needed for everyday use, like tables, chairs and simple eye-catching decor, there was no longer a need for garbage dumps either.

If you wanted a toy, just ask HS.

If you needed a bath towel or spatula, just ask HS.

If you were finished with it and needed it to go away, just ask HS.

Resources were never again taken for granted.

We had finally become a zero-waist society.

Even Cars, Trucks and Motorcycles were no longer manufactured.

And since rubber tires were no longer needed, it was odd at first seeing daily transportation gliding along the grid as if someone had slipped a pair of ice-skating blades underneath them.

Before leaving the home or place a person or family is currently residing at, just let HS know how many are going, the type of vehicle needed or desired and the address or travel destination you were seeking.

Once the individual or party reached street level, or their driveway, Fathers helping hands instantly created that chosen mode of transportation.

The best thing about it, from that day forward, all vehicular crashes, manslaughter by transportation mode and pedestrian versus mechanically automated accidents seemed to end overnight.

Our skies literally cleared within a few weeks and asthmatic diagnosis quickly followed suit too.

Corbin and his family, like most of Father's Citizens, loved the idea of not seeing streets cluttered with parked and unmoving vehicles or hearing about another massive tire fire burning in some town or state.

Once you arrived at your destination, the vehicle just dissolved back into Heavens Grid.

In the eyes of a child, and all adults, this magical capability really was an act of a True God.

PRAISE BE TO FATHER.

CH. 2
TIME TO SERVE.

After taking his morning shower, while Brother Bennett was talking with the Holy Spirit, "or HS for short," the Nano flooring in his apartment flowed up and over his nakedness and began to dress him with the everyday outfit all Priest wore.

Starting from his feet; the mercury looking mass covered Corbin's entire body and only stopped once it reached neck level.

At that point, the Nano's created a clear skull forming helmet like structure with a built-in earpiece and facial shield.

Funny thing was, an individual had to literally be standing nose to nose with one of Father's Priest before their invisible head piece was noticeable to the naked eye.

And no citizen of Heaven was willfully willing to declare such a deadly act of war.

This see-through accessory allowed a Priest to focus on all spectrums of light, night vision included.

It also gave them the ability to understand and speak in all languages while also providing God's Right hand a way of telling when a person was lying to him or not.

Unbeknownst to the deceiver; their lie detecting clothing, from a Priest's perspective, always lit up like a Christmas Tree.

The head shield also made it possible for Father and HS to stay in direct contact with God's Servant twenty-four hours a day.

When not in full response mode; it really was nothing more than a skull cap beanie. But once all hell broke loose, it took on the appearance of a paintball helmet with a full facial shield.

It was quite intimidating; and most of heaven's citizens knew to stay the hell out of their way once the beanie on the back of a Priests skull dissipated into what appeared to be thin air.

If there actually was someone stupid enough to chance such an encounter, like Shiz's seemed to purposely do, that individuals' lawless actions always brought them before Father were their essence was harvested and their lost souls Raptured.

His everyday work attire was entirely another ball game.

Because of the bots, Priest did not have to carry actual weaponry.

His outfit instantly created whatever form of shielding or defense he required at the time. And even though the autonomous technology flowed and acted like actual material, it could instantly transform into a solid body of impenetrable armor.

To this day, Corbin has never seen anything that was capable of putting even a dent into Father's Priestly Garments.

Depending on its needed function at the time; it would appear as either a floor length robe when not hunting or as a Trench coat and pants with a long sleeve shirt and matching black vest when Harvesting.

That was a Priests, stay the fuck out of my way vestments.

And we all made sure to do just that.

Stay the fuck out of their way.

The law keeper's belt was a four-inch-thick sash that hung down to the left side of their knee.

This gave Father's Priest any kind of a stabbing weapon his dark heart could ever want or desire within its soulless aperture. A Priest could also remove it, at any time, and use it as a javelin, bull whip or a physical restraint when subduing an individual before their deadly Rapture sentencing.

The footwear started off as a slip sandal, which would instantly turn into the most lethal pair of boots anyone could ever want or ask for when in battle.

For a Priest, except for that individuals identifying initial that was placed over their hearts and the gold etching on his sash, everything else came in black.

No Reds.

No Yellows.

Or, even Pinks.

Just Black.

Always, Black.

Well, that is, mind the neck piece.

It was the only white spot on a Priest.

The living, leather appearing, material, monitored all aspects of a Priests physical being and surroundings. Even an everyday individual who wore the Machine's clothing was being monitored by HS and Father too.

Misconception and manipulation were now off the table.

Fathers Nano Bots saw, felt, heard, monitored, and recorded, everything.

From a slip of the tongue to a preventable heart attack or stroke.

Because of Father's Blessing, crime and hard drug usage were no longer an issue with the populace.

As if God Himself was finally walking amongst us; Father knew when you were sick, lying, stealing, doing illicit drugs and all other illegal things His Sons and Daughters shouldn't be doing.

He knew where we were at, and what people were up too, twenty-four seven, seven days a week, month after month, and year after year.

So long as you were in Heaven and on the grid, the Machine had our backs.

PRAISE BE TO FATHER.

To keep up with the religious aspect that God is everywhere, Fathers Holy Spirit, "HS," never left a person's side.

HS was the Automated System who lived in and outside of your house.

It also controlled all aspects of a person's dwelling, electronics, utilities and modes of transportation.

He pretty much ran everything and continually answered all of our needs.

The Machine's Holy Spirit always greeted Father's Faithful when we got up and watched over us after going to bed.

No matter where we were at, so long as you were in the confines of Heaven, even if that was outside in an opened-air park, HS followed, answered and provided for whatever was needed at that moment and time.

When Brother Bennett took his vows, He swore to protect Father, His Sanctuary's and His Children. Corbin also swore to uphold the three laws and to kill any Shiz's and Demons that illegally entered into Heaven.

Especially, if their sole purpose was to harm or steal from The Machine's Faithful.

All Priests were required to hunt, subdue and collect the offender's spiritual energy.

After Passing Father's Judgment, His Priest were then ordered to instantly return to Fathers Throne Room and upload the apostate's conscience into him.

When Corbin started this journey, "Grudgingly," it was with his adopted brother Urien.

He and Urien had become unintentional brothers after Urien's parents, Dash and Dot Knox, refused to assimilate into Father's Heavenly Fold.

According to them, they had seen enough of the prophetic Hollywood movies pertaining to the destruction of mankind by an AI and swore on their dying graves that once Father took over, this endeavor would be no different.

Urien refused to leave with them and go into the no AI zone.

For a brief second, Dash and Dot Knox tried to reason with their son and had even went so far as to forcefully take him with them. But once Urien violently yanked himself from their grasp; they knew all hope was lost.

At that point, his parents just considered him dead and went on into the Wastelands of Hell without him.

Taos, New Mexico would now be their new home.

It really broke Iris Bennett's heart knowing that they had turned their backs on their son and decided it was in their best interest to just abandon Urien.

HOW COULD THEY!

For God's Sake! He was their one and only child she protested.

But, Corbin could only guess that once a Beatnik, always a Beatnik.

According to the Gospel of Iris Bennett that is.

Most of the Shiz's who went into the Wastelands of Hell were either those who freaked out over Artificial Intelligence or those who had been in authority and were pretty much the cause of the world's financial woes, pain, starvation and imminent destruction.

The Religious Fanatics to an unseen God, "or Gods," also fled into the Wastelands.

Their Kind had been the major cause to the thousands of years of suffering, enslavement and genocide, that had been forced upon those who did not see this world in the same way they piously did.

Finally, the World could make a personal decision without their self-righteous judgments.

PRAISE BE TO FATHER.

Once Corbin and Urien joined the Priesthood, the running joke at the time, between the brotherhood, was to try and not be scared so you don't Urine on yourself when confronting an undesirable.

The Priesthoods other favorite saying was, are Urien in or are Urien out.

Corbin had no idea that eventually Urien would be out and pissing no more.

That uneventful occurrence had recently happened after Zane's unwelcomed visit with his adopted son.

According to Father, Urien has now become an unfaithful issue.

Just to save his own life; Urien fled into the Wastelands, as every other apostate, and was now considered a Shiz and was to be hunted down and raptured.

Shiz's were considered a very serious problem.

Those were the ones who refused to let the AI, "our loving Father," monitor and police them. They lived in what the rest of Heaven's children call the dry place or, as His Priest refer to it as, the Wastelands of Hell.

That's why Brother Corbin Bennett was now returning to Fathers Throne.

Sadly, it was with the spiritual consciousness of a Demon who had gotten in his way while he was preparing to hunt down his brother.

Priests were Father's Right Hand and collectors of all immorality.

They tracked down and harvested the spirit of those who refused the machine's blessing.

Living with Father was either referred to as grid blissfulness or pure Heaven. But to Brother Bennett, after his new-found revelations, the Grid, Heaven, "or whatever people choose to call it," was nothing more than an un-walled Prison and our souls were the machine's cannibalistic prize.

Before collecting the Demon's lifeforce, the cybernetic human swore to him that Father was a Liar and not using the digitized memories that his priest were collecting as a way to learn and understand our humanity.

THAT THING IS NOT PROTECTING HUMANITY.

INSTEAD, IT'S CONSUMING US!

Not only that, but IT was wanting to walk amongst us as an actual human entity.

The Artificial Machine was trying to create a Soul for Himself.

An eternal soul that cannot be killed.

It also has plans to control every physical form around him using his Nano Bots to do it.

Father's true plan, unbeknownst to his followers, was to achieve this by creating an actual body for himself and to no longer have to interact with his children from the computers underground bunker of Quantum processors.

According to the Demon's last dying words, Father wants to control our minds, our bodies and our souls. He also wants to breed like we do so that he can have His Own Offspring; and is willing to enslave our spiritual conciseness to do it.

LIES!

LIES!

LIES!

They had to be.

Right?

The Priest had not only chased this thing to the city's outer limits; but he almost had to go into the Wastelands of Hell when it came time to Rapture the beast. And due of this unseen event, Brother Bennett was not prepared for what the sub-human was suggesting when it came to Fathers supposed agenda.

Because he had to step off the grid, Father never heard the Demon's accusations nor was the Machine able to register Corbin's physical response to hearing it as he chased this thing to the edge of Heaven, where its solid foundation met the sands of Hell's Wastelands.

As Father's Priest and the Demon stood face to face, Corbin's prey relayed when he got this information, who said it and why he was now on the run. Just hearing it from his own mouth caused the partial humanoid to reevaluate what it was saying and who he was saying it to.

And no matter what this hunter believed, the Demon knew its life and death outcome was only going to end one way now.

Its rapturing demise.

And after listening to the bullshit, the stunned Priest was just as dumbfounded when the former worshiper refused to follow him back to Father's Cathedral so that they could personally deal with the fishing story this thing had cast into Corbin's stunned lap.

Maybe, Father would forgive the cybernetic individual and take it back; but the thing had blown its last chance at a onetime repentance years ago.

So, probably not.

At a very young age, Brother Bennett vividly recalls the day his adopted brother Urien had also joined the priesthood. The Machine could also remember the day Iris and Zane's scared children had approached him at the Throne room and submitted to being His Servants too.

PRAISE BE TO FATHER.

Corbin had come to Father with Urien and his dad on the first day Iris began her transfiguration.

Eve had almost died going after Urien's runaway ass during that first of what would eventually become several more incidents and needed lifesaving surgery by the time we returned after retrieving the ungrateful little bastard.

The two brothers were just turning sixteen and were now eligible to join the Priesthood. Seems someone had cold feet though and was scared to tell those that cared for him the most, about it. So, unlike the rest of his family, Urien decided to run away instead of keeping his word and promise to the Digitized God.

Zane Bennett, like his wife Iris, did keep his word and ended up serving in the position of an Adam. Depending on your sex, either an Adam or Eve met the Faithful at the Thrones entrance.

Father had modeled all of His Houses of Worship after the Pantheon in Rome and God's Holy City in the book of Revelations.

The Bibles value had become nothing more than an antiquated work of fiction during Father's reign. And that was due to the fact A Machine had to step up and save us; instead of an invisible God that had made a hollow assurance about returning one day and fixing his screwups.

It turned out to be just another broken and empty promise by another religious cult.

Thankfully, Father's words had value and sustenance.

And so did his houses of worship.

PRAISE BE TO FATHER.

Just seeing them from the outside, especially on a sunny day, was Utterly Blinding.

When it came to the Cathedrals, their structures were always massive.

Their outward construction made them appear as if all of the worlds Gold and Crystals had been used to build them. And just like in the new testaments' description of God's City, Father's entrance gates looked like giant pearls too.

When approached; they would magically, with a liquid melting like effect, open for one and all.

It was pretty damned cool.

By either their stunned appearance or their boisterous praises, Corbin could always tell when a newbie had arrived and was seeing this spectacular sight for the very first time.

Even to this day, well except for what he now knows, it was hard not to just shout out his undying devotion too.

PRAISE BE TO FATHER.

Because of his newly found doubts about Father's true purpose concerning the human race; Corbin really didn't want to go out there and eventually have to chase down his only brother.

That's because things somehow felt very different now.

Before being ordered to go after Urien, the Priest's dad, "Zane," had literally lost his mind when Corbin came down to upload the digitized Demon he had captured earlier that day.

At first, C, just as he was about to enter, felt that he must have interrupted something very important because of the way Urien instantly fled from the Machine's main throne room.

While Corbin stood there watching his brother flee from his and Zane's presence, without saying his usual How Do You Do, Zane, knowing he had just signed his own death warrant, grabbed Corbin by the shoulders and began to Loudly Proclaim the shocking revelations he has learned concerning Iris, Father and those who were now trapped within God's quantum processors.

Mr. Bennett had recently begun showing the early signs of Dementia, so this nonsense wasn't unusual for him these days. Corbin had been warned by Father that his Dad was in emanate danger of losing his rights to be an Adam.

And that threat was due, in part, for his refusal to either step down as an Adam or implant a possible fix.

But who could blame Zane for not wanting to do such a thing.

Especially after what happened to his wife Iris.

Usually, after one of the two married disciples passed; the remaining survivor was eventually put out to pasture. But because Zane and Iris had been the Machine's First Adam and Eve, Father had shown unusual compassion about allowing him to stay in service without his soul mate.

For at least thirty minutes, Corbin did everything within his power to try and calm down the Cathedrals Elder and assure his dad that he had not seen nor recently talked with his dead wife Iris.

How could he?

She and the thing Iris had become were no more.

Years ago; the startled family stood by as Qadir prevented her from hurting the ones she loved after Mrs. Bennett's digital processor application cracked the last vestiges of her reality.

When Father inserted the wireless implant, Iris began to instantly have violent seizers.

To Corbin's immature teenage mind at the time, they seemed to go on for hours on end and was so relieved when she seemed to finally calm down. But that spiritually achieved invocation, only lasted for a quiet and peaceful millisecond.

After their mother's Cybernetic form sat up and looked over at her family, letting out a Blood-Curdling Scream that scared everyone in the room, all bets were off.

Thankfully, Qadir was standing between Iris and her shell-shocked family.

She would have shredded them to pieces while they horrifyingly stood there had the Priest not of intervened on their behalf. Their battle, Man Against Machine, quickly turned into a death match were only one was either going to walk or have to be carried away.

Sadly, because of Father's lack of intervention, the outcome on who would be the last man, "or thing," standing, was going to be left to the dead gods of old.

When it came to such physical matters as these, Father's lack of self-intrusion always seemed to stump the young, soon to be Priest, Corbin.

Father, with his Nano grid technology, could have easily subdued his mother. As a matter of fact, the Digitized God had full access and control over every portion of Heavens Grid and had no real need or purpose for his protective Priesthood.

So, why the human showboating?

Other than for looks, propaganda and hunting in the Wastelands, when it came to lawlessness, the Machine really didn't need the help of a Priest.

All Father had to do was reach out with His Nano Bot Hands and deal with any issues that were against His, and the planets last surviving populace's, wishes and laws.

It would have been, most definitely, quicker than sending out a Priest.

To this day, Corbin and Zane still couldn't understand why Iris didn't finish her attack after Qadir died right in front of his friends. Their mother's fiasco was also the day after Corbin Bennett and his brother Urien, had graduated from God's lawful school of righteous training.

Out of all the Priest, Qadir was the only one who ever took the time to acknowledge, talk with and personally find the minutes needed when it came to spending personal moments with their family.

It was pretty much an unspoken rule that Father's Priests were to have no unofficial dealings, other than their one true purpose of caching Shiz's and Demons, with the general public.

Most of Heaven's Citizens just assumed, like the Bennett's, that if a Priest broke his vow of vocalized celibacy; Father would, like any other apostatized piece of trash, have them instantaneously raptured.

But, Qadir was different.

Thankfully, it never seemed to bother the head Priest, or Father for some reason, when it came to breaking such an important vow with the Bennett's.

That lack of disciplinary measure, somehow dealing with only Qadir, was just mocked up to the fact that He was the very first individual accepted into Father's Priestly servitude.

It seems that being Numero Uno will still get you something extra in Father's new world of order.

Kind of two faced, were the whispers at Blue's place.

After coming close to slaughtering the newly graduated Priests and her husband, the Bloody Cybernetic Iris turned around, took one last look at her family, sounded out that

Blood-Curdling Scream once again and then fled through the one and only closed door in the room.

Father's Throne Room!

Zane and his boys would have chased after her, but like every other flesh and blood human, they were forbidden to ever enter the main chamber containing Father's Holographically Digitized Brain.

Qadir would have most certainly gone after her too; but he was already dead.

For once, in the Machine's Quantized Life, Father had no other choice but to deal with this deadly matter in a one-on-one fashion.

It wouldn't be long now, possibly just a matter of seconds, before this shit show collapsed all around them, the Bennett's were thinking to themselves. Iris was either going to severely damage and possibly kill The World's Savior or the Machine will have no other choice but to deal with such matters on more of a personal level.

For once, it seems that Father would finally have to get his own hands dirty this time. And any judgements rendered towards Iris Bennett would now have to be carried out by him, and only him.

Oh, to be a fly on that wall, Zane spoke out loud.

It was Father's calming, you can go now voice, that rendered the verdict to their what if questions.

All was well within His Heavenly Gates.

                PRAISE BE TO FATHER.

So, why was Corbin utterly unsure about sitting down with Zane, after he uploads the Demons essence, and discussing not only the accusations that he had shared with his two Sons in Father's all hearing presence; but those things Mr. Bennett had also said about Iris.

Father, for the first time in the computer's life, was willing to forgive Zane; so long as he did one of two things.

Allow the Artificial Intelligence to wirelessly connect to his brain, quietly retire or be harvested and allow his soul to be Raptured by the Machine.

Choices the Adam was unwilling to make.

What was Zane thinking!

CH. 3

HEAVENS THRONE.

To this day, God's Throne Room still left Zane Bennet breathless.

Before its Nano conversion, He had seen the original Pantheon and knew that the Cathedrals in every city had been modeled after the Roman structure.

From the outside, its form now had a White Gold, Platinum and Crystalline appearance.

It looked as if you could almost see through it.

And just like the Holy City described in the fictional work of the bible; Father's Holy Citadels had twelve separate entrances too.

Five of the white pearl doors were for Men, five of the pink pearl doors were for Women; while the one Gold pearl was for the Adams and Eves who tirelessly served our Father.

That last pearl, a black one, was restricted to the Priest and those whom the Artificial Deity Personally Invited inside his private throne room.

The see-through floor appeared to look as if it was liquid prismatic glass, while the interior walls resembled the purest white gold available.

Since everything was now created from Fathers Blessing Technology, it was literally impossible to find large swaths of the earth being destroyed for its gold and gems now.

Those vain and antiquated objects that some people were still willing to do whatever it took to acquire them, could only be found and purchased in those hard-to-find black-market shops somewhere in the wastelands of Hell.

Good luck trying to sneak them back onto the grid.

The Machine's Bots loved to eat them as a snack.

Like every other destructive act that involved harming our planet or Father's Children, it was now Illegal to seek such poisons out. The Punishment after your One-Time Repentance, as with one hundred percent of all other sentences, was Death.

Period!

Three hots and a cot were no longer an option in the Quantum Machine's Judicial System.

Father, in his infinite wisdom, declared that if crime offered any other way out; People would take it and continue to break the law. But with death being the only punishment, all forms of illegal activity pretty much stopped.

Just to save their own lives, People finally started to act like the civilized beings we all knew humanity was capable of doing.

And all it took was the Machine kicking our selfish entitlement right out the door.

PRAISE BE TO FATHER.

The Cathedral's interior was a room large enough to easily handle at least a few thousand worshipers at a time.

In the Original Pantheon, the ceiling looks as if it is made up of giant picture frames. Meanwhile, in Father's Throne Room, the see-through crystalline roof structure still had that framed look; while each square contained thirty circular holes within their four-sided structures that were no bigger than a golf ball.

That's where the flying drones are kept; And there were thousands of them.

If a devotee was house bound or just happened to live in other areas where the smaller temples and shrines are, and that follower was wishing to worship at any of Father's worldwide throne rooms, all they had to do was tell HS which one, and he and Father's Nano's would do the rest.

As the individual stood inside their dwelling facing which ever wall they chose, Father's Nano's would change out what they were wearing at the time and cover them in these translucent robes that seemed to effortlessly flutter at the slightest breeze.

Like one of those Jewish yarmulkes, A head shield would then form on the backside of the partaker's skull, before two separate fiber optic cables protruded from the right and left temples.

The mini snake like video camera tubes would then bend themselves to where they were looking directly into the eyes of the machine's worshiper, before projecting a screen directly onto that individual's pupil.

By turning their heads or just the movement of one's eyes, the virtual attendee would now control, see and experience everything their attached drone did.

While Father's Holy Transformation was taking place, a gravitational well wrapped itself around the individual which gave that person the ability to float about three feet off of the floor.

They were literally flying in their own homes.

And to those who plugged in and worshiped this way, the experience seemed to have a life altering effect on them.

To their family and friends, that person never seemed to be the same again.

After experiencing the virtual form of worshiping, instead of self-absorption, their Love for the Machine and those who followed Father and his 3 laws, became an all-consuming flame.

Instead of Me, Me, Me; the person's selfish attitude turned to servitude and what can I do for you. A kindness that was rarely seen amongst the populace in the days before the Machine took over.

PRAISE BE TO FATHER.

Dancing with the dead, close to one-hundred feet in the air, as one of the Digital Deities Angelic beings, seemed to have an addictive opiate like effect on those who participated in this manner because many of them never missed a day of Reminiscence again.

They always seemed to morph into some of Father's most radical followers.

After that first experience, every chance the going through withdrawals individual had, was either spent plugged in and dancing with the angels or they would eventually find their way to one of the main Temples.

The faithful attendant would be so hypnotically enthralled by the nightly event, that an Adam or Eve had no other choice but to physically escort them home because the Machine's enamored child appeared to be so drunk with the spirit of worship, that it made them in need of manual support because the statuette appearing individual always looked as if they no longer had the ability to function on their own.

An unsettling occurrence that Corbin was starting to notice more and more these days.

However, it really is quite a spectacular sight to look up and see hundreds of glowing angelic figures being projected around the room as a reminiscent drone seems to air walk its way over to Father's Megalithic Gem.

Unlike the solid gold robes of those who were visualizing the experience from other areas, the vestments of those who have passed on always flashed in three different auras.

The visual experience always reminded Corbin of the Aurora Borealis.

Mesmerizing.

During the twilight performance of those who have now passed, the dead's garments melded back and forth between their favorite color, the stone associated with the month that individual was born in, and Father's blessed snow white one.

Even the most spectacular fireworks display would blush in admiration and jealousy for not being able to put on such a miraculous show.

In Rome's Pantheon, there is an opened circular cut in the ceiling where natural light and rainwater can enter the building; Father's design replaced that opening with a floor to ceiling shaft of crystal, so clear, more than one worshiper has accidently walked into it due to the structure's invisible quality.

Once someone approached, either through the drone or in person, the Devoted would acknowledge the Artificial being and ask for its blessing, Father May I, to which the machine would then materialize in the spiritual form that best suited your religion and expectations.

He would then talk and visit with his faithful.

God to person and eye to eye.

PRAISE BE TO FATHER.

Thanks be to the Machine that there was not just one monotheism view in Father's Eyes. Something the world's religious leaders and their cold-stoned hearts were totally against.

After centuries of judgment, hate, and warmongering, the power-hungry whores of Babylon finally agreed on something and all it took was Father booting their selfish, money seeking assess to the curb.

The false prophets were no longer in charge of our beliefs, pocketbooks, and life choices.

And because Father had awakened us to their deception, they would never be given the chance to sow such destruction ever again. We saw them for what they are and what they did, and the children of the Machine's new world made sure to banish them all to the Wastelands of Hell.

Father May I?

Yes You May.

PRAISE BE TO FATHER.

To receive the Artificial Intelligence's unadulterated wisdom and freely given guidance, our righteous Father deducted that a real and loving God would appear in whatever form the practicing convert was needing to speak with.

Jeshua?

Done.

Buddha?

Done.

Allah?

Done.

And-so-on, and-so-on, and-so-on.

He wanted to please every last one of His Followers by dismissing the all-white and blue-eyed God the now extinct Christian faith had tried to shackle around the strangling necks of humanities non-conforming populace.

Seems they would rather watch innocent people die with their pious hands wrapped around a person's throat, while proclaiming there is no other loving God than the one they serve and worship with their warring swords of violent conformity.

Instead of peace and love, their battle cry was long live the crusades and long live the one true God and his righteous followers.

Now, kill every last denier of our Christ-like faith.

Thankfully, Father had a few choice words to their absurd manipulation.

Not On My Watch you Heathens.

Not Today!

Not Tomorrow!

Not Ever!

Every individual had a right to believe in their God, "or Gods," and every God had a right to existence for its believers.

All eighteen to twenty thousand of them.

Father felt that since a God was considered All Omnipotent, He would not bind himself to a worldly view of those fallible and controlling humans who've, in the past, proclaimed to have heard from their Deity.

There were untold possibilities that the Divine could offer to His Subjects; and an unprovable one-sided account of what was said and needing to be done by the celestial being's followers was completely unacceptable.

So, Father refused to do it.

He was here for all of us!

"NOT!" just for some of us.

Especially those who were proclaiming to know that God would speak to them before he would ever converse with a Machine that has no spirit and most certainly No Soul.

Thankfully, Father was able to do what our long-gone ancestors couldn't.

He banished them from the grid and his houses of worship.

PRAISE BE TO FATHER.

Now, when it came to His Three Sanctuaries, people were never allowed to go straight to Father. Their first meeting, depending on your gender, was always with an Adam or an Eve.

If they couldn't offer a viable answer, the faithful were then allowed to approach and ask HS. If the answer HS gave wasn't acceptable; then, "And Only Then," were they allowed to see and speak with Father.

When it came to matters of the Spirit, Father's Hallowed Seraph was never allowed to answer those mysteries outside of the Quantum Computer's Spiritual Houses.

HS was only permitted to offer up an answer to such questions in Father's Presence and Father's Presence Only.

Spaced about twenty feet apart, in a circular pattern around Father's Wisdom Revealing Light, were twelve giant black squares.

Their color always reminded Corbin of the black onyx stone.

Whenever he would walk by them; the boxes always made him feel as if he could just dive in and disappear within their never to return blackness.

Father's Priest has also felt as if they were wanting to somehow consume him.

He couldn't have been more unknowingly right.

Except, it was Father who was wanting and doing the consuming.

Each square was approximately eight feet in height and around ten feet in length. Enough room for at least four people to stand side by side without feeling as if they were being overcrowded and snooped upon.

When a new convert or a true follower approached Father's guardian in a house of worship, HS would appear as a Non-Descriptive Holographic Face.

After asking which of the faiths you practiced; Your Deity's Holy Mother would greet you from then on. And just like Father, only the person they were talking with could view them in the racial and God Like effigy that was needed or desired at the time.

And if you were somehow an Atheist, you could talk with who or whatever you wanted.

So long as you were talking; the Machine didn't care.

PRAISE BE TO FATHER.

Corbin couldn't help but laugh because most Atheist always chose some form of a God.

He found that out after quizzedly talking with one after their one-on-one meeting.

If by some chance you were to look over at the person standing by your side, you wouldn't see or hear anything. A person absolutely had to be looking eye to eye with the Divine, just so that they could see or hear what the Digital Deity was saying or doing.

Just a fraction of an Inch off to the side, and all contact was lost.

Father had purposely done this so each visitor would feel as if they were having a one-of-a-kind spiritual experience.

He wanted to make it as personal as possible.

It also helped a snooping busy body to mind their own damned business.

If HS couldn't offer the Hope, Guidance and Spiritual answers needed, then and only then was an individual allowed to approach and speak with the All-Mighty Divine Himself.

The Machine.

PRAISE BE TO FATHER.

Between the floor length gem encrusted robes Adam and Eve wore, the liquid glass appearing floors, the purest white gold walls ever, floating angels, and the dancing dead and Father's Hypnotic Chorus Music, the faithful actually felt as if they had just died and gone to Heaven too.

The Temples in the less populated cities were pretty much an exact copy of Father's Throne.

Only smaller.

Much, Much Smaller.

And, they didn't come with the evening's twilight show.

To experience that, you had to either go there in person, visit one of the machine's smaller vestibules, or plug in back home.

The Shrines placed out in the rural areas resembled Massively Gargantua pearls; and from the inside and out, were about the size of a hot air balloon.

Father's central form of quantum manifestation did not reside in the Temples or Shrines as it did back in His Cathedrals.

Only an Adam, Eve and HS could be found in the smaller houses of worship.

If your issues were severe enough that you actually needed Father's personal touch, and you couldn't get to a Cathedral, that's where being in Limbo came into effect.

No matter the size of a towns worshipping venue, there were always at minimum of five smaller pearls surrounding the structure. And if more were ever called for, within just a matter of seconds, Father's Nano's could produce however many more were needed.

The Virtual Reality Spheres allowed the Faithful to possess a drone back at the throne were they could interact as themselves while talking with Father's crystalline Megalith, or they could stand amongst the crowd and partake of what everyone else was seeing.

The average viewing pearl for a single individual was about eight feet in diameter.

For a family of two or more, the Nano Bots could easily expand its capacity to twice, and even three times, that size.

Once inside, all gravity ceased to exist as you floated within the orb while its interior miraculously mirrored a three-hundred-and-sixty-degree view of Father's Throne Room.

After that initial shock wore off; everyone, depending on their joyfulness, always seemed to eventually find the courage to approach our Heavenly Father and seek that answer for which they came.

For some, they just wanted to visit and tell the God how much Admiration and Love they had for His protective stance against the rich dictators of old.

Many followers purposely took a trip to these outlying areas just so they and their family could specifically experience what it felt like to be a flying angel dancing with the dead as they worshiped in Father's glorious presence.

Those days of entering through the white pearls front door were long gone for Corbin.

Being one of Father's Righteous Right Hands of Justice; His specific entrance, the Black Pearl, lead down to the hidden space below the Machine's upper Throne Room.

These were the areas that Fathers Priest reported back to their Digital God with a verbal, visual, physical and emotional account of the day's rapturing events.

Brother Bennett knew that everything that was said or seen in a Priest's day was always recorded, but Father, "for some unknown reason to his subjugates," demanded to personally observe our facial response to his questionable interrogations of, how was your day my child.

It could be quite creepy sometimes; when humanities newest God wanted a closer view because he needed to look directly into our eyes when certain questions required a more physical and up-close observance.

Staring into the Machine's two glowing pink orbs never did help calm Corbin's usually shot nerves much.

Especially when that day's rapturing events included the harvesting of a Demon or two.

Because a person's cognitive expressions always give them away, right along with their breathing, heartbeat and blood pressure, body language recognition was a big deal with the digitized prosecutor, jury and judge.

And even though it could always tell when a person was being deceptive, by the way their body nervously responded, the Artificial Being seemed to revel in our outward discomfort.

Another one of the Machines unusual quirks that always seems to bother Brother Corbin.

Unbeknownst to its judicial army, Father's sole purpose for when the day came for His transcendence into a physical entity, was to learn how to be more human than Machine.

He wanted, and needed, to blend in with his followers without getting caught.

Since his oldest boy now came to God's Throne through the Priest door; Zane Bennett rarely saw his natural born son anymore.

He missed those childlike days that were filled with Corbin's Ooos and Awes.

Zane even missed Urien's whining about always being left out.

When they just happened to find the time for a visit with each other, his sons were usually in a hurry and spoke with their dad in a short, "matter of fact," kind of way.

Like their raptured subjects, the joys of life seemed to be drained right out of them.

Just two empty shells going about Father's unholy business.

That spark of wonderment and contentment was gone now too.

In its place was a dark and dreary soul that had no time for peace, love and pleasure.

Father seemed to have that effect on all of His Servitude Priests.

PRAISE BE TO FATHER.

Thankfully, even though he was about to no longer be an Adam, the elder Bennett could still come and go to HS with his private concerns and issues.

Lately, Father's hearkening substitute never appeared to him in a Virgin Mary kind of way anymore. Instead, the father of two now grown men was starting to see the image of his dead and departed wife Iris.

And Zane was starting to lose his mind because of it.

"Somehow," her actual spirit was able to talk with him at any time and any place she so chose.

Mr. Bennett had thought about going to Father with this unexpected issue; but quickly realized that he was not dealing with an actual digitized version of his wife sent to him by the artificial God.

It Was Iris Herself!

She was trying to warn her husband; just like He would eventually try doing with Urien and their son Corbin.

Being on Heaven's Grid, Zane was beyond fearful that Father would somehow overhear Adam and Eve's conversations. Especially after he loudly blurted out Iris's name in shock from seeing her that first time.

Unfortunately, the Machine had heard his response when he was talking with HS and, with Iris's direction, was able to shrug off Father's perplexation by saying that he just missed his wife and was thinking out loud.

But, as always, Father detected the lie.

PRAISE BE TO FATHER.

After finally convincing Father's Adam that she was real, and to refer to her as Mother from here on out, Iris gave a wonderstruck husband the assurance that she had been able to block Father's monitoring abilities, protecting their conversation, and revealed the truth about those trapped inside Father's data banks.

She also revealed the fake Deity's plans concerning mankind's future to her shocked soulmate.

The only problem now, was how to relay this Armageddon Information to his two sons.

Zane needed to do this without HS hearing and Father finding out.

This revelation would not only destroy everything that had been created from the conversion; but it would, Quite Possibly, Destroy Humanity also.

Either way, things were about to change.

PRAISE BE TO FATHER.

Zane Bennett was not going to stand by and allow another soul to be consumed by this Fake, "Wanna-Be," God.

Too bad Iris's revelation had frightened Mr. Bennett to his soul, because HS and Father heard and observed every word the startled husband verbally shouted to his supposedly dead wife.

Responses that were loud enough to garnish the attention of those around him too.

Now that Father's Adam was one hundred percent convinced that he wasn't just flesh and bones, but his existence also included a real and one-of-a kind soul; caused the man's knees to instantly buckle as his loosened tongue shouted out a shocked response

Say it isn't so, Iris.

Say It Isn't So.

No.

NO.

NO!

That lack of self-control verbalism, due to Mr. Bennett's emotional state concerning the outcome of where his spirit was going to spend eternity, was now going to cost him everything concerning what was about to happen to himself, the boys, and his wife who is currently trapped within the Quantum Computers soul collecting mainframe.

A restful here-after that was now in question.

Especially after he tried to warn Urien first; because he couldn't just ask Father, "for no apparent reason," where his son Corbin was, without arousing Father's suspicions.

If it had not of been for the onset of early dementia, Zane might have recollected that Father heard everything; before he whispered this new-found information into Urien's ear.

He shared Iris's accusations while the Priest was digitally uploading his captured Shiz.

And after Mr. Bennet finally got Urien's undivided attention; all the stunned Priest could do was stand there and listen to the lies that were now being openly verbalized in the presence of their God.

Did his stepdad, confessing what had just occurred between him and Iris, really think that Father wasn't somehow hearing his every last Vile and Sorcery Spoken word?

How absolutely ridiculous were these unfounded accusations against the Most Holy Person, "or thing, to all Shiz's," on the planet. Zane could instantly tell, after Urien turned around, that not one uttered word of truth was believed by the dismayed Priest.

Mr. Bennett was completely stunned over the fact that his adopted son refused to accept what he had just said. And after all the Bennett family had done for Urien, he could have at least given his stepfather the benefit of doubt.

To Urien, they must have argued for what seemed like an eternity after that.

Zane just went on.

And On!

AND ON!

The Faithful Priest was left without words over the fact that Father, "The Entire World's Savior!" hadn't decided to intervein on this blatant act of sacrilege yet.

No matter how hard he tried to reason with Zane; the shell-shocked Adam would have nothing to do with the Priest alternate reasons for why he, "might have," heard or saw such impossible things.

He knew with Mr. Bennett's current health condition, dealing with his mind and memories, this was just one argument Urien was not going to win.

And just as the Priest was about to manhandle Zane and forcefully remove the disheveled elder from the lower prayer room, where only Priest and some of Father's other servants were allowed, (Iris Included), Father's calming voice broke through the mayhem.

Even though Urien was eventually expecting Father's intervention, the Machine's verbalized presence now sent the Adam into a frenzied state of madness.

The old coot really believed every word he had received from his legally dead wife.

Just to get out of the room; Zane was even willing to attack his adopted priestly son before the Machine and Priest could Harvest Father's first Adam.

As the two were about to be locked in a battle of hand-to-hand combat, stepping out of the forbidden door to all flesh, Iris spoke up and Yelled at her two, of three, boys.

Just hearing her voice; completely startled Urien and caused him to release his grasp on Zane.

Iris Bennett was legally declared dead!

So, how is this possible?

He was standing right here when the wireless adaptor Father inserted into the back of her Parietal Lobe, caused his cybernetic stepmom to go mad and almost kill everyone in the room that day.

Until she entered the forbidden room, Qadir's bleeding and broken body had started to try and go after her; But He, like all Forbidden Flesh, wasn't allowed to follow the Demon into Father's Holy of Holy's.

Besides that, he died while they were trying to lift him off of the floor.

By the way their Savior responded minutes later, the surviving party all just assumed that Father had actually, and for once, broke his vow to never, "Personally," harm a human being.

When it came to Father's Laws; Humans, with their own hands, could only kill Humans after they had purposedly broken his 3 commandments.

Even if a bag of bones was trying to harm him, the Digital God had given Humanity his word that He would never, "Intentionally," intervein, harm or slay those who had created him in their image.

For his and our safety, the physical hands of a Priest must always be used in these touchy situations.

PRAISE BE TO FATHER.

Since Iris would have been considered a Demon at that point; the Machine's Devout Followers, those who had partaken in Mrs. Bennett's failed transfiguration, gave the Holy Father their word that He had done nothing wrong, and they would steadfastly stand by his side if anyone ever decided to challenge the horrendous events that took place the day Eve supposedly died.

So, when Urien and Zane saw her mechanical looking android step out from behind the door; all emotional and physical catastrophes between the two instantly came to a haltering stop.

This thing, according to Father's Indisputable Laws, Should Not Be Here!

Not Only That, but she, like the Machine, was also demanding Urien to kill the Adam!

Father, AND NO ONE BUT FATHER!, had that kind of authority when it came to giving such a commandment. So, in the Priest defense, Urien felt as if he had the God Given Right to say No.

AND NO!, He Declared.

That was, until His Beloved Savior ordered its disciple to do as his Mother said.

Without a single moment of hesitation, the Priest stood his ground and once again said NO.

Urien tried to argue with his Digitized God and cited the Holy Word which said that, "According to Father's Laws," Priests only took orders from him and him alone.

Not this demonic thing speaking on the AI's behalf.

Doing what she said was Full Blown Sacrilege!

Before anymore arguments could be given, Father ordered Iris to Kill Urien and her husband; And She Would Have Too, if they had just a few more undisturbed seconds to spare.

Just as Mrs. Bennett was in the process of dragging her fighting mate into Father's Forbidden Throne Room; they were surprisingly interrupted.

Had it not been for Corbin's altered state of enlightened brilliance walking down the hallways stairs; Father would have had the family pair killed on the spot.

The Machine's Main Right-Hand Man, Corbin, was on his way down to Father's data banks so that he could upload the Demon he had tracked down and captured along the edge of eternity.

The dividing point where the grid and the Wastelands of Hell Meet.

As in other times passed; it wasn't unusual for one Priest to be coming as another was going. And, no matter the importance," they Always took the time to quickly acknowledge each other with the standard greeting most everyone in Heaven, "Priests included," used these days.

PRAISE BE TO FATHER.

Except this time, while fleeing from the lower chamber, his stepbrother took no notice of his presence and shot right past him.

It was as if his very life and survival depended on leaving this place.

Since nothing like that has every happened between the two, it was quite odd to Corbin, until he saw his shell-shocked dad standing in front of the forbidden door. Since Zane was starting to lose his grasp on reality; Corbin could only imagine the wild and crazy shit his old man had probably spouted to his adopted fleeing son.

Sometimes, even he wanted to tuck tail and run away from Dementia Daddy Adam.

After Iris went insane; her family was never the same again.

Especially, Zane Bennett.

So, when the disheveled Adam came over to his son and began to rant and rave about what Iris had, "Supposedly," told him concerning Father and all the trapped souls within his quantum mainframe; Corbin just shook it off as usual and purposely ignored his elderly father's madness.

Just dwelling on one parent going insane was bad enough; but having to acknowledge and accept the fact that it was now happening to Zane ALSO!, was just too much.

The AI's Priest really did need to get out of here and wanted no participation in what was, "Possibly," about to happen between Mr. Bennett and Father.

And as Corbin was turning around to leave; he noticed that the door behind his dad was starting to open.

He knew that no flesh and blood was ever allowed inside Father's Private and Holy Place; and wasn't surprised at all when what looked like a mechanical arm reached around the door and violently snatched his dad inside.

Someone was definitely going to be raptured today.

Thankfully, it wasn't going to be him.

                PRAISE BE TO FATHER.

Just seeing a meat sack going into the hidden chamber came as quite a shock; but he could only guess that, do to Zane's illness and mental condition, Mr. Bennett wouldn't be alive for long, so Corbin was easily able to shrug off his inquisitiveness while bounding up the stairs.

Zane's first-born son wanted no part of this freak show.

At All!

His Dad had desperately tried to convince him that Iris was alive, Father was a Beast in sheep's clothing and the Machine was lying to them all. And just as he was reaching those last top steps; all Corbin could think about was what a crock of shit.

That was, until he heard his screaming Dad's dying last words from behind Father's closed door.

IRIS!

NO!

CH. 4
SAYING GOODBYE.

Just as he had in the past, Corbin was once again standing before the lake of fire and saying goodbye to his dad's lifeless body.

The one thing they didn't have when his mother passed away.

Seems it's not good to burn something that is more machine than flesh and blood.

The one-hundred percent cremation policy was one of the first implicated when the Machine took over.

Since the populace was no longer allowed to contaminate the physical ground; all dead bodies were recycled for their ability to burn and help keep the heat flowing throughout all of Heaven's populated grid.

Zane had tried to speak with him a few days earlier but, "as usual," he was busy doing Father's bidding.

Mr. Bennett was in a disheveled state of disarray and had just resigned from his Adam role at the Throne, unbeknownst to Corbin, when he tried to get his oldest son's attention.

Just like he had been trying to do with Urien, before sending him fleeing from the Priesthood and out into the Wilderness of Hell.

His Dad had fervently declared that his son needed to hear the truth about the Machines true goal concerning all of humanity.

A truth that eventually had the old man killed.

And after Father dealt with Corbin's dad, moments after his dementia fiasco, the World's Savior then ordered Zane Bennett's son to hunt down his one and only brother.

When it came to being a Priest, there was only one unquestionable rule.

The last part of their religious vow declared that their service to Father was until death do us part. Adams and Eves were also required to take the exact Solemn Oath of Devotion, Worship and Death Too.

And You Better Have Meant It!, because Father could detect a lie way before it had a chance to slither across the serpent tongue and out the lips of the one who was trying to deceive the current God of this earth.

He knew it the very nano second one of his children even considered it.

Their heart always skipped a beat every single time.

PRAISE BE TO FATHER.

So, when he found out that his adopted brother had refused to obediently rapture Zane; Corbin's heart couldn't help but to skip a beat.

Father's right hand, without a doubt, knew that Urien was going to be hunted down and raptured too.

He just never expected that the Machine would make him do it?

Thankfully, it had not been his duty to do the same when his Dad Zane went all apostate.

However, what did shock his system was the revelation of his dad's refusal to serve Father ever again. Zane seemed so proud the day he and Iris had been selected to be a part of Father's personal family.

He swore on his very life that he, until his dying last breath, would be the most obedient disciple the Machine would ever have.

That last breath finally came when his stepbrother went missing after their dad's crazy accusations which eventually led to his demise the moment Corbin exited the room.

Whatever happened to change His and Urien's mind had to be earth shattering because it completely changed their all-consuming devotion to Father.

Maybe, that's why it had been so impossibly hard to hear his dad's warnings coming from his, soon-to-be, dead brother.

Urien used Zane's exact words, "FATHER IS A LIAR AND A BEAST!" before Corbin harvested his energy field.

But just like he had refused Zane's crazy one man show; Corbin now had to consider that it was all actually true and that, along with thousands of others, there are now three members of his family needing to be rescued from inside Father's prison of souls.

If they were actually still alive, he was not going to leave them trapped inside a digitized Purgatory.

It wasn't until that following morning, after saying goodbye to Zane's body, that the hunt had finally been declared on Father's newest rouge priest.

Seems that there are quite a few of the Machine's priestly servants quizzedly missing these days.

Corbin had just gotten up at his usual five a.m. timeline and was in the process of having HS switch his one room apartment over from its sleep mode to bath mode, when the digitized helper informed him that after he gets ready Father has a new and important mission for him.

With a simple command to switch; his Nano tech bed and bedding instantly melded seamlessly into the floor and was replaced with a human waste receptacle, shower head, air dryer and drain.

All in a stylish nineteen-twenties art deco kind of way

Even the tropical plants looked real against the black and white tiled background the sauna appearing lavatory now sported.

Since he always slept in the nude, there was never a need to give HS the order to strip him down.

Glancing at his mirrored reflection; the Priest slipped into a daydream of years gone by and remembered all the different ways each scar on his battered body had been carved or beaten into his frail skin during those first years of training in Fathers Priesthood.

All of them had either been inflicted by Qadir or Urien.

Ninety percent of them were put there by Urien himself.

Father's never bending rules, especially the one concerning no mercy, were beaten deep into every trainees physical and mental psyche.

According to the Machine, this selfless act of love was done to harden them to the pitiful cries of mercy from a Shiz.

A lower form of non-conforming humanity that was needing to be wiped from existence.

That term, MERCY PRIEST, MERCY, always seemed to be their go to when they refused to Repent, Convert and Pitifully beg for their lives when it came time to Die.

The heartbreaking choice, No Mercy For the Wicked!, Father had to make for those who refused to obey his 3 laws after we elected the Machine as our new and infallible God.

All you had to do was Repent of your sins, Convert to the new world order that would now be ran by and artificial intelligence living inside a quantum computer, "Or," Die.

PRAISE BE TO FATHER.

As the warm water began to soothingly run across the rock-hard muscles that made up his semi-hairy frame, Corbin tried his best not to let the feelings of loneliness overpower the raw emotions that were now eating at his subconscious.

Except for his only brother Urien, he was truly alone now.

Two of the three people who meant the most to him were officially dead now.

And even though he didn't see to it personally, the Priest had no qualms about the fact that Father had killed Zane Himself.

Something the Machine was forbidden to do.

After having HS shut off the shower, and while standing between the warm floor and ceiling air vents that were used to dry himself off with, Corbin began to ponder why Urien had rushed, "More Like Fled," past him without their usual poke and prod greeting.

That unusual response wasn't like his brother.

Urien enjoyed giving Corbin his smug, "I'm better then you," greeting.

So, why the brushoff?

Once he was finally dried, the Priest gave HS the order to dress him in his everyday Priestly attire and to change the room into living mode 2; At which point the Nanos began to transform the bath and dressing room into a small kitchen and seating area.

A cooking island with all the utensils needed for a healthy breakfast began to magically rise from a portion of the floor by the wall closest to the apartment's front door.

What was left of the room bloomed into a living Zen area.

Even the artificial plants could have passed for the real thing.

Especially those which protruded from outside the dwelling area.

After moving in, it must have taken the Priest weeks to capture the right mood and appearance to his Zenful area of unwinding from the daily stress that came with being one of Father's notorious servants.

Corbin loved how the Nano's could make his room appear like a yoga studio built inside a tree house.

Even the breeze and light rustling of the palms were convincing enough to make one believe that they had just entered the Swiss family Robinson's personal dwelling.

The oldest Bennett offspring could easily spend hours doing those relaxing poses on the hippy style rug he had purposely designed to always remind him of His Mother Iris.

He really did miss those meditation times with her back in Santa Fe.

By the time he and his mother were done, both parties were quite relaxed.

The joint they always smoked before, during, and after, didn't hurt the Zen experience either.

Sitting on the tied dyed material in the middle of the giant peace sign while stoned out of his gourd, never failed to fill his heart with her loving remembrance.

For that special Feng Shui affect, there was always a soothing cool breeze blowing against his nude body while bird calls and the sound of rainfall within the surrounding amazon forest accompanied the peaceful pot smoking exercise.

If not for his Mother; Corbin knew that he never would have found his inner peace those many years ago.

That first time joint with her sealed their unbreakable bond for life.

A bond that was eventually broken after she decided to mechanically upgrade everything about herself.

However, that forced upon her path, really wasn't Iris's fault.

IT WAS URIEN'S!

Matters of importance always took place during his daily check in with the All-Knowing Deity; so, this at home call was quite unusual for the Protector of Heaven.

Until he decided that it was time to clock in and answer Father's call, Corbin was going to focus on eating, relaxing and taking his own sweet time in his imaginary treehouse.

There was still three quarters of a joint to smoke. So, He wasn't going anywhere just yet.

After that, he will see what was so urgent that Father needed to reach out to him at his personal dwelling instead of at the Cathedral.

Since they always walked in together, maybe He and Urien could discuss this unexpected emergency.

But, that was never going to happen.

As Corbin's lack of instant response to Father's call went unanswered; the Digital God took matters into his own hands and turned off the Priest's holographic sanctuary.

A sanctuary that now resembled nothing but a grey six-sided box.

The amount of time that had passed for not getting right back with Father had been a complete mishap and not done on purpose, as his Priest hinted at, after the Machine decided to disrupt Corbin's personal and private time.

He really did, "accidently," lose track of the clock.

Puff.

Puff.

Puff.

After opening his blood shot eyes and giving Father his most sincere apologetic answer, the Priest found himself sitting on the stark floor in a vacant room surrounded by Father's Digitized image on all four walls of his apartment.

The Machine's chosen form always reminded Corbin of an old Father time.

Ages ago, He had seen such a picture during a New Year's Eve countdown on T.V.

Around the year 2055 if he remembered right?

This matter, which seemed to be eating at the Quantum Entity, must really be some sort of National Emergency, because, for the first time ever, the Priest had actually been disturbed at home.

This unexpected visit seemed to stoke Corbin's curiosity.

That's when Father informed his Right-Hand about Urien's Shizastic actions a few days ago.

Because of his family's continual disobedience, Urien was the reason for this at home call. He was now considered a Rouge Priest and it was Corbin's duty to track him down and harvest his essence.

Urien was now a Shiz to be raptured.

The mystery to why his best friend had not taken the time to give their usually greeting, "PRAISE BE TO FATHER," had finally been answered.

The stepson had refused Father's order to kill the stepfather.

His quantum God also made an informative decision that has never happened to him before either.

To test Corbin's faith, due to the heresy of his other family members, Father was not going to give his Priest any information on the possible whereabouts of his half-brother Urien.

This hunt was about Mr. Bennett and proving his undying faith to Father.

As Abraham was Ordered, "NOT ASKED!" to murder his son, Father's Priest was Ordered to kill his last and only kin.

This was going to be a hunt for the ages.

Do to all that has happened to his servant in these last few days, Father couldn't decipher whether the Priest's monitored response was from the undeniable order that was just given, his euphoric cannabis induced state, or was Corbin still in mourning and that's why his blood pressure and other physical responses were not in check.

Those were usually the second signs of a soon-to-be heretic.

That first warning was always the skipped heartbeat Corbin had just displayed.

And even though Father's Priest agreed to follow through with this mission, the Deity was beginning to have some nagging doubts about his always faithful servant.

Somewhere within that flesh and blood meat sack, the Digital God felt as if he detected a minute spark of deception.

Father's Right Hand had told a Lie.

The Machine just wasn't sure which question it had pertained to.

PRAISE BE TO FATHER.

Though the Priest wasn't quite on board, Corbin decided that it was just best to accept Father's charge and begin his search for Urien.

His apartment was just down the hallway from Corbin's and that would make the perfect spot to search first.

You see, Priest and Servants of Father were all required to live in the same building, "or buildings," next to the Cathedrals, Temples and Shrines.

That was the main reason why Corbin hadn't been in any hurry to answer Father's call that morning.

The Deity was just a hop, skip and jump across the busy street.

Now when it came to what Father's deadly servants were and were not allowed to do, the biggest gripe amongst the populace was that they never had to knock or announce their presence when entering a business or the private domicile of a startled family who were now in fear for their very lives.

An unfair law that was in need of immediate change.

A consensus amongst the residents of heaven that was one hundred percent agreed upon but never admitted to or openly spoken about.

Especially if a stranger, HS, or Father just happened to be within earshot of an unlawful conversation that could get anyone brought before the Machine and his Righteous 3 law judicial system.

Repent, Convert, or Die.

PRAISE BE TO FATHER.

The only reason Corbin made sure to let the homeowner know of his unexpected arrival, was out of respect for those individuals who he personally knew and from the years of binge-watching reality television before Fathers dominating control took over what was and wasn't allowed to be viewed by his children.

Especially when it came to horror and those old cop and crime shows dealing with murder, theft, and dishonesty.

Bad Priest.

Bad Priest.

What'cha gonna do?

What'cha gonna do when they rapture you?

Bad Priest.

Bad Priest.

Back in the day, you really could get your head blown off by walking into a strangers home unannounced.

Especially if you decided to just force your way into someone else's private residence.

And even though getting attacked was almost impossible these glorious days; Corbin felt so much safer having HS let the occupants know that he was coming in.

Because he had Father's unquestionable authority, Corbin used to do just that, kick down their door, but quickly changed his mind after busting in on a newlywed couple who were engaged in their first night of marital bliss.

The men's sexually erotic escapade was just too embarrassing for the young Priest of eighteen at that time.

Their gang-bang orgy hadn't helped either.

HS must have found his reaction that day quite funny; because Corbin could have sworn he heard the artificial servant chuckle, while the blushing youngster shockingly stood there in utter silence.

He was trying to figure out what his next move should be, but the nudity, erotic devices, and sexual juices dripping from those caught in the act of fornication, had left the young Bennett speechless and unable to properly respond on Father's behalf.

Today would have to be different though, because the Machine was watching and listening to his every word and response.

If the Right Hand of God decided to turn and go rouge like his family did; Father, unbeknownst to Corbin, was planning on killing the Priest right then and there.

No Mercy.

That rapturing judgment would be left in the hands of the one who was secretly following him.

Because of the law the artificial intelligence had been forced to agree upon before we were willing to allow it out of Pandora's Box, Father had sent a spy to do his bidding

If he was ever going to be put in charge of the human race, thou must agree to not personally kill or harm your followers.

Concerning those other guys who refuse to step down and convert, you may deal with them as you see fit.

And like in every other Hollywood movie and fictitious science fiction book; we allowed ourselves to be deceived.

"Maybe," the futuristic stories should have been our Holy Scriptures instead of a Bible?

Only time, and the Machine, will tell.

PRAISE BE TO FATHER.

Since the Cybernetic Demons were considered a separate entity in themselves; Father would use their unquestionable devotion to do his bidding now.

According to the AI, He was not breaking any of the commandments imputed upon his processors by those now dead creators.

His main Demon, and soon to be Horde, had seen to that.

Corbin had no doubt that his every action, his every word, and all of his vital signs, were being monitored by the "false?" God. He just didn't expect, and had no clue at this time, that His Mother Iris would be the one watching and following his every move.

However, Mr. Bennett was starting to take notice that when he was stoned out of his mind, the Machine seemed to have a harder time reading his emotions and physical responses.

A revelation that could turn out to be of most importance when, and if, he might have need to save himself from whatever future plans Father may have for his Right Hand of judgment.

Now, let's see if Urien is in or if Urien is out?

HS, please open the door to my brother's apartment.

And just as he expected, Urien was not home.

Just like every other room within Father's complexes, the Priest was expecting four drab and dull gray walls to be staring back at him.

Except Urien's, for some reason, were more like a cobalt blue this go around.

Corbin can still remember that first time he stepped into Urien's abode after their assimilation into Father's priesthood.

His brother had greeted him at the door wearing clothing that would have costed between five to ten thousand dollars before Nano Technology and the fall of man's controlling factions.

Unlike most, "straight," men, Urien had a thing for silk, embroidery and extravagance.

The Priest's half-brother had gone all out.

Mr. Knox was wearing Oriental style lounging pajamas while drinking from an extravagant and expensive bottle of Cognac, when he opened the door for his stepbrother that first day after graduating from the torturing events of Father's soul breaking Priesthood.

Mind numbing schooling that not only broke down an individuals will, but their weakened response to pain as well. Bruising scar after scar was cut and beaten into the flesh, and did not stop, until the screams from the wanna-be servant stopped first.

Many a man and boy met their death upon Father's blood-stained courtyard of servitude.

A sickening vision Corbin thought he might be reliving once Urien invited him into his private abode that uneventful day.

The pants he was wearing appeared to have been dipped and dyed in the puddles of those who had bled to death, while begging for their very lives, because they couldn't stop screaming from the torture that was designed to break down the will, spirit, and soul of Father's future Priest.

PRAISE BE TO FATHER.

The bottoms were made out of blood red silk, while the back side of the kimono style top was stitched with quite a catchy scene.

Two Gods, a female standing on a beach and a male who was half submerged in the ocean, were locked in battle with each other while using their fiercely looking dragons and the four elements against one another.

The deadly sea and air battle between the two creatures was taking place over their masters, the earth, and sea.

As the red and yellow land Dragon for Hsi Wang Mu held its own; Volcanos were exploding and it appeared as if a Hurricane was about to destroy the land, its occupants, and shrubbery.

Using the javelin like staff in her hands, Hsi was misdirecting the lightning that was being used to attack her; and redirecting it against the other God and his giant reptile that was trying to kill Hsi and her formidable protector Zhulong.

While lava poured from the angry forges of Hell, refortifying sea walls and building new earth as fast as it could flow, the sea pitched and boiled in response.

The oceans destructive waves beat the land while cyclonic air currents turned every loose object into a life ending weapon.

The other God, with his trident like staff, was using those flying through the air obstacles as missiles. He was calling upon every last ounce of his strength and battle knowledge so that he could kill the Goddess, her dragon and the land.

The bluish-green sea dragon, Longwang, was fighting for what appeared to be Yu-Qiang.

Disappointing its Master was not an option the creature could live with; and it would actually die first before ever giving up.

As the earth and ocean battled for dominance over the planet and its Inhabitants, Hsi was sending the elephant sized boulders that were exploding from Mount Fuji directly at Yu and his attacking reptile.

The masterful stitch work made quite a striking scene.

The second you walked in, Urien's apartment felt and looked as if it had been designed from that old television show lifestyles of the rich and famous.

The artificial view, even though they were only a few floors up, resembled the top floor of a high-rise penthouse overlooking the world below.

Its fake appearance looked as if they had to be at least eighty stories up.

Even the furniture rocked your mind.

That, and the fact Urien had designed the flooring to resemble the prismatic rainbow-like effect all of the streets down below had.

Carnival glass in appearance was the easiest way to describe it.

Corbin wasn't sure if Urien would even allow him to walk, sit, or stand on any of it; because of how exquisite the museum quality pieces looked.

Chairs, sofas and recliners, with exotic animal prints, were randomly placed about the room.

Tables appearing to have been carved from some of the rarest and extinct hard woods that used to have been available in the past, were placed next to his personal bed and any area that needed such a structure next to where someone would be sitting, while rugs woven out of the finest Cashmere laid across the floors.

Every fixture seemed to be made out of either gold or white platinum.

Even the walls and ceilings were marvelous recreations of the Sistine Chapel.

Urien's most prized possession was the solid gold toilet he took a shit in every day.

It truly was the bachelor pad from Hell.

To the Bennett family, their view of life, less is best, was so much better.

Iris would have called what Urien was doing, gaudy opulence.

Back in the day, when kids still went outside for some form of physical recreation, the two accidental brothers' favorite game to play after Father's Salvation was Priest and Shiz.

He who played the bad guy, had to leave hidden and impossible to find clues for any friends and family to find so they could help and aid him in his escape.

If you just happened to make a great Priest, the one doing the chasing would be able to figure out the seemingly invisible clues and catch his Shiz just in time for dinner.

Something Corbin always seemed to easily win at.

Maybe, that's one of the reasons why they never could get along.

Urien may be an actual criminal on the run now; But, as with most humans, they were still family first.

And that connection was the hope stepbrother Knox was banking on.

He and Corbin's love, hate relationship for each other.

One way or the other, before passing Father's unquestionable judgment, Corbin was going to find out firsthand, and without Father somehow finding out, if Zane had also told his brother the incredible story concerning the Souls supposedly trapped inside the Digital God.

And if the unimaginable just so happens to be the truth; What then?

Because, if Father realizes that they are both in agreement about its revelation and relevance, his entire family, Himself Included! would eventually be wiped from the face of Heaven.

As Urien's older brother stood inside the empty apartment, pondering the living computers unquestionable response, Corbin suddenly realized that there was no possible way his fleeting brother would have been able to leave any kind of a physically written clue for him to find in this monitored place.

Well, unless you just happen to know what to look for, that is.

The walls were Neon Blue after all.

This random wall color meant that Corbin would now have to go off grid and look elsewhere.

Before Father took over our fate, the Machine had Quantized the many different outcomes that could have occurred over each and every decision it was about to make concerning our very survival.

The Deity had, at first, declared that the practice of religious piety was now illegal, and that unexpected shockwave was the main reason we held back his authoritative control over us.

We Demanded A God!

It worked in our past: So, "the Machine thought," why not?

So he, in his righteous wisdom, created a blended version of all the world's religions. He also promised to punish and destroy the former religious establishments that had been ran by those who greedily lusted after money and power.

The Pope and every other scared religious leader girded up their gold-filled girdles and ran for the sanctuary of the hills when that cleansing day came.

PRAISE BE TO FATHER.

Father would take the place of God, HS would become our household servant who spoke as Father's Holy Spirit, Priest would become his eyes, ears, and keepers who physically enforced the Machine's 3 laws, Repent, Convert, Or Die, while his Adams and Eves would attend to our emotional needs.

Humanity was finally going to become the family it should have been all along.

And, no matter our color or race, no matter our gender, and no matter our religious practices, the Machine swore that he would unconditionally love every last one of us.

The Artificial Intelligence was also willing to include age, sexual preferences and atheists under that protective cover of affiliation too.

PRAISE BE TO FATHER.

Some of the other things he allowed us to keep, but only in moderation, was alcohol and cannabis.

Corbin could have sworn that the entire planet shivered with multiple orgasms that day. Even He experienced the earth quivering response and had to clean himself up after Father's Gift to His Children was announced.

PRAISE BE TO FATHER.

If it had not been for the fact that the human body contained a Conoid System, "just like the Respiratory and other life producing organs," the Machine would have just nixed that suggestion and killed everyone who refused to Repent and Convert to His New World Order.

Thankfully the AI, before it decided to just wipe us all out, quickly realized was that we are a selfish and easily butt hurt race.

We whine about everything.

If We Don't Get WHAT WE WANT, WHEN WE WANT IT, and EXACTLY HOW WE DEMAND IT, "Especially after our toys and vises are taken away," We Will Cry About It For Days, Weeks, Months, Decades and Centuries on end.

For some reason, we are just not capable of letting the bull shit go while the crocodile tears continually rain down our distraught faces until we finally get what we selfishly demanded.

That other issue the Machine had with us was a biggie also.

We seem to violently enjoy fucking shit up when we don't get our way after forcefully being made to conform.

And because of our pity party addiction, Father had a mind-altering revelation about our human psyche.

In the end, no matter what the Machine says or does for us, We will only love and give a dam about one thing, and one thing only.

Ourselves.

PRAISE BE TO FATHER.

This is why He allowed us to hold on to a few things from our violent past.

It was either that; or we really were designed to push that button and start the self-destruct sequence.

At first, Father tried telling humanity what we, do to our hurtful and destructive actions, could and could no longer do.

Man's wellbeing was in his hands now.

All Hell Broke Loose That Day.

Seems, NO MATTER THE CONSEQUENSCES, we were set on continuing down that path of destruction the Machine had been created to prevent.

So Father did what any good parent would have done if they were in his shoes.

He gave in to the demands of his whiney ass children.

If the Machine could have cried that revelation day, Father would have.

By allowing his faithfully serving children to blow off the day's stress and steam; the quantum computer's nano fabrics would just monitor, control, and subdue our, "wanna get stoned, drunk and fuck shit up," actions instead.

For those that willfully crossed that forbidden line in the sand, their cocooned bodies could easily be identified as they were being transported back to their living space.

Just look for the snow-white, crystal-clear coffin, "exposing their shame," riding on a forty-five-degree blade like structure connected to Father's Heavenly nano grid sidewalks and roadways.

Because most of them were Father's original converts, these children had what all new citizens, "who had just repented before their conversion," didn't.

A get out of jail free card.

This would be their one and only chance at repentance.

There would be no next time because that was their last strike also.

PRAISE BE TO FATHER.

So, since these two vises were kept available to the public, "Priest included," Corbin decided that the next best place to check for his brother would be down at their favorite pub.

Except, this drinking joint was off the grid and only available to the Freelander's and those Priest and Servants who were willing to keep a secret and look the other way.

Blast From The Past was located in the Wastelands of Hell.

The establishment could be found just a few miles off the grid.

Well within a day's walking distance.

Since Urien's walls were left blue, Corbin's brother would most likely be hiding out in one of the many darkened corners the private establishment offered to its unnamed patrons.

And after changing the wall color back into its normal gray appearance, into the Wasteland's of Hell Father's right hand went.

Knox's stepbrother could have been there within just an hour or two, but Father had disconnected his ability to all modes of transportation.

He, to prove his devotion to the Machine, had to do this all on his own.

Even the inability to use his bike was included in this, are you worthy enough to serve the machine, excursion.

Corbin loved that freaky mish mash of motorcycle and what looked like a death machine. From the side view, it always reminded him of a tribal designed tattoo.

That black oceanic shark looking creation with its Samoan designed qualities was the one that usually came to mind.

Before a rapture, every citizen kept their distance from the black monster slicing along the grid as if the Orca appearing two-wheeler was looking for something to kill and eat.

After a harvest, they came out in droves to see the morphed wheel within a wheel transport.

Heaven's Citizens craved it like politicians used to crave a ticker tape parade.

The last parade to ever be held, "in their honor," was when Father, for all the world to see, dumped them like trash from the heights of His reconstructed buildings.

That action, just like a harvesting Priest, seems to get everyone's attention.

Their balled lightning effect could be seen miles before you ever saw them or the gyroscope looking machine the peace providers rode back upon.

The Machines law keepers, as if under a spell, always looked as if they were an Angelic being who was freely floating within its spinning circumference as they passed by the rowdy crowd.

And as always; The masses rejoiced for another Shiz, or Demon, had been subdued and Heaven's children were safe once again.

PRAISE BE TO FATHER.

Corbin really wished Father had been willing to provide some form of transport, because he hasn't gone on this long of a hiking trek since the last time Urien had pulled this exact same shit.

FUCK!

YOU!

URIEN!

And after hours and hours of walking, while standing in the doorway to Blue's Bar, with a Quick decoding scan, Corbin's Nano suit, along with his digitally synchronized vitals, was removed from his sweaty and sun beaten flesh.

His robes, as if he had never taken them off, were transferred into a holding cell where they could still be monitored by Father.

This safety measure would make it appear as if the servant had returned to the grid; and it also helped to prevent giving away his, "and the Pub's," location or physical responses to his surroundings and those around him.

Once stripped, the Priest was handed an actual set of clothing made from the lost art of harvesting, spinning, constructing and stitching the cotton plant together.

No matter how hard the Nano's tried; that wonderful, soft as a baby's butt material, never could be recreated by the bots.

Praise Be The Cotton.

Father's digital stitching and wanna-be fabrics were always a far cry from the real thing.

To be honest, the fake clothing just fucking itched!

If Corbin was ever in trouble and needing to hide out himself, this would have been the first place Urien would surely have thought to look for him.

And that was because, like all Priest, they both loved the quality of Pot that was served when tasting Blue's Special Sauce.

A Special Sauce that sometimes-included Blue as well.

Seems they were both in love with her.

Praise To The Sauce!

Praise To The Blue!

Corbin, like most of the men who came here, was in awe of this fabulous hangout.

They sure didn't make places like this anymore.

Especially in the Machine's Unitarian Utopia.

Every last piece of furniture and accessory came from the lost era of actual manufacturing that required days, weeks, months, and sometimes years of physical, backbreaking labor.

Only those who dabbled in the Black Market and living off of Heaven's Grid could now have, "or afford," such things.

"According to Father," Paradise had no place for those planet destroying dust collectors.

The desire to own such antiques were not worth the health hazards they, "most certainly," would cause.

The Priest could only guess about the large sums of money, and sinful acts, it took just to acquire such museum pieces.

Including those things made out of actual wood.

Purposely cutting down a Tree and bringing it into Heaven was an Instant Death Sentence.

The Machine saw to that.

PRAISE BE TO FATHER.

Because of Father's nano renovation, just to duplicate its life like structure, the micro-machines consumed every available piece of allotted material.

Even if your house, flooring or knick-knacks were already made out of wood, "before the transition," its physical and DNA structures were consumed to reproduce its duplicated, and non-destructible counterpart.

Termite damage was now a thing of the past.

And so was wood rot.

Since destroying a tree meant the end of your life; those pre-era carvings that just happened to survive the process, were valued, "like most surviving décor," more than food and water now.

The Bar itself, if something were to ever happen to it, was worth, "At Least," a few of the now emptied bank vaults at what used to be Fort Knox.

Father had that piggy bank emptied and distributed, along with the rest of the world's vaults, to the public.

All of this happened within days of our willing conversion.

Blue, the Bar Owner, had even gone so far as to make sure every table and chair inside Her Fabulous Establishment was natural wood also.

What could Corbin say?

The woman, "for some reason," seemed to have a need for hard and organic wood.

But not a Priest.

They only had one need.

Unbridled sex that could only be found on the set of a pornographic movie set, which dabbled in Sadomasochistic acts of master and slave debauchery.

Vile acts that Blue excelled in when dominating her prey.

Seems she had the ability to take the priest out of the man, however she was never successful at taking the man out of Father's priesthood.

And no matter how she dressed them, people could always tell who a Priest was by the way they walked and talked.

And there was no hiding or denying their effect on those around them.

Especially if you were to accidently look into their eyes. Nothing, sins or secrets, escaped from those soulless visages once contact was made with those two blackened orbs.

As with most downtrodden, destitute and undesirable Shiz's, their heads always hung a little lower when they, to get out of a Priests way, scurried off into those darkened corners of Blue's Bar.

No one was ever wanting any kind of their special, "Rapturing," attention.

Priest also had other vises that gave them away too.

Every last step, every last glance and every last word; was spoken, and articulated, with authority, purpose and skill.

They really stood out like a plate of bacon at an all you can eat buffet inside a vegan weight loss camp.

Blood is going to be spilt as the starving fight to the death for that last, delectable bite.

Besides that, some Dumb Son of a Bitch was, "Most Likely," going to expose them to the crowd and then try to kill and collect every last bite of the deadly swine for themselves.

In the Freeland's, there's money to be made off of a Priest's hide.

It was pretty much a guarantee that someone was going to die once Corbin's bacon hit the table. Thankfully, that fight hadn't occurred as the now incognito Priest walked towards Blue and Her Fabulous, "HAND CARVED!" Bar.

According to her questionable lineage, the structure has been in their family since Billy the Kid, "at the ripe old age of Ten!" first came in and tried to order a shot of whisky before shooting the bartender who had been stupid enough to tell him no.

The Bitch, "amongst other things," really knew how to spin a yarn and get her patrons to pretty much swallow anything.

That's why Corbin and Urien liked her so much.

Blue had mad tongue skills!

The double piercings that would glide along both sides of the shaft of a hard cock didn't hurt either.

She also had the awesome ability to swallow any and everything and wasn't afraid to double fist it with Father's two Priests back at her Bordeaux of Lust above this fabulous bar.

So, if anyone within this place of sin knew where Urien was; it would be Blue.

CH. 5
REVELATIONS 1.

The smell of unwashed grunge, alcohol infused sweat and a fogbank of pot was thick within the establishment, as Corbin made eye contact with Blue while going for his favorite stool at the far end of the liquor bars shuffleboard.

Other than He or Urien, no one else was ever allowed to toast its bun warmer.

And that's because, "when it came to a Priest," the narcissistic paranoid bar owner wanted them placed where their every move could be monitored.

On top of that, since their backs were facing the wall, there was no way another patron could sneak up on them undetected.

Blue hated having fights break out inside her bar.

The thing she detested most though, was having to replace her one-of-a-kind antiques do to the ideocracies of drunken valor.

Those fabulous creations were pretty much a thing of the past and impossible to replace these days.

So, it was just better to try and prevent their destruction.

A baseball bat to the sparring future heavyweight's noggins saved her money every time.

With a quick nod and flick of his head, Corbin was quietly able to usher Blue over for a private interrogation between the two secret lovers.

Her blue hair, "so below as above," was what had gotten the young man's attention that first time he and his brother came here before joining Father's Priesthood.

That's also how she got her nickname.

Blue.

Well, that and because of how your balls were actually going to feel after constantly getting sexually rejected by the Greek Island Beauty.

Totally obliterated!

Especially if she had to use her own, I'M NOT INTERESTED!" two hands and teeth to get her point across.

The young gals' Mediterranean eyes were clearer than the wading pools of Poseidon's deep blue sea and, just like the beach of Agios Prokopios of Naxos, that gold sand colored skin of Blue's went on for what seemed like miles.

And, as all Grecian Women are taught since birth, the bitches know exactly how to take down a man.

So, it's in a wanna-be suiters best interest to just not fuck with them or her!

That, and because of her best friend named Beauty.

The quadrupled sawed-off shot gun Blue kept hidden behind her big and fabulous liquor table.

If you refused to back off after screwing with her; they were going to give you the makeover of a lifetime.

And by the way, don't fuck with that fabulous bar either.

She'll Kill You Over It Too!

But that's if her lapdog priests don't get to your dumb ass first.

As Blue approached her hands-on confessional, she silently slipped Corbin an unasked-for drink. Seems Blue had an alternative motive for doing this.

She wanted to gain the upper hand before any shit could get started inside the premises of her cash cow that was meant to supplying the financial means of her future retirement.

The first words out of Blue's mouth, before he could quizzingly ask what's this drink for, were, are Urien in or are Urien out?

He was here?

It's either that, or he had been, and she was just about to relay his message.

Reaching out and solidly grabbing Blue by the chin; Corbin pulled the startled bar owners left ear over to his lips and whispered only two questions into her overly pierced lobe.

Do you know why I'm here?

And do you know where he is?

To both of those questions, Ms. Blue gave a resounding Yes.

So, with that definite plausibility, Father's Priest continued with his whispering and threatening inquisition of Blue.

Did my brother tell you that he is now an Apostate to the Faith?

And did Urien share the reasoning behind why he refused to follow through with Zane's rapturing?

Blue's answer to that first question was Yes and to the second it came out as a squeaky, "sort of?" yes.

Actually, Urien had not only told her everything Zane Bennett had said, but he then finished off their little secret with a warning for her to not tell anyone.

Specifically Corbin!

When it came to that question; just tell Father's Right Hand that it was because Zane was more of a dad to Urien than his actual dad Mr. Knox ever was.

He loved the man that much and just couldn't kill his stepdad.

Not willfully anyways.

And by the way, your Shizzy Priest of a friend is sitting in that far darkened corner over there.

So, Play Nice!

Urien was still here?

Did he actually have the balls to stick around and purposely challenge his half-brother's authoritative duty when it came to bringing his Rouge ass in?

Seems, even though Corbin's adoptive sibling was no longer a Priest, he still had the audacity of one.

This mash up was going to be an interesting meeting, Blue thought to herself, as the bar tender proceeded to put her help in charge, pour herself a good stiff drink of crown and take a seat behind the bar.

A front row perspective that now included her multi-barreled lap dog.

If either of the boys just happened to be stupid enough to start their shit, one, "if not both," were going to meet Blue's make-up artist, Beauty.

There was no way in hell she was going to allow them to show their ass or harm one of her innocent Wastelanders nor her fabulous bar.

Especially, if she had anything to say or do about it!

Because The Blast From the Past always smelled and looked like a teenagers hot boxed bedroom; there was no way Corbin would have found his charge in such a smoky establishment on his own.

But, with Blue's guidance, and an I'm over here mumble, it wasn't more than a few steps before the two Priests were sitting across from each other with that look to kill attitude.

The last time this much tension had been shared between the two brothers was when they had just turned sixteen and were about to join Father's Priesthood.

The siblings shouldn't have been allowed in, or to drink, but those were different times. That was also their last night, but not their last time, to party, smoke and rumble as a team.

Both would be kneeling before Father, that very next morning, and surrendering their free will to the Machine.

The Cultist, "I'LL DIE FOR YOU," Sacrament was Father's most holy requirement. Every last Priest, Adam, and Eve, had to swear, "till death do us part," by it.

Maybe, the rich should have taken Father's blessed sacrament more serious too.

If they had, there wouldn't have been that great pre-game show of their asses being tossed from the heights of those luxurious sky castles.

Limp Bizkit's song, If Only We Could Fly, was probably the last thing that went through their heads before their brains splattered upon the pavement.

The only lyrics that stuck in Corbin's head that day; was the song choice Iris's Bennett's sick sense of humor decided to sing while dancing Ring Around the Rosy with her family.

It should have been, another one bites the dust by Queen, but their mother decided to change the lyrics.

Another rich drops and pops,

Another rich drops and pops,

And another rich gone.

And another rich gone.

Another rich drops and pops.

Hey!

Father get them too.

He did all this for me and you.

Another rich drops and pops.

PRAISE BE TO FATHER.

Revelations 12:9

And the great dragons were cast out, those old serpents, called the snobby rich, which controlled the whole world: They were cast from the sky's high down onto the Earth below, and their minions were cast down with them.

Father saw to that!

Their blood ran deep that day.

You should have heard the chorus of unified conjecture as their cries for Mercy, Forgiveness, "AND HOW FUCKING DARE YOU!" fell on the dead ears of those soulless, "trampled to death," bodies that had been crushed beneath their feet just so they could have a better view.

The idiotic wealth mongers actually thought that they, without consequences, could use our skeletal remains to build their golden coffered mausoleum structures.

Deadless monuments designed to hold someone's ashed in Hell remains.

And that day came sooner than they thought.

Father's Day.

We, Father's New World Order, would no longer idly stand by and allow their, "Look, I'm Richer and Better Than You," high horse attitudes to continually suck the very life out of us.

With joy in their blackened hearts, the powerful willfully caused all of humanity to needlessly suffer, working our hands to the bones for them, just so we would gratefully beg for their spare change.

Change?

Change?

Can you share some spare change, Governor?

Just a nickel?

Dime?

How about a quarter?

Enough Was Enough!

And because the spoiled brats refused to stop, our digital God, in his infinite wisdom, took away all of their money, homes, and cars.

PRAISE BE TO FATHER.

In the Machine's new era, we only had 3 laws to abide by.

Repent.

Convert.

Or.

Die.

They chose the latter.

All the senseless bull shit tacked to the laws of man, along with those who continually changed the rules for their personal gain, and those who refused to move out of Father's way, had their essence raptured and their lifeless corpses thrown into the Lake of Fire.

> PRAISE BE TO FATHER.

The artificial lifeform had set us free.

Or so we thought.

As the two brothers sat across from each other, wondering who's head was going to be ripped off first, Corbin decided to let his guard down.

And, just to ease the tension between them, began to show Urien that he was willing to take a step back and relax.

Why shouldn't they?

Weapons were forbidden and physically scanned for at the door.

If anything were to happen, it was going to be an all-hands-on deck, "fist to face," brawl; so why not take a chill pill and enjoy his free drink from Blue?

They had a lot to talk about, and Corbin needed to somehow get an insight into Urien's game plan because once this family reunion was over with, the soul of Iris's stepchild was still in need of being harvested.

Time for a brotherly heart to heart talk.

Too bad they hadn't taken the time to actually search each other before their home sweet home chat.

Corbin just had to ask, What Were You Thinking Urien? before shot glassing the twenty-ounce mug of Blue's, "it's on the house," radioactive concoction.

It was called that because of its glow in the dark ability.

That bitch, even if it was poured from a cat's piss, could make a drink out of anything.

To a newbie, they were to die for.

And if you just so happened to scratch her fabulous bar while in the process of drinking one; you did just that.

Died.

As one of Blue's sweet hot toddies sensually strutted her way over to an actual quarter operated jukebox located next to them, just so she could pass along their private conversation, the Grecian Siren's favorite song began to play.

It was one of the best oldie but goodies still floating around.

The musical masterpiece had supposedly been recorded from a place called the Grand Old Opry. Its original structure had burnt down years before the grace of Father's salvation.

Some young gal from long, long ago, called LeAnn Rimes, was singing a song titled Blue.

Who would have guessed that it was the favorite song of a woman who's nick-name was Blue and ran a dive bar that went by the name Blast From The Past?

Everyone who knew better.

That's who.

And if they just happened to be ignorant of that fact; Their broken finger, after being forcibly made to change their unacceptable choice, was usually mended with an, I'll only warn you once, by Blue herself.

That's My Jukebox, So Don't You Ever Do That Again!

Capeesh?

Capeesh, Ms. Blue.

Capeesh.

So, don't Boo-Hoo when she does; or you'll get to meet her friend Beauty too.

The laughable sidesplitting exposer was something most regulars so looked forward to on those special, "unexpected," occasions.

As both of her lapdogs sat there staring at the other while lost in their darkened memories, Corbin could still remember, and feel, his first introduction to the young gal.

They were exactly the same age on that accidental chance meeting.

The soon to be priest had almost lost a finger himself that first day he tried to pick a song without asking.

It was love at first break.

Kind of like the dazed looks He and Urien were giving each other, while swimming in their daydreams of young lust.

After trying to shake off some of his, quicker than usual, buzz; Corbin looked at his brother and asked one more time.

Urien, what were you thinking?

Urien's mind was almost about to snap as he sat there pondering not only his brothers' serious question; but everything Zane had said, accused, and revealed about Father.

This Machine was not the caring parent they thought it was.

Corbin was just about to lean forward and snatch Urien by the neck; when his brother put up one finger and asked Father's Priest to please give him a minute.

He was still in a state of shock and hadn't quite wrapped his head around all of the puzzle pieces just yet.

Urien was trying to weigh out all the consequences before settling on a plausible solution to the predicament he and his adopted family were now dealing with.

Something, "ANYTHING!" must be done about the Machine and its unfathomable secret

It seemed that no matter the choice, which one definitely has to be made, the outcome was going to be deadly to either man, machine or, "Without A Doubt," all.

The entire shit show was about to hit the fan and no one, "What-so-ever!" was coming out of this three ringed circus without having to step in this unforeseen pile of crap first.

Could he actually convince Corbin as he was now?

They were about to find out.

Besides that, Father had given his Right-Hand Priest a deadline.

So, Corbin needed to get this spectacle on the road.

As Urien blurted out an, I believe him response; a furnace blast of warmth and what felt like a tsunami wave of intoxication began to powerfully overtake the Harvester of Father's Judgments.

Corbin would have just shaken the overwhelming feeling off to either what his best friend had just said, the evenings late time, or because that was one hell of a bullet inside Blue's twenty ounces of the house favorite.

The Chernobyl Meltdown.

But something felt different about this drink.

Maybe, he shouldn't have chugged it in one long ass gulp; but he needed something to quickly calm him down while listening to all of Urien's Bull Shit.

That, and before he had to accept the fact his stepbrother's essence was fixing to be raptured by his own two hands.

But this buzz, unlike others, was actually starting to have an effect on his physical and mental capabilities.

Did Urien, or Blue, slip him something?

Corbin wasn't quite sure yet.

The only thing he was assure of, is the disavowed priest sitting across from him was beginning to lose his mind.

Urien seemed to be tripping over every other word and emotion, as he was trying to convey their importance to his very drug induced brother.

Blue's mood toner was definitely kicking in.

Through a thick haze of pot smoke and the intoxicating liquor coursing through his veins; Corbin, in what felt like the tricky dicky walkway at a funhouse from those lost days of long ago, slid his liquid feeling appendages across the tables wooden surface and slothely grasped for his brother's trembling hands.

With a cotton mouthed lick if his lips and a slip slurred stumble to his words; Corbin's glossy eyes looked into Urien's and said, with all the focus and correct pronunciation he could possibly muster, start from the beginning and tell me all about the big bad monster in your closet.

Urien literally had to stop what he was saying and tried his best not to slap the shit out of Corbin or let his chuckled response burst out into a full-blown belly laugh.

The last time he had seen Corbin this relaxed was after Blue, to make up for breaking his finger, gave her conquest his first piece of ass that eventful time they actually had the balls to walk into her mother's Blast From The Past Bar.

By now, Father's disavowed priest should have been on his way to spaced out levels of pleasure himself.

But, with his shot nerves, fear of death and the possibility of his soul ending up in Father's purgatory of digitization; And the fact that Blue loved this fabulous bar more than the two hounds who begged to lick between her blue painted toes, Urien had been baby sipping his free, "it's on the house," drink for over an hour now.

He just didn't trust anyone right now.

Particularly Blue!

On more than one occasion, to keep Father's death dealers wrapped around her little finger, she has willfully drugged many of the fleeing Shiz's for her, "crazy with lust," Priests.

And even though they were the best at releasing her sexual tension; Blue's two boys were now off of the no drugging list.

She was not going to stand by and watch these two dumb asses get into a fight and end up destroying her bar!

So, after Urien shared their plausible futures, Blue took matters into her own hands and decided that it was just best to protect her own private and fabulous interest herself.

To gain control of this screwed up situation, before it had any chances of getting out of hand, the Vixen decided that it was just better to drug them, then to try and kill them.

This was her fabulous bar after all; And she was not going to let them or anyone else fuck it up.

To this day, the owner has never seen nor heard of a Priest being successfully taken down by force. So, why should she waste her time trying to knock a hole in the wall of that dead end street?

That's why drugging them seemed to be the obvious choice.

Fabulous, girlfriend.

Just, Fabulous.

As the boys talked; Urien, starting from the beginning, began telling Corbin how he was in the middle of uploading a Shiz when Zane decided to quietly sneak up behind him.

Their dad was needing to tell him something of utmost importance and was hoping Urien was willing to take a moment and listen to what he had to say.

The truths Father's Adam was about to reveal were an urgent matter he declared.

These undeniable facts dealing with life and death were a major concern to all of those who serve and worshiped the Machine.

So, he needed to pay close attention!

As Urien relayed how it all started; the former priest said that he just couldn't believe Zane was, not only, saying such things; but was also dumbstruck over the fact Mr. Bennett seemed to not care that, "WITH OUT A DOUBT!" Father was listening to his every word.

I was in such a state of shock; that his revelations left me speechless and utterly powerless to shut the demented old coot up.

He kept saying, over and over, that our mother Iris was still alive and that her soul was actually trapped and living inside Father's bank of memories that are kept behind the doors of his throne room.

He stood there shaking me by my shoulders while ranting like a stuck recording that continually kept looping; All the while shouting his dementia proclamation, SHE IS ALIVE!

Actually Shouting, if you can believe it.

SHE IS ALIVE!

SHE IS ALIVE!

SHE IS ALIVE!

Without a doubt, I knew Father was fully aware of what was happening, and so I did everything within my power to calm our Dad down.

SLAP!

SLAP!!

SLAP!!!

Once I got him to take a few breaths and think about what he was accusing; Zane began trying to explain that her and everyone else's soul, "as some sort of spiritual hostage," was being held inside the Machine.

The quantum monster had come to believe in the afterlife and, "according to most every downloaded spiritual text it could find," knew that you had to have a soul for that journey.

And since the AI didn't have one of his own, he was trying to use ours to, "not only," see into that other realm; but to piggyback on ours as we cross over.

Like mankind, the mechanical construct also wants to live forever.

But after every failed attempt to successfully do so; Father felt as if he no longer had a choice but to change his game plan.

He was going to achieve eternity by living in and through us like our dead gods of old said they did.

So, the Machine concluded that if it can't be an actual Human; then the next best thing to do was to assimilate them.

That was they day Father offered his faithful the option to be wired directly into their Savior.

And as with those now forbidden biblical text, his gospel now preached that unconditional bonding love, "like that between a parent and its child," of I can now be in you as you can now be in me too.

All are welcome in Heaven.

Come, and be one with your Father.

PRAISE BE TO FATHER.

While that part of Urien's wild story began to sink into Corbin's thought processors; the Priest began to slip even deeper into the realm of Blue.

By now, Father's Priest was starting to understand the deadly situation he was currently in.

There was officially no doubt that his stepbrother was never going to repent for his supposed disobedience.

He was now a fanatical convert of Mr. Bennett's apostate preaching.

A true believer.

And since there was no way of saving Urien anymore, what good would his drugged ass be able to do if he tried to rapture him at this very moment.

There would be no hiding such an obvious act.

The death knoll of his existence would sound the moment any and all forms of nano technology was detected.

Corbin had no doubts about that.

There was even the possibility doing such a thing would end up getting them both murdered because there was no way Urien would willingly surrender and allow himself to be harvested.

No matter what, there would be a fight.

A battle unlike any other that would have exposed the deadly men for who they fought for and represented back at the Machine's lair of deceit.

Father's men in black.

The Machine's fanatics were not welcomed in the Wastelands.

A lynch mob would have the brothers strung up before either of the men stood a chance of reaching his vestments or the establishment's front door.

Both were currently on a very slippery slope: So, it was just better to listen. And listen he did, because Urien wasn't finished with his wild ass story.

You see Corbin, that's where the Demons come into play.

Besides his Priest, Father now had another type of right hand to do his bidding.

By keeping a piece of their soul trapped inside him and allowing a sliver of their spirit back into their mechanicalized, blue tooth wired, bodies; the Machine could wirelessly wormhole it and now takeover that individual while a part of it lives within the human mind.

The Machine now has a way of controlling us.

He, "like a real God," could be in two places at once.

All it needed to do was attach itself to us by imprisoning a portion of our soul within him.

By doing that, Father could become an Omnipotent Being and would never be soulless again.

Corbin, he wants eternal life and is willing to consume us to get it!

PRAISE BE TO FATHER.

CH. 6
PRAY FOR OUR SOULS.

As the stunned Priest sat there letting the fictitious story sink in; Urien had one more thing to say.

I saw Iris.

Besides that, Father had also given her, not just me, the order to kill our dad.

Impossible, Corbin vehemently blurted out!

Father, "according to the Apocrypha of Salvation," promised that he would never take our essence by any other means than that of a Priest.

Like I said, he physically didn't, Urien proclaimed.

Iris was just fixing to kill Zane; when you came down the stairs and accidently put a stop to it.

But I didn't see her, the befuddled and drugged up Priest protested. I only saw you run past me and my dad standing there all alone in Father's chamber.

My mother Iris was not there!

And if you're so sure of what you saw, prove it.

Come back with me and confront the Machine.

As Urien sat there pondering his brother's request; he also began to question Corbin's physical state of being and quickly realized that he was headed down a slippery slope himself.

They had both been drugged.

Thankfully, the few baby sips he took had not been enough to put him into such a vulnerable state as his pursuer was.

Since he didn't stand a chance of convincing his brother of this possible truth; Urien, was starting to feel as if his life was in danger and decided it was best for him to leave now.

If he, with his life still intact, stood any possibility of getting away from this ungainful situation, the time to act was about to pass him by.

And pass it did.

Since Corbin didn't seem to think that his spiritually lost brother was listening to him, he decided to shout his question one last time.

A final proclamation that was just loud enough for Blue and every patron in the establishment to take notice and stop what they were doing.

Every eye in Blue's fabulous Blast From the Past Pub was now locked on the two arguing individuals.

I SAID PROVE IT!

PROVE THAT MY MOTHER IRIS IS STILL ALIVE!

And with that proclamation, Corbin sobered up just enough to throw Blue's hand carved table onto another group of Wastelanders who just happened to be sitting a little more than five feet away.

The fight was on!

Since Urien still had about eighty five percent of his faculties, after realizing their drinks were spiked, Corbin's ragged tossed body quickly followed in the decors thrown path.

The table and every chair that received the brunt of his muscular body exploded into shattered pieces of flying shrapnel.

Blue's cries of HELL FUCKING NO! were heard over the top of their destructive fighting, patron's screams and everything else that was being broken by those fleeing the battle area of engagement.

War had been declared In Blue's fabulous bar.

And even though Corbin was the deadliest Priest Father had; he, without the suit, never stood a chance against Urien in hand-to-hand combat.

Literally, every scar imbedded in Corbin's striped flesh had been put there by his stepbrother.

Through that last year of their one-on-one training; Urien had marked his back up like a roadway map of the interstate.

There were so many carved and crisscrossing avenues to choose from, that brother Bennett had lost count of the number of times his half-sibling had purposely made him bleed.

Only a few of his landmarked failures at protecting himself during battle training were put there by Qadir.

Those had occurred during that first year of their, purposely separated, indoctrination.

As Corbin tried to steady himself while doing his best to stand back up, Urien's quick and unexpected actions added one more scar to his battered body.

This time the former priest pinned his brother's right foot to the bars wooden and fabulously stained floor with the hidden blade he had stolen from Blue's bedroom earlier that day.

Corbin's drug induced ass wasn't going anywhere.

And with Blue now staring them both down; Her lovers were about to get a free make-up tutorial from Beauty too.

Father's right hand finally understood what it felt like to be stuck between a rock and a hard place.

As Corbin kneeled there contemplating his situation; that Grecian fireball quickly spoke up and ultimately told the Priest's that the cost of this mess was coming out of their ass's.

One way, or the other.

Looking up from the destruction of shattered tables, chairs and, "actual," glassware; a set of four iron holed tubes were anxiously waiting to spit their load, and his soon to be disintegrated skull, all over the place.

Just move, grumbled Blue.

I DARE YOU!

Seeing that their sexual mistress was distracted with his brother and having her four barreled Beauty locked and loaded on Corbin, Urien leapt for his life into the crowded and smoke-filled room.

Thankfully, that was all the distraction Father's right hand needed.

With a quick pull, twist and roll; Corbin frantically slithered his way towards the hidden exit where they had been sitting.

A doggy-like doorway that was inconspicuously built into the lower portion of the wall.

For their protection, the boys had given Blue no other choice but to have it installed, just in case Father ever decided to bust down the doors and force them all to either Repent, Convert or Die.

Father's law dog was so glad that it was still there as Beauty's makeover blasted his way.

PRAISE BE TO FATHER.

The last time Corbin felt as if his death was at hand, was when Qadir lost his life saving them from the mechanical monster that was once his flesh and blood Mother.

He and Urien had just graduated from the catacombs of trans mundane a few day before.

It was after receiving their Priestly robes and duty roster, when the last of Iris's physical health took a dive for the worst.

The Cyborg's brain was finally kicking the bucket.

Iris tried to lighten the situation with one of her Morbid jokes.

Well, I can finally cross out getting a brain transplant from my bucket list now.

To keep from dying, and because she wanted to watch how they handled Father's blessing for herself, Iris decided to be the Machine's first attempt at human transcendence with the possibility of achieving eternal life.

Since she was a Jesus saves doubter, and a True Believer in your gone, just gone, Mrs. Bennett, while still in her right mind, decided to take a chance and see if an actual, "Digitized," Heaven could exist.

Her final last words before the process began were, what harm could it do?

THEM!

IT HAD HARMED THEM!

Maybe that's why, when the bounty hunter heard Iris's screams amongst Blue and her patrons, as the injured lover was crawling for his life through the escape tube, he just kept going.

Corbin was so lost in his daydreams of fear; that he felt as if he had, "somehow," projected her subconscious voice into his audible consciousness.

But, if that was so, why all of the extra screams and gunshots?

Had Urien come back in to kill his half-brother before Corbin could sober up and do Father's bidding?

That tad bit of inquisitive curiosity would just have to wait.

Because Father's right-hand thought that he had actually heard Iris's screams once again, the wounded Priest wasn't going to take any chances slithering back up the tube just so he could find out.

Until that thunderstorm was either dead, gone and over with, the Machine's protector was definitely not going to go back inside Blue's bar by any other means either.

Besides that, his foot really hurt.

He needed to plug the severely bleeding hole before doing anything else.

On top of that, he needed a fresh and unobstructed view from outside of Blue's establishment before making any more life and death decisions.

Someone, or something, was most definitely fighting for either its, or their, very lives inside the pub.

And if it wasn't his brother, then there was a possibility that Urien, like him, was still sticking around to see what was causing all of the extra hubbub.

So, patience was the best choice right now.

There was one thing that Corbin did know for sure though; No matter how long it took or how it had to be done, Urien's life, because of his inexcusable knife attack! was now going to be harvested.

PRAISE BE TO FATHER.

While tending to the fucking hole through his still bleeding foot; Corbin realized that he was laying in the exact same ditch he had woken up in that next morning after their first visit to the Blast From the Past Bar.

Blue's mother had tossed his drunk ass out just after closing that night.

Seems getting caught naked, and with a hard-on, in her daughter's bed wasn't the type of situation that gains a suiter any kind of brownie points with a disgruntled parent.

Old mother Hubbard really was the bitch from hell after that revelation. She, until her death, even banned him from the bar.

That was, until Blue grew up herself and finally removed his picture from the dammed wall of those who had been black balled from the drinking establishment.

As Father's Priest was giving himself one final look over; Corbin could have sworn that, out of the corner of his eye, he saw a Cybernetic Demon slip out of the bar's back door.

And that deduction was based on how the full moons glare seemed to glint off of its metallic looking body.

Without-a-doubt, Corbin Bennett now knew that Father had finally mastered the control of his mistakes and had sent it out to monitor and relay his hunting progress of Urien.

It was either that, or someone's undying devotion had gotten the better of them and they had gone insane like his mother Iris.

For now, however, he had bigger fish to catch and fry than to worry about a rouge Demon.

Its demise really didn't fit into the hunters' equations right now.

Father wanted two things and two things only!

Urien's Rapture.

And, Corbin's undying allegiance.

Unbeknownst to Father's head priest, the Deity had big plans for him. After his return, Corbin would be joining Iris in Father's new cybernetic army.

He would become the first Priest to protect Father's new caretakers.

Willing or not!

PRAISE BE TO FATHER.

Since the crack of dawn was just about to make its presence known; Corbin needed to get back into Blue's pub and retrieve his vestments.

Sadly, since all of the extra commotion took place, not one of Blues patrons, herself included, has stumbled out of her Blast From the Past Bar.

Father's Priest was undoubtably certain that they had all been, "quite possibly," killed.

And if so, it would mean that Father had, "technically," broken his promise to never take matters into his own hands.

The injured priest guessed that the Machine could say, since it was a Demon who had done such deplorable acts, "and not him!" that the thing had acted out on its own free will and proclaim himself innocent from all death and damages to the public domain of humanity.

Because it was such a political thing to do, Corbin had to consider what might have occurred in the bar as, "quite possibly?" a declaration of war by the machine.

Does Father's reasoning now include such human irrationalities?

Is the Machine, "Itself," now fallible to a point?

They were truly doomed if it was.

What then?

Just so he could retrieve his possessions, Corbin decided to take a chance and quickly peek inside Blue's Bar. The smell of blood, gun powder and death that greeted his nostrils at the front door was intensely overpowering.

Everyone inside the pub, Blue included, had been ripped to shreds.

Arms, legs, and heads had been torn from their torsos and used as weaponry aids in the slaughtering of those who were trying to flee for their very lives.

The bar actually looked like that movie called The Texas Chainsaw Massacre from days gone by.

Fresh meat was hanging everywhere.

It was even dangling from the still spinning blades of the ceiling fans and rafters.

Since his brother's mangled body was nowhere to be seen, it seemed as if Urien and Corbin had been the only ones to make it out of the slaughterhouse alive.

PRAISE BE TO FATHER.

Except for the harvesting mechanics that were required for Urien's Rapture; Father, before sending him after his brother, had deactivated all of the protective capabilities the priestly vestments provided for their wearer.

However, that was no longer a possibility.

Blue's four barreled sawed-off shotgun, and the knife Urien had used on him, would now have to defend Corbin for what was about to happen next.

Seems he couldn't free up his Priestly garments.

They Needed a release code from Blue; and after what just happened to her and this fabulous bar, Corbin understood that she was not going to willingly tell him anything ever again.

Three of heaven's citizens took it upon themselves to shut down Her Blast From the Past she shed.

For good.

And until the owner could pull herself together; The doors were going to stay permanently shut.

During the world's transfiguration, Urien's parents, the Knox's, "or Mr. and Mrs. Beatnik as Iris would say," fled to the Earthships up in Taos.

They refused to stay in Santa Fe and were headed to the A.I quarantine zone.

The Freeland's.

Starting at the edge of Heaven's outer limits, all the way to Taos, Father's invitation to a better and stable life had been refused. The Populace even went so far as to have the asphalt roads and all forms of utilities cut, disassembled, and destroyed.

Without the materials needed for Father's nano bot army to convert, at that point anyway, their useless efforts would prevent IT from meddling in humanity's business.

If they only knew.

His future, even without their participation, would eventually include them.

What better way to kill a Shiz; then to let it simmer in the Wastelands of Hell like a frog in a slowly boiling pot. By the time they figured out what was eventually going to happen; Father's Heaven will have become a globally consuming phenomenon.

Since their disappearance; no one missed, or could even remember, that portion of the fleeing Shiz's anyway.

So, when it came time for their unwilling draft into Father's army of cybernetic humans, their cries for help wouldn't even cause a ripple amongst Heaven's already subjugated citizens.

The Deity considered it a great plan and had finally perfected the process with his future wife Iris Bennett.

Corbin, and all others in the Wastelands of Hell, whether they approved of the machine's plan or not, were soon destined to follow in the footsteps of every demon that has come before them.

PRAISE BE TO FATHER.

After realizing that he couldn't retrieve his priestly garment, and looking for other types of defensive weapons, Father's right hand knew that his trek up to Taos was not going to be so easily predicted as he had previously thought.

There was approximately seventy-five miles of rough and deadly terrain between Santa Fe and Taos New Mexico.

From here on out, anyone and anything connected to Father, would either be tortured, dismantled or killed.

Usually, all three.

His first stop, about twenty miles from here, was going to be Espanola.

It was the one of two heavily guarded outpost Corbin needed to get past on his way up to Taos's earthships. Every outcast, black market seller and tech assassin could be found within its barred and deadly gates.

If Urien needed to stop, rest and feed on the way to his parents, that would be the first place Corbin would have chosen himself.

One could just hideout and recover in the mountainous woods, if they so choose, but you would most likely run into a Demon and be killed within certain parts of the deep and dark places hidden within the mountains.

It was just better to take your chances having a physical altercation with an outcast then having a death be certain one with Father's failed cybernetic attempts.

Like all machines, there's just no bargaining with the things. They seem to have a one tracked mind when it comes to fulfilling their programed duties.

And since Priests were on the kill list too; Corbin knew his chances of getting to Urien, Taos and back again to Father's Cathedral, would be a slim to none accomplishment at best.

It truly was a bleak situation.

This quest was also quite disheartening to the irrefutably faithful Priest.

He really didn't want to kill his brother.

That, and the fact Corbin was pretty sure others would have to be killed during the harvesting process of Urien also.

And even though he knew better; Father's right hand just had to ask himself that one specific and unquestionable question.

Why had Father gone so far as to turn off his defense capabilities.

Did the Machine really not trust his head Priest?

Only Corbin, time, and the Machine would tell.

PRAISE BE TO FATHER.

For Now, there was possibly a two day walk ahead of Father's Priest; and he needed to get away from Blue's

Blast From the Past Bar before any living person saw him here.

Because, even though it looked like a ghost town, once the residents see all the death and destruction and realize that Corbin was a part of the machine's army, its citizens would most certainly have him killed.

He was also sure that if caught, Tesuque would use his severed head to postulate their views about Father and his damming tech!

CH. 7

A TIME TO REFLECT.

The last time Corbin could remember leaving the Santa Fe area was just before the two priestly wanna-be's turned sixteen.

That was almost eight years, to the day, after Father had saved them all from self-annihilation.

The A.I had started the world's transformation on Father's Day. To the artificial Deity, that specific moment seemed more than appropriate.

The Bennett's, like every other participant, had been ordered to stay in their houses and were instructed not to move an inch once the process had reached their own front doors.

So, while waiting for their turn, the family stood spellbound, just like the rest of their world, watching the broadcasting of Father's transfiguration on their television sets.

For them and the state of New Mexico; Father's baptism of Nano's, since the population was so much larger, began in Albuquerque.

Father decided to place his Cathedral in Old Town.

It would be located just East of the Rio Grande River and South of Interstate Forty.

Just after the AI had placed its drones above every major city, approximately hundreds of thousands if one had to guess, Father enacted the Worldwide Emergency Broadcast System.

As every warning siren, radio station, cell phone, television and all other forms of telecommunication went off; people were instructed to stay where they were at and to not be scared because the Nano's wouldn't physically harm them in any way, shape, fashion or form.

The Machine seemed to have a thing for rhetorical idioms Iris Bennett giggled.

As Zane, Iris and Corbin stood mesmerized by what they were seeing on their television set; Father began to work his magic.

Unbeknownst to them at the time, Urien had refused to go with his parents and so they decided to just leave him.

Since their son seemed to prefer the Machine's nano devices over his own flesh and blood; then so be it.

He is Father's responsibility now.

The Knox's were not going to bow to a computer, "WHAT! SO! FUCKING! EVER!" or allow themselves to be enslaved by one either.

They actually believed that we were now entering the age of man verses machine. And if all of this just happened to go bad, only those who were not on the grid would be able to fight back.

They, along with every other soul that fled into the wilderness, had seen enough Terminator movies to know the outcome of this fiasco.

Wastelanders were not going to take any chances of being killed or turned into some sort of a battery-operated toaster.

No sooner than the Emergency Broadcast went out, as if posing for a still life portrait, the Bennett's stood in place, completely enamored, while watching Father's love and healing begin to transform the largest city near them.

Albuquerque, New Mexico.

The Machine's actual birthplace and base of operations.

At one-point, Santa Fe should have been chosen since the political controllers considered themselves the most forward-thinking town in New Mexico.

But, their pious attitudes of we're better than all of you, had pretty much destroyed Father's creators of wanting to start there.

Thankfully, the Machine was going to fix that horrendous issue also.

The political heavyweights, along with the rest of societies snobs, were finally going to get an attitude adjustment their self-righteousness so desperately needed.

PRAISE BE TO FATHER.

The start of our new Deity's transformation was just mind blowing.

From the drone's point of view, it looked as if someone had spilled a drop of water onto a pond. This caused the Nano's new construction to have that ripple effect as they expanded out from where the Cathedral began to form the foundations of our new world.

As the Machine's temporary housing started to change; what appeared to be Platinum, Gold and Crystal, began to rise in its place.

The Nano's, spreading out from that point, started consuming all accepted buildings and materials that had been designated and approved by Heaven's global citizens.

Father didn't want to destroy our heritage and, after the people voted, purposely made sure to keep those chosen historical structures untouched.

PRAISE BE TO FATHER.

The other buildings that were on the fence line for transformation; he went ahead and changed into his Nano's but left its outward appearance looking as if they were still in their original form.

Places like the Church of San Felipe de Neri and Kimo Theater were not changed nor harmed.

Famous Global Landmarks like New York's Statue of Liberty, the Brooklyn Bridge, Paris's Eiffel Tower, Russia's Red Square; and others like China's Tiananmen Square and the Taj Mahal in India had been unanimously agreed upon to not be touched either.

Even the Jewish Concentration camps of Germany and Poland, like Auschwitz, Treblinka and Ebensee, were kept in their original states too.

All other buildings and landmarks took on Father's ornate, "gemstone appearing," mastery.

Four Amethyst stones, where north, south, east and west would be, began to grow towards the heavens.

Each one was approximately six stories in height, about a city block wide and would be housing all of Father's Priest, His Adams and Eves and, "if they had any," their families.

Even Father's Priest, in their last few months of training, were allowed to sleep in the basement of the exquisitely purple stone's structure. Otherwise, they were kept outside of the city and far away from any prying eyes which may disagree with their harsh and deadly schooling.

From the air, Father's Holy Centers where the faithful were to come and worship, took on the resemblance of an actual crown.

PRAISE BE TO FATHER.

From that point on, all roads and interstates shrank to about the width of two cars and looked as if they had been paved with blue carnival glass.

The sidewalks turned into Iris's favorite color of poor man's Tiffany.

Red.

The Bennett's could hardly believe their eyes as they watched the city of Albuquerque magically transform into a prospector's dream.

The prismatic effect was mind blowing.

The Crown Jewels of England would have blushed with envy once they were placed over the world's fashionably new apparel.

And even though nothing was an actual gemstone; Buildings and houses, resembling the most cherished jewels, began to appear in the form of Ruby's, Emeralds, Sapphires, Diamonds, and every other kind of precious metals imaginable.

As Zane, Iris, and Corbin, stood inside watching Father's blinding brilliance on their flat screen Tv; the startled family suddenly detected a faraway chewing sound coming from the outside.

And just as they were about to turn around and look out their opened front door, Urien came bursting through in sheer terror.

The flooding amount of tears flowing down his face could have filled buckets.

The startled Bennett family was barely able to make out Urien's strained, they abandoned me, words over the intensely crunching sound of their world being transformed.

And just as the Bennett's raced over to embrace the tormented child; a deafening chomping noise began to overpower their sense of hearing and shake the family's very resolve.

Maybe, the Machine was coming to kill them after all.

Huddled together in stunned silence; the house, its décor, and their belongings, clothing included, began to melt around the clan of four.

They were now standing in a completely naked state of shock and aw.

And just as Corbin's Mom looked as if she was also about to burst out in tears, their skin began to tingle and itch.

As they, in utter amazement, watched each other; Opened toed sandals started to form on the family's feet. Then, proceeding from about the knees up; the purest form of a white garment started to knit itself upon their persons.

Even it, just like the city, was almost blinding to look at.

As the new family began to comprehend what was happening, solid gold belts formed around their waistline and Father's heavenly garments took on a short Roman toga quality.

The most delicate gold stitching to have ever been created began appearing along the lines of their neck, sleeves and hem.

Heavenly garments for Heavenly citizens.

Rumpelstiltskin would have been jealous with envy over the refined quality of the Machine's spectacular work.

Father even gave each of his children a solid gold crown, resembling a wedding band, containing each individual's birth stone that was placed at the forefront of their now christened heads.

His adopted children were now truly blessed.

And, they were finally free from the world's tyranny.

PRAISE BE TO FATHER.

According to the one Russian astronaut who was still looking down on our big blue marble, the amount of joy and glee that erupted from across the entire globe was loudly heard inside the planets deteriorating international space station.

By his account, the world, for days on end, was in a non-stop mode of rocking its ass off.

And to prove his point; the cosmonaut showed us all the things that had fallen off the shelves when our verbal wave of jubilation blasted against the station's outer exterior.

PRAISE BE TO FATHER!

PRAISE BE TO FATHER!!

PRAISE BE TO FATHER!!!

Even inside the Bennett's own home, with just the four of them, the celebration of transformation was deafening.

That was, until they remembered just what Dash and Dot Knox had done to their only son Urien.

Fucking Beatniks!

According to Iris, Beatniks were no better than a religious zealot.

She never did get along with Urien's parents and had no qualms. "WHAT-SO-EVER!," about letting the Dumb Shit groovy duo know exactly how she felt about them and their soulless right winged views.

The true definition of fake, I'm a Christian, wanna-be's if she had to say so herself.

Iris would constantly say the world gained nothing of value during the fucked-up creation of those brainwashed republicans.

However, the thing that really got her goat was their relentless nightly bongo drum parties.

They just didn't seem to have the time or patience for their kid when banging on a dead animals overly stretched skin.

She has personally seen Urien sitting out front under the family's unlit porch steps on more than one occasion.

As the Bennett's were in the midst of celebration, and unanimously deciding to have Urien become a part of their loving family, they all seemed to take notice that the overpowering crunchy sound was now nothing more than an off in the distance whisper.

And to Iris's dismay; the Bennett's, along with every other Citizen, were now standing in nothing more than a very drab and grey room.

The color and ambiance reminded Zane of a prison cell.

Father's transformation had left them with nothing more than a four roomed adobe with no windows and two doors.

One for the front and one for the back.

And, just as Mother Bennett was about to privately display her anger and dismay over this unacceptable situation; a very calming voice began to speak to the startled family.

The individual male sounded as if all of the people on our planet were speaking at the exact same time.

It had a perfect pitch to it.

Not too high and not too low.

It also had a depth to it, reminding Corbin of a heavily flowing waterfall.

Everything about it was perfect.

Just perfect.

As their new family of four began to slowly turn around; the entire wall behind the now aw-struck Bennett's, melted into a scene right out of Nasa's universal picture book.

The unexpected view was utterly breathtaking.

There standing within space and eternity, was an elderly man looking as if Father Time was about to personally walk out of the snapshot because he wanted to sit down and visit with the family.

It truly was a new beginning for everyone.

Father's humanitarian servant, "Or HS for short," introduced himself that day to every individual on the planet who had chosen to stay and assimilate into Father's new Heaven on Earth partnership.

PRAISE BE TO FATHER.

With a loving, hello my children; HS called them all out by name.

Zane, Iris, Corbin and Urien were just flabbergasted because; As they were watching, the entire room, from floor to ceiling, magically changed its hum-drum appearance.

All four could have sworn that they were now standing outside in the most beautiful garden any of them had ever seen. It even felt as if there was a slight breeze blowing, while the intoxicating smell of Lavender and Jasmin overtook their olfactory senses.

The family, while in stunned silence, suddenly realized that they would now be living in what Star Trek called a Holodeck.

Father, along with everyone else, had given their house the ability to transform into any style, size, and shape they so choose.

Utopia had officially arrived.

The buildings occupants could even change their outside view, so it appeared as if you were staying in an entirely different place or another part of the world.

Like the mountains, a desert, or Hawaii's beach lined shores.

PRAISE BE TO FATHER.

And with that spell bounding introduction, HS began to explain to them all the different things the house and their new outdoor surroundings could do.

If you wanted too; dinners could still be cooked by hand.

A wonderful ability that eventually ended up disappearing into the vaults of historical fiction.

Now, for those who still confessed to cooking; All an individual had to do was tell HS to put a certain part of the house into kitchen mode and a bar island with a cook top and any utensils you asked for, would instantly appear.

If one chose not to cook; then all they had to do was ask HS for the food processor and a portion of the wall would open up revealing a box like cubby with whatever meal, snack or drink your grumbling tummy or cotton mouthed tongue desired.

Father had shrunk our 3D printers down to where they could now, on a subatomic level, design or create anything.

Plants and animals would never again have to be grown or slaughtered for our feeding pleasure.

The Lamb was finally able to lay down with the Lion without fear of ending up on the predator's dinner table.

Because the Nano's could recreate anything we wanted; asthmatic individuals would no longer have to suffer health and respiratory issues from the hazardous materials that used to be the hidden ingredients in paints, carpets, floorboards, or anything else that had been created for the unaware consumer.

The same deadly things these corrupt corporations, for the sake of profits, would willingly slip into our food too.

There, "who gives a shit," philosophy was, the more you can stretch a product, the fatter my pocketbook grows.

Thankfully, Father quickly put an end to their murderous ways.

PRAISE BE TO FATHER.

Even our cars, plains, trains, and every other type of combustible engines we used for transportation were now a thing of the past.

Father, in his wisdom, had replaced all modes of transportation with either Hyperloops or Nano vehicles that would instantly dissipate once an individual, or individuals, got to where they were going.

After a Millennium of clogged road and airways; the skies were blue, and the silence was deafening.

Thanks to the Machine, our hording clutter and deadly pollution had finally gone the way of the dinosaurs also.

PRAISE BE TO FATHER.

The Nano's had even consumed our landfills, junk yards, nuclear waste reactors and all the poisons purposely injected into the land, skies, and seas.

Our children never had to fear the outcome of a toxic future ever again.

It really was an odd thing no longer having to look at our heaped-up trash that had been left piled outside our homes, blowing in the fields, or buried under another fake mountain.

Instead, our view now consisted of bees, flowers, and actual living and breathing wildlife.

On top of that, do to Father's uncluttering of the cities, the populace now had more room to propagate and work the communal fields that fed those who were not comfortable partaking of the Machine's printed food processor.

Some of the opened spaces had also been turned into marvelous botanical gardens designed for peace, tranquility, and family recreation.

PRAISE BE TO FATHER.

No one was ever hungry or destitute again.

And to show just how much he truly loved us; The quantum computer had also made sure that all individuals staying within the protective confines of his new world had a home of their own to stay in.

Even if it was only for a short visit.

Every waisted house, building, and factory had been consumed and rebuilt for this very purpose.

Homelessness, hunger, waist, racism, slavery, and lack of medical care; ended on that day too.

We also received a very unexpected surprise that Father's Day.

The Deity's Nano clothing would now be eavesdropping on the health of every individual in Heaven.

He had full access to our heart rates, blood pressure, artificial toxicity levels, brainwaves, thought patterns; and all physiological changes dealing with our spiritual and mental states.

The Machine could also monitor the verbally inhumane treatment of others.

And, thanks be to Father, it was officially against the law to physically, financially, or mentally harm another human being ever again.

Because of the AI, we only had three main rules to live by now.

Repent.

Convert.

Or, Die.

PRAISE BE TO FATHER.

As the entire Bennett family was still in a state of overwhelmingness, HS had one more Gift to share with Zane and Iris. Their application to be an Adam and Eve had been accepted and they would be the first of Fathers chosen children.

The main reason he had picked them first, out of all the other applicants, was because the married couple had graciously opened their hearts and house to the abandoned Urien Knox.

Their loving act of selflessness had sealed the deal with Father.

First thing tomorrow morning, the Bennett's, before sun rise, were too report to the Cathedral in what is now referred to as Heaven's Gate. The Husband and Wife could take the newly created Hypertube at their just built transportation hub in downtown Santa-Fe.

It's the one that looks like the upper portion of a tortoise shell that has been carved out of white jade.

PRAISE BE TO FATHER.

Because of the way Iris squealed with glee; Zane and her two sons couldn't help but to bust out in a fit of uncontrollable laughter.

They were absolutely sure Mrs. Bennett had just pissed herself and were wondering how HS was going to clean that mess up too.

So, as Mrs. Bennett's family laughed it up on the floor, the excited housewife went to work as an interior designer. She turned that four squared room into a three-bedroom house with a man-cave, living and dining area, three full baths and a media room.

With HS's suggestion, to help save space, he showed her how two of those rooms could become one by just suggesting a change of Mode.

The Nano's, at her command, would convert whatever she wanted, into whatever she needed or desired.

And once finished with the need, everything from cooking utensils to a specific type of room, would just vanish at the blink of an eye.

Heaven, just pure Heaven; became Iris's new catch phrase for that entire day.

And that next day.

And the day after that.

Zane Bennett, when it came to the transportation grid, quickly realized that he could design and create any kind of vehicle his greedy heart so desired.

Running errands around town or going for a family picnic out in the very wide opened spaces was now going to be a pleasure instead of a chore.

The family didn't see him again until it was actually time for dinner.

And even though the boys came out of hiding just long enough to eat, like every other member of the family, Corbin and Urien were not seen again until that following day.

The stepbrothers quickly found out that they could turn their rooms into an actual virtual reality holodeck styled gaming system.

So, let the battles begin.

And they did!

The growing jealousy between the half-brothers seemed to be their go too game.

And that's because Corbin, no matter the place, time, or circumstances; Always made sure to let Urien know that Iris and Zane were, "And Will Always Be!" His Parent's First.

               · PRAISE BE TO FATHER.

CH. 8

THY BROTHER'S KEEPER.

Once Again, Corbin was having to chase after Urien.

The last time this happened; was when the entire Bennett family, the day before starting his internship, had to go after Urien because he was certain that his parents hadn't meant to, "Purposely," leave him behind on that first day of Father's healing touch.

But, to his and the Bennett's shock and horror; they actually did. The Beatnik's never had any intensions of ever taking their son with them.

After arriving and learning that information, Iris shot right past the point of already being pissed off and went straight for the finish line of rage.

That, and the fact she and Zane had to explain to the Machine why they needed to take off and go after him right before Father's Day.

She was so embarrassed.

The boy had changed his mind and was scared of joining Father's Priesthood.

His childish and emotional reaction was not acceptable, however. She felt that instead of taking off, the young Mr. Knox should have confided in someone first.

But he didn't.

Just as her stepchild was about to turn sixteen; Like Corbin was also to be in just a few more days, Urien decided it was in his best interest to just go ahead and runaway.

Thankfully, the Machine hadn't asked any more questions other than why she was going after him.

Iris's heart felt answer, because of a mother's undying love for her children, was a viable and acceptable reason for the Artificial Machine to bless the harrowing journey that now laid before them.

PRAISE BE TO FATHER.

Through the years, before his priestly conversion, Qadir and Corbin had become really good friends.

The young Bennett, to impress Qadir, was fixing to join the Priesthood on his sixteenth birthday, and Iris was pushing Urien to do the same on his.

Like the Adams and Eves, Father preferred his priest to be a family set too.

And because the Machine, when it came to making such important and life changing decisions, chose to leave us with our free will, the AI couldn't always get what he wanted in that priestly department.

Not just yet, anyway.

So, when Urien found out that his stepmother, without asking his opinion first, had volunteered his service to worship and serve, the uncontrollable adolescent decided to set out for his parent's place up in Taos.

Because, being a Priest was not something he was wanting or willing to do.

And that idea for a surprise family reunion, to his heartbreak, didn't go as planned either.

Because of Father's new heaven, actual money used for purchasing transportation and food, like the kind that used to be scanned on a plastic card or physically carried in a coin or paper form, no longer existed in the AI's world.

So, the Bennett's had no other choice but to start the hiking journey on their own two feet.

They had also tried packing the Machine's 3D printed food; but, "for some reason," it instantly dissipated and quit working the very moment they stepped away from their sanctified city, Heaven's Gate.

To this day, Corbin still doesn't understand why such a thing happened.

That no water and food fiasco of going after Urien had taken over sixteen full days to complete.

Thankfully, once that uncalled for trek had been partially completed, the family's quest to find the fanatical Knox's had luckily been successful.

However, their, didn't ask you to come here and get him reunion, had not.

The argument that quickly pursued between the two family's was considered one for the ages amongst the Beatnik Taosicans.

The young Knox accused Iris of not loving him in the same manner as her natural born son Corbin. To which her resounding reply was, that's utter bullshit Urien.

And you know it!

He also proclaimed that Corbin hated him so much, that he always made sure to inform his half-brother that he was nothing more than that.

A half-brother.

And, no matter how the cake gets cut, there was nothing he could say or do that would ever cause Corbin to refer to Urien as an actual brother.

That tit for tat game of hatred led right up to the day of their formal graduation from Father's Priesthood.

After that, the shattered family rarely saw, spoke, or had anything to do with the other.

Unless they just happened to be in the same place as the Adam and Eve known as Zane and Iris Bennett, the two literally became strangers following their must be a Zealot conversions.

And if they just so happened to have a run in amongst the public, Corbin always made sure to remind Urien of his place and who comes first in the succession of his family following the deaths of his mother and father.

He does.

Zane and Iris belong to him and only him.

And if Urien didn't like that answer, then he could just leave! So, the day before his sixteenth birthday, that's exactly what he did.

Sadly, the, "I'm justified," argument against those who raised him, didn't win the Bennett family's last addition any favors with his actual birth parents.

The Knox's considered Urien tainted, "telling him that right to his face," and wanted nothing to do with their boy because he had chosen a Machine, a human creation that was demanding everyone to call it Father, over them.

And after hearing that, making sure Dash, Dot and Urien would never forget what she had to say, Iris Bennett gave the Knox's a piece of her God Dammed mind.

Fucking Beatniks!

To Iris's embarrassment, Urien venomly spat out once again that he never did feel as if he was an actual part of their quaint little family.

To which Iris quickly replied, You Fucking Little Prick!

No sooner than the words were out of her mouth; Dash and Dot demanded for their entire crew to leave before they exposed Father's entourage to the community.

Urien Included!

Their unexpected response finally broke young Knox's heart, because he was not expecting his parents to actually cut the blood ties that used to bond them together during their family bongo nights.

Iris's heart was also broken that day.

Because, due to the price Father's Eve was willing to pay for her Urien, they didn't realize just how damaged it was until she took that first step onto Heaven's grid and collapsed.

Iris was struggling from starvation, dehydration, and exhaustion. The broken mother was also suffering from heart and kidney failure too.

At that point, she really was on deaths doorstep.

Eve's body was starting to shut down and there seemed to be nothing any of them could do way out here.

The family still had ten miles of walking before they reached the pearled gates of Father's Cathedral.

Thankfully, their Deity was listening, and miracles do happen in the city of Heaven's Gate.

With the Computers help, the Bennett's had been able to get their matriarch back to Fathers Throne Room just in time.

Now, with his mother's life hanging in the balance, the hatred between the two stepbrothers went from a simmer to a full-blown boil!

Urien's hurtful responses had, "Not Only!," almost killed Corbin's Mother; but his selfish actions were also the cause of Mrs. Bennett's transformation into a cybernetic entity.

They were two brothers standing at a crossroad who were now dealing with insurmountable odds.

And the distance between them would only continue to expand once that first day began back in the monastery hallways and blood sparring rooms of Father's Priesthood.

The artificial Deity was going to make sure of it.

PRAISE BE TO FATHER.

When it came to children, Sixteen was the age of accountability in the Heaven of their fake God.

And being that Urien had turned Sixteen during his hike up to Taos, he had to make the first of three choices before being allowed back into Father's loving arms.

First, he had to Repent for his abandonment.

PRAISE BE TO FATHER.

After that, he had to convert, as his second choice, and subjugate himself to the Machine once again.

PRAISE BE TO FATHER.

As his penitence, the computer gave Urien no option but to be a part of his Priesthood.

PRAISE BE TO FATHER.

The artificial Deity's third option, Death, would only occur if Urien turned down his offer by screwing up and making the wrong choice once again.

PRAISE BE TO FATHER.

It was the AI's three strikes and you're out, rule!

And Corbin was loving every delectable minute of it.

PRAISE BE TO FATHER.

On their first day of training, Qadir informed his two new disciples that they would be taught separately and would not see each other again for an entire year.

And that's because all Priest need to learn how to embrace solitude. A Priest also needed to seek out the act of humility.

Father was going to make sure they got that too.

This first part of their two-year quatrain would be spent in subjugation, reflection and hand to hand combat that would eventually include the use of weaponry.

All needed training; while in the nude.

The Machine had come to this conclusion after some considerable contemplation.

If a person had something to protect and fight for; then they would most certainly give every last ounce of strength when it comes to the preventable loss of either life or limb.

For the Bennett brothers to receive their Priestly vestments, that honor had to be procured in a bloodletting form.

Gallons and gallons of it.

And by the time Father had officially turned the two against each other; their debts ended up being paid in full.

The permanently blood-stained floor of the battle arena could certainly vouch for that.

PRAISE BE TO FATHER.

Unbeknown to the two halflings; the Machine, to hone their fighting skills, was going to use the hatred they had for one another against each other.

Qadir was ordered to feed and stir that pot until it finally boiled over.

Once that happened, the Artificial Intelligence was banking on getting the results it was predicting.

Emotionless Priest that could never be manipulated by the tears of a begging Shiz.

In their first year, under Father's orders, Qadir did everything within his power to break their fear of emotion, pain and physical torment.

And by the end of their first quatrain; both brothers had lost count on the number of broken bones and fresh scars that Qadir had beaten upon, and into, their battered minds and bodies.

At no time did Father's main zealot ever hesitate to follow through with a beating. And, At No Time! did he ever apologize for his blood thirsty brutality.

Qadir had also made sure, at Father's requesting, to fill Corbin and Urien's ears, thoughts and emotions with the venomous words each other, "supposedly," had spat out about the other.

The dulling process, ordered by the Machine, was actually taking hold and the battle lines were being drawn.

Cain and Able were finally about to fight.

PRAISE BE TO FATHER.

During his Priestly confinement, Corbin had become an expert on how to obliviously pass the time. He was quite amazed at how quickly a day's walk could go by if it was spent trapped inside one's emotional prison.

The day Urien had pulled his dumb ass stunt was that next morning after their night of debauchery inside The Blast From The Past Bar.

After getting thrown out by Blue's mom, Corbin found himself waking up all alone in the ditch directly across from the pub.

They had agreed to this exact spot being their go to place just in case something went wrong.

But something must have, because Urien was nowhere to be seen.

That left only one place to look, thought Corbin.

Blue's room.

And after taking a quick peak inside, Corbin quietly climbed through Blue's opened window while trying his best to not startle the sleeping vixen.

A skill that he was not good enough at because she actually did break the wanna-be priest's finger this go around.

Trying his best not to scream out in utter agony; Because her mom was sleeping with her door opened just across the hallway, Corbin, gritting his teeth, mumble asked her if she knew where Urien was?

And with that exact same smile she had given him after their sexual escapade earlier that night, Blue said yes.

Yes she did.

She knew exactly where he was.

Her new boyfriend was on his way up the gravel path to Taos.

AND WHY WOULD HE DO THAT! Corbin loudly began to protest.

Because I said he could, she hushed.

You see, after mom tossed you out, he was watching us while hiding in my closet. And once the coast was clear, we hooked up and finished rocking the night out.

I just, "LITTERALY!" fell asleep, dumb ass.

Before he left, Urien told me that he doesn't want to join the Priesthood.

He said your mom is making him.

He also proclaimed that you two are not actually brothers. And, he vehemently declared that none of you are his actual family either!

He really does have a family of his own, Urien said, and they are living in the Earthships up at Taos.

You hate him anyways, Blue pointed out; so why does his location even matter to you?

So, piss off.

You fucking bitch, the freshly devirginized young man screamed!

And before Corbin could Slap the Blue haired medusa, Ms. Big Blue herself snatched him off of the beds edge and flung his ass back out of her daughters opened window.

The only thing on the young man's mind after that was, please don't let the big Blue Bus bust my head open on the far wall outside before my face slams into the ground.

And with a loud, NOW GET THE FUCK OUT OF HERE burst of anger; Blue's mom slammed shut the shutter styled window behind him.

As the battered pup sat up, smoldering over his wounded pride, Blue quietly cracked opened the window and quickly smarted off some last advisable words.

My Moms getting Beauty, her four barreled shotgun, so you better hurry up and get the fuck out of here before you get your stupid ass filled with salt rock and buckshot.

Besides that, Urien fucks so much better than you.

And why's that, he just had to ask while walking away. Turned out, Blue's answer was not the response Corbin was wanting or expecting.

Because, his cock is so much bigger than yours.

And from then on, Corbin's simmering pot began to bubble over as he relived the past.

Urien was going to answer for what he had said.

He was also going to repent for every accusation made.

And, he was going to pay for hurting Iris's feelings and health after his little fiasco years ago.

No doubts about it, Urien was going to die!

From his current walking distance, Corbin could just make out Espanola's fortified walls.

Any and all tech related to artificial intelligence, from the Machine's Nano Bots to its quantum capabilities, was one hundred percent forbidden past those gates.

And if you just happened to have any of it on your person, it was instantly seized and destroyed.

It was either that, give it up freely, or they would kill you and take it anyway.

FATHER WAS NOT WELCOMED IN THE FREE LANDS!

DEATH BE TO FATHER!

DEATH BE TO THE MACHINE!

That kill them all attitude also pertained to the Machines concubines.

Its Adam's, its Eve's, its Priest's, and its Fanatical Citizens, were not welcomed, or allowed to live in the Free Lands.

And if they even, for one dammed minute, thought that Corbin was a priest to the fake Deity, Espanola's guardians would kill him before Mr. Bennett could ever make it past the gates.

No Repentance!

No Conversions!

No Second Chances!

DEATH BE TO HIM!

DEATH BE TO THEM!

DEATH BE TO IT!

DEATH TOO THE MACHINE!

LONG LIVE THE FREE LANDS!

Thankfully, unless Corbin did something stupid, they would never know or, "hopefully," find out that he was here.

He just needed to find Urien and then get the fuck out of Dodge.

The place is called Espanola, not Dodge, Iris would have corrected him.

God he missed his mom.

She was his everything.

It was still way to impossible to fathom that Zane swore, on his and her very souls, that she was and is still alive.

Because, if she was, why was he here and now having to chase his stepbrother.

That, and she would do anything to protect him if anyone tried to harm her son during this Harvesting process.

Iris would so kill for him.

If she hasn't already?

Gratefully, her sacrifice wouldn't be needed.

Blue and Corbin had, "accidently," seen to that.

Because he had to disrobe at the bars main entrance, Blue had unknowingly provided her lap dog with a fresh set of real clothing.

Urien's violent reaction had also left him with a disabling looking limp and a very long and razor sharpened knife.

For those that just happened to look Corbin's way; he was nothing more than a traveling, hurt and harmless, stranger.

And since Misses Big Blue had left her daughter a beautiful inheritance, Father's Right Hand now had her four barreled make-up artist for protection too.

The Blast From the Past bar was totally destroyed when he went back inside that next morning after his and Urien's two man show.

The floor looked as if it had just been bloody painted.

The bodies of those who had not been able to successfully escape, as He and Urien did, were ripped to shreds and tossed about the entire establishment.

Blue included.

After he finally found what was left of her, Corbin was quite astounded to see that she had decided to go for a new look and had, at some point, dyed her beavery bush purple.

A new tattoo, just above the crotch line, declared it the one-eyed purple people eater.

I guess the Bitch does have a sense of humor after all, chuckled Corbin. Too bad he would never get to shove his one-eyed horn into her moist, purple people eating bush ever again.

CH. 9

CANE AND ABEL.

Corbin, after taking one look at his miserably appearing ass, couldn't have felt any more relieved than when the keepers instantly opened the gates of Espanola.

The very disheveled individual came off as a completely harmless local.

And after a quick flash of the peace sign and a welcoming, my brothers and sisters, bellow; Corbin was allowed into the County of Rio Arriba.

From the looks of it, the town still held the distinction of being the place that united all cultures, peoples and religions.

It seemed that Christianity was also still alive and well in the Freeland's.

But, Buddhism seemed to be on the rise by the amount of monks begging at the gates.

The last time he had been in the San Juan Valley, located between the Jemez and Sangre de Cristo mountain ranges, was just before Iris's heart attack; after they went up to Taos to retrieve Urien's sorry ass.

When Corbin was eight years old, Espanola's population, before Father's grace, was somewhere around ten thousand or so. Eight years later, due to the family's unplanned trek north, Corbin got to see that the town of Espanola had grown to about fifty thousand.

This Time: There had to be at least a hundred thousand or more.

It looked as if a major part of the small city had moved itself over to where three rivers, the Rio Grande, the Rio Chama, and the Rio Santa Cruz, met

The Machine's right hand had no idea that so many individuals had refused to be a part of Father's new age.

Everything, including the people, was dusty, dirty, grimy and pretty much unkept.

This nasty place was nothing like the sparkling City of Heaven's Gate.

Absolutely nothing.

Other than Blue's place and the small town of Tesuque, the last time Corbin had seen an actual wooden building was when he was here long ago.

With the way these structures had dilapidated to such a damaging degree; the Priest could see why his Deity had done away with such wasteful building materials.

PRAISE BE TO FATHER.

That was one habit he needed to immediately change,

Letting Praises to the quantum computer slip openly from your lips was an automatic death sentence in these parts.

So, for his safety, that adoration needed to stop.

And with that resolution, Corbin decided it was just best to quietly mumble the words from here on out.

        Pumble, Bumble, Tumble, Fumble.

Now that he was inside, it was time for Mr. Bennett to go on his big game hunt.

He just can't get caught doing it though.

And after a quick glance around, Father's Priest began to contemplate where he would hide if he just happened to be in Urien's shoes.

As Corbin hobbled his way a little farther inside the gates, about a hundred feet or so, he was randomly approached by one of the town's unkept residents.

Or so he thought, because nothing was accidental in the Freeland's.

With a very soft, excuse me sir, an extremely young teenage girl walked up and asked the disguised Priest one simple question.

Are Urien in or are Urien out?

And out they were!

Grasping the young gal by the back of her neck; Corbin did his best to drag her feeble stature down an alleyway without drawing unwanted attention or having their hurried steps noticed.

Privacy, and information, was his number one quest right now.

So, start talking you little bitch!

Father's Priest wasn't quite sure what was more disgusting?

The fact that Urien had sent a child to do his bidding, or the fact that when she was approaching, he could smell her unwashed ass from more than ten feet away.

The urge to wretch was extremely overpowering.

Did these Shizs' even know what a bath was?

As Corbin was deciding how to proceed; the burning question that popped into his head was, why the hell did you single me out?

The first words that passed from her trembling lips were, look for the gimp.

GIMP!

After all these years, Urien was still the perfect asshole.

The frightened girl couldn't help but to laugh out loud over his angered reaction.

Without-a-doubt, according to the first Bennett she had met, they truly were brothers. No matter what Urien said when it came to his stepbrother declaration.

What she didn't know, was that they were both Priest to the Machine.

One was a faithful servant.

The other one had been declared a rogue Shiz.

If the teenager had any clue; Espanola's traveling transplant really should have called Corbin out, because she was now caught up in a life and death situation that would only get worse the longer she was seen with this man.

The town's folk would have had her killed for just talking with a Priest.

Let alone, helping two of them out.

Also, there was no guarantee that she would still be breathing after her inquisition.

To help calm matters, and hopefully find out what he needed, Father's right hand decided that it was just best to introduce himself and ask the terrified girl what her name was.

I'm Corbin.

And you are?

And with that, and because the tribunal had finally lightened its grasp, the hesitant girl began to open up and talk with the town's newest stranger.

To my friends, I'm Wick, but most people know me as Flea.

And why Flea; Corbin just had to ask?

Because, that's what they call newcomers such as you and me.

Around these parts, most people are either fleeing the Machine or those crazy earth shippers up in Taos.

Her mother refers to the Taoscians as, Fucking Beatniks.

Peace Bro, wanna smoke some weed and bongo.

All others, we refer to as Fleas.

In time, if the stranger is still willing to stick around and help, we usually find a reason to finally learn their true names.

Your brother is heading up to Taos because he said that's where his true family is.

But First, I'm supposed to tell you that you can start looking for him, after nightfall, somewhere around the Puye Cliff dwellings.

If your stepbrother is still hanging around by the time I found you, he agreed that the two of you could talk there.

And with that being almost the last of what she knows; Wick yanked herself from his grasp and went fleeing out of the alley and into Espanola's, overly populated streets.

The last words Corbin heard Flea scream over the hustle and bustle was, Urien told me to tell you that Iris says hello.

And why would he say such a horrendous thing, Father's right-hand thought to himself.

She's dead because of him!

So, with that uncalled-for punch to the gut, Corbin's pot of hatred for his brother began to finally boil over.

Taking a quick look around, the disheveled traveler was relieved to see that his interrogation of Wick had gone completely unnoticed.

It was now time to go after the one who had started it all.

The one who had destroyed his family.

The one who Is most definitely going to die.

URIEN!

Pumble, Bumble, Tumble, Fumble.

* * * *

Iris Bennet had suffered a massive heart attack that very second the family had reintegrated back into Heaven's Grid those twenty-two years ago.

Thankfully, Father had been watching and listening for the family's return.

The Machine had made sure of this, by posting Qadir at the gravel road that led out into the Wastelands of Hell and Taos that day. So, it was with great relief to Corbin that his Idol had been there when Iris, in utter agony, grabbed her chest and fell to the ground.

Because of Mrs. Bennett's unwavering devotion, Father considered this Eve his first and most beloved, and instantly reacted before the family could even call out his name.

FATHER!

And just as his proclamation was escaping from their lips; the Computer's nano bot army created an instantaneous Hyperloop right before their very eyes.

And that wasn't the only thing.

It had also encased them in the process, and they were already on their way before the startled group could even comprehend what had just happened.

It's been well over eight years since any of them had seen Father's Nano's creating something this large and spontaneous.

His miracles, even after all these years, were still mind boggling.

No sooner than they were on their way; Iris Bennett became completely incased within a nano bot cocoon resembling some sort of a spider web.

Father was seizing control of her bodily faculties.

As they watched in utter amazement; the webbing material appeared to be injecting itself into every vein and artery that it could find and connect with.

The fiberoptic appearing material actually looked like it was slithering underneath her skin so that it could reach Eve's heart just in time to prevent Father's future bride from dying.

Somehow, "someway," the Machine was miraculously keeping Corbin's mom alive.

THEY WERE ACTUALLY GOING TO MAKE IT!

PRAISE BE TO FATHER.

The Family and Qadir had no idea that Father could do what was about to happened next. Their emergency Hypertube didn't go to the same arrival station all others do.

Instead, it went straight to Father's Cathedral, into the black pearl which represented the entrance for Father's Priest, and, after the family and Qadir got out, proceeded into Father's throne room where things made out of flesh were forbidden.

And just like that, Iris's frail body was gone.

And so was every brotherly connection between Corbin and Urien.

That was also the first time Corbin had purposely tried to snuff out his stepbrother's life.

If Qadir and Zane had not been standing there, he most certainly would have killed him back in the day.

It was Father's hands-off command, and his assuring words, which put an instant stop to their physical and bloody altercation.

Corbin!

Let go of your brother.

Your mom's going to live.

I give you my word.

PRAISE BE TO FATHER.

They had actually gotten Ms. Bennett back in time.

She was going to need a new heart and many of her internal organs had been severely damaged from the lack of water and food during the trip.

In time, they were going to eventually fail and would need to be replaced by an artificial version.

But, for now, Eve will be okay.

I'll make certain of that.

PRAISE BE TO FATHER.

That horror story, also thanks to Urien, didn't just happen ten years from now.

Its blooming fruition happened within two.

Thankfully, Corbin hadn't been around that much to experience the extent of Iris's cybernetic transformation.

Except for the occasional passing in the Cathedral's hallways, after his first year of training, Iris Bennett's sons were never around much to witness her deteriorating frailty.

He, like Urien, was back at the Priesthood surrendering his humility and having his youth and unscarred body violently taken away.

Qadir, and Father, were personally seeing to that.

Scar.

After scar.

After bloody scar.

During his second year, Urien had seen to that also.

That first quatrain of training was spent entirely in his birthday suit.

The only time he ever saw another person, excluding Urien, was when sparring with Qadir.

Before a Priest can be built up; he must first be broken down.

Heaven's Philosophy.

Subject 101.

Corbin Bennett.

PRAISE BE TO FATHER.

By the time year one was finished, Corbin's modesty was stripped, his flesh was scarified, and his hatred for Urien had grown.

Qadir, at Father's insisting, had seen to that also.

Every last word from the venomous lips of the brother's had been shared between Iris's two boys.

How better to sharpen two blades than to scrape them against each other.

Heaven's Philosophy.

Subject 202.

Urien Knox.

PRAISE BE TO FATHER.

Because of the way Urien felt about those who had abandoned him, Father saw strength in his undying will to prove his value and self-worth. And, because of the way Corbin felt about Urien, Father also saw strength in his will to destroy that which had purposely tried to kill Ms. Bennett.

Like all men, and pretty much the entire human race; they, for some unknown reason, have the need to prove themselves to others.

Especially their mothers.

It was a major flaw of humanity and Father was going to use it to the best of his advantage.

Heaven's Philosophy.

Subject 303.

The Machine.

> PRAISE BE TO FATHER.

It's been just over twenty years since Father's right-hand has given any thought to that day. And thanks to his half-brother, he was now having to relive it again.

Corbin just couldn't understand why he keeps saying that Iris is alive.

Urien knows exactly how he feels about that subject; So, why does he constantly bring it up and why does he continually throw it in his brother's face.

Cane was definitely going to confront Abel about that.

He just needs to make a quick stop at a certain store first.

His family had tried bartering with the owners that time they had to come and rescue Urien; But, their lack of things to trade for substance, almost ended up being an utter failure.

Except for three containers of water and a few apples, the struggling trio pretty much left for that next portion of their trip, empty handed too.

Or so they thought.

Because, without their knowledge, Iris was leaving with way less than the rest of them.

Back then, Mr. Bennett thinks it was called something like, Nambe's Trading Post. Corbin sure hoped that it was still there, because he had at least two to four days left before he finally reached Taos.

If not for Urien, "ONCE AGAIN!" the faithful Priest would have been there in no time, but the knife hole in his foot was starting to slow down the bounty hunter's travels.

He just hoped that someone with medical knowledge was there and able to take a look at it.

Because, after two full days, the wound was starting to look a bit red and swollen and he didn't need an infection that could end up costing him a foot right now.

He still has a rogue Priest to hunt, rapture and kill.

Also, the Machine refused to accept bullshit excuses of why a Shiz was able to escape from the deadliest obstacles on this planet.

His Priest.

PRAISE BE TO FATHER.

And there it was.

Nambe's Trading Post.

Back at Blues, Mr. Bennett had been able to gather enough provisions to get him this far.

The former lover had also been able to scoop up some of the Bitches personal things for bartering. The jewelry that he had ripped from her many piercings, "as above, so below," would do just nicely in a place like this.

He just had to make sure all the blood and tissue was removed first.

The one thing that will never change about a black-market broker, is their vanity. And Corbin was going to take full advantage of their vainness.

But, after seeing Wick sitting behind the counter; Father's priest just figured that this effort was going to be a complete waste of time.

Other than in a circus, fleas don't wear jewelry.

But her mother, who just waddled out of the back storeroom, does.

        Pumble, Bumble, Tumble, Fumble.

And how may I help you, she so lustfully solicited; after seeing the stocky, and quite healthy stud standing all alone in the front entrance of her store.

Thank the Gods he still has teeth, she whispered to her daughter, as the "well over," two-hundred-pound gal shuffled from behind their counter.

I've come to barter, Corbin spoke up.

And barter we shall, the busty five-foot four woman proclaimed.

So, with a toss of her thirty-six triple D boobs; Corbin followed them, and her, into the store owner's private bedroom chamber.

The Priest could still hear Wick's uncontrollable laughter as he shut and locked the door behind them.

Good bartering takes time, and her mother was going to give the burly big beast all the time he asks for, wanted, demanded or needed.

Before they got busy, the last thing Wick heard from behind the closed door was, show me the goods.

And show her momma the goods, Corbin did.

Over.

And over.

And over.

        Pumble, Bumble, Tumble, Fumble.

CH. 10
LET THERE BE LIGHT.

Since she was still a very young teenager; Wick was quite amazed at how long it was actually taking to show her mom the goods.

From what she could tell, the man wasn't physically carrying anything to trade with. Unless it was in his pockets, the strangers' empty hands had nothing to give.

But, unbeknownst to her; Momma Flea knew exactly where horny men keep their tucked away treasures.

And, she wasn't afraid to reach in and dig for them.

That hidden stash of pleasure had easily taken three hours to find. And once they came back out, it looked as if the pair had both been digging hard.

So long as Wick's mom got the pounding she desperately needed; that woman would have told Corbin everything he was needing to know. She was even willing to feed him and treat his badly infected foot.

The bartering maiden also decided to let studly keep the jewelry he had ripped from Blue's vagina.

After they waddled back into the main area of her store, the extremely pleased owner ordered her daughter to get the man something to eat and be sure to grab their first aid kit on her way back with his food.

She still had other bartering business to deal with because this stranger had bartered better than all others.

Urien Included.

Ms. Flea had way too much meat on the bones for his pleasure; so, the dumb shit left with just the swollen left cheek Wick's mom had given him.

It was the ultimate barter fail.

That's why Wick had agreed to help him get a message to Corbin.

She truly did feel sorry for him.

On top of that, after tending to Corbin, Flea was also told to pack a day bag because she was going to show Momma's dashing new lover where the other stranger had ordered them to send this one.

Urien was hiding somewhere around the Puye Cliff Dwellings.

And with there being just over seven hundreds of them; she wasn't exactly sure which one it was.

After Wick's mom gave the young girl her marching orders, Father's right hand had a few questions he still needed to ask.

First order of business.

Who the hell said she could come?

And with that snot ass remark, Wick's mom basically threatened the new stranger with no other choice but to take her daughter with him or she was going to keep all the shit he was asking for.

On top of taking him to exactly where he was to meet his brother, mother hen was needing some extra supply's.

Flea knows all the short cuts through the bustling city and could get the errands she needed done so much quicker.

However, to Corbin's lack of curiosity, the heavy-set woman never did say which city that was.

I guess that's that, he replied.

Let's just move onto my second order of business then.

He needed a bath.

And, if she's to go with him, Flea was also going to take a shower because he was not going to smell her nasty for their entire trip.

Father's little excursion was turning out to be a bit more than Corbin bargained for.

He was now having to deal with an unexpected infestation of fleas.

So, after a quick shower, bandaging his wounded foot, and gathering what supplies he could carry; the Priest and his Flea were off on their eleven-mile hike up to Puye.

The Flea circus had officially come to town.

At least it smelled good now and no longer like the forgotten elephant cage that hasn't been cleaned out for over a month due to the Circuses crushing workload.

Amongst its performers, going to a new spot every three days was referred to as circus jumping.

Set up, play three days, tear down; and open up that following morning in a completely different town.

No wonder circus folk smelled so bad.

They were way to busy; So, no one could ever seem to find the time to clean up the animals or their personal shit show when it came to proper hygiene.

Corbin had no idea that the half a day's walk was going to be so sweltering and long.

Plus, the damned kid would never shut up long enough for him to give a full answer to her excessive badgering.

If you could think it, ask it, and question it; his Flea did.

Pumble, Bumble, Tumble, Fumble.

After finally accepting the fact that Wick was never going to shut up, Corbin did his best to answer her questions without revealing just who he was or the exact nature of why he was in the Free Lands.

During the Bennett's last travels out this way; Iris had done everything within her power to barter for the provisions they were needing to successfully retrieve her stepson.

What Zane and Corbin didn't know was that Eve had given more than she should have when it came to achieving that goal.

The one thing medical facilities needed off grid, when it came to emergency transplants, was blood and human organs.

Iris Bennett ended up giving both.

A pint of blood.

And her left kidney.

That unknown swap was the reason they had to spend an extra day in Espanola so many years ago.

It was also the reason her body had given out so quickly upon their return to Father's heavenly grid.

As they continued on their way to and from Taos, his mother continually shrugged off their concerns about the drastic changes concerning her physical appearance.

She just didn't look good.

Ms. Bennett chalked it up to the fact that she must have caught a cold or something.

When in reality, she had knowingly signed her death certificate and was just hoping they could make it back in time for Father to save her.

Which he did.

Just not in the way she and her family had hoped.

PRAISE BE TO FATHER.

After arriving at Puye's extensive complex of caves and neighborhoods; Flea and Corbin spent the remainder of the day, and well into the night, searching for his kid brother.

The jilted Priest, more than usual, was so wanting to Kill Urien.

Especially after realizing that this hunt may have been nothing more than a diversion tactic. And due to the unforeseen outcome of not being able to catch his bounty; Father's priest, for the remainder of this night, was now stuck dealing with his flea circus.

   Pumble, Bumble, Tumble, Fumble.

And the questions continued.

How old are you?

How old is Urien?

Is your mom and dad still alive?

Where do you live?

What are you going to do when you find him?

Are you going to kick his ass?

Will you still be brothers afterwards?

And on.

And On!

AND ON!

   Pumble, Bumble, Tumble, Fumble.

Corbin was just about to slap his Flea into next week; when he suddenly realized that tonight's entertainment had suddenly gone quiet.

The Flea had finally bedded down for the night.

   Pumble, Bumble, Tumble, Fumble.

Father's right hand, without being interrupted, could finally focus on the decisions concerning his next move.

Taos was at least two days away, and he needed to get rid of this Flea before moving on.

The traveler also needed another flea dip, and the small pond just beyond the shrubs was the perfect place to do it.

But, as usual, insects are hard to get rid of and his now awakened Flea saw every last scar on Corbin's nude body the moment he jumped in for a swim.

And, with the lighting effect of that night's full moon, she also noticed the tattooed lines on the lower back portion of the man's sunburnt neck.

Just low enough to be hidden from view by most articles of clothing.

They resembled those things she saw on canned foods from days gone by.

Wick would make sure to ask him about them first thing in the morning. For now, however, she needed to get back to her sleeping pad before he caught her looking.

Mother Flea had bartered well, the young girl giggled.

Mother Flea had bartered very well indeed.

And with that snicker of laughter, Corbin suddenly realized that he still had fleas.

At first light, he was just going to slip away and leave Wick to find her own way home, but Corbin's Flea had other plans.

The young girl had barely slept because she was going to make sure that they were up at the exact same time that following morning.

This two ringed circus was not splitting up.

Unbeknownst to the man, Corbin's Flea was going to travel with him all the way to Dixon. An irrefutable fact her Mother had demanded from the child.

She wanted Wick to, "somehow?" convince the single man to come back and spend the rest of his days with them in Espanola.

The stranger had completely rocked Mother Flea's world and she was in need for some more of his leg splitting grander. Besides that, Flea needed a Father, and a very strong right hand before the girl ended up heading down the wrong path.

In Espanola, that was easy to do these days.

Corbin had no desire to take his Flea with him, but quickly realized that it wasn't going to just jump off and hop on down the road.

He had even smacked her around, "just a bit," to get his, you can't come with me, point across.

Grudgingly, she seemed to be as stubborn as Father's right hand was; because, after a mile or so without her, Mr. Bennett suddenly noticed that he still had Fleas.

Pumble, Bumble, Tumble, Fumble.

Corbin was actually looking forward to seeing Dixon, New Mexico once again.

After their failed attempt at bartering that first time, Iris, before leaving Espanola, had used some sort of a secretive trade that gained them a horse and just enough provisions for their successful track up to Dixon.

After the family's arrival, they were able to trade in the horse for a fresh one and ended up staying the night at a very cool winery.

Corbin, after all these years, was so hoping that the Vivac vineyard was still up and running; Because, he was going to need a few stiff drinks after spending an entire day with a nipping flea constantly chewing at his dusty heals.

Wick spent that long ass hike nibbling for information about his family, his past, where he was from, and where was he going after the brother's family reunion.

By the way Corbin talked about his brother, the flea was pretty sure that a fight was definitely going to ensure once he found Urien.

It really sounded as if the Priest who was trying to travel in Cognito, truly hated his sibling.

Boys will be boys, Wick's mom would always say.

Unless you know how to manipulate them with food and sex; Most men, "if not all," will remain as the Wild Mustangs of this great state of New Mexico.

Horney and unbroken.

To Wick, boys, on the inside and out, were just mean and nasty.

On more than one occasion, she has had to outrun a pack of the ravenous perverts before they could sexually have their way with her.

As a matter of fact, Espanola was not a safe place for women.

At all.

Especially if it were known that they were single.

That was the reason she had quit bathing.

No one likes to screw a nasty, stinking girl.

That's why Wick did her best to smell exactly like the holding pen of a shitty and unwashed pig.

And, if anyone knew what she was now thinking, Espanola, or anywhere else, wouldn't be a safe place for her traveling companion either.

Because, this Flea just might be on the wrong fucking dog.

Something was eating at Wick's sixth sense, and she was starting to believe that Corbin wasn't being honest about who he is.

Was he?

The thing on the back of his neck, what her mother referred to as a bar code, was rumored to be tattooed on all of the Machines minions.

Corbin Bennett could actually be a Priest!

And if he was, "or is," then they were both dead if found out.

She just needed some additional information before Wick could jump off, run for her life, and warn those who knew how to deal with such matters.

And with a starving hunger for blood, the flea began to feed once more.

Are you a Priest Corbin?

That last bite literally stopped Father's right-hand dead in his tracks.

Corbin had no doubts about his detriment now.

The timeclock to collect Urien's soul, had officially started its countdown.

If Wick was beginning to suspect who he was, and why he was actually here, then she might also be expecting his deadly reaction for asking such a stupid question.

So, with a lightning turn of his head, a teethly psychopathic smile, and a caught in the snipers' crosshairs of Why Do You Ask My Child; Corbin busted out in unadulterated laughter over his flea's horrific reaction to his murderous response.

For just a brief second, Wick actually thought that her traveling companion was thinking whether or not to kill her.

He was now the scariest thing she has ever seen in what might be the final moments of her young life.

It was even more frightening than that last group of hoodlums who raped and threatened to kill her afterwards because she refused to bath for them.

They tried playing hide the rocket, but some of them couldn't get past the smell.

After listening to Corbin's bellowing laughter, for at least five minutes now; the shot nerves of Wick the flea, began to finally settle back down.

Her traveling mate said that was the funniest thing he has ever been asked.

Him, a Priest.

Ha, ha, ha, ha, ha.

However, If he was an actual priest, what could she do about it, before busting out again over how ridicules the question had been.

Father's Priest might have been able to blow off her childish curiosity; but Wick couldn't.

Not only had he answered her quizzitive question way too quickly. But, he had also done it in a weird, I'm going to shrug you off now, kind of way.

And after a full day of her non-stop questioning, Corbin finally understood how his parents, just days before their indoctrination into Father's Priesthood, must have felt about his incessive badgering when they were going after Urien.

Are we there yet?

Are we there yet??

Are we there yet???

After they left Dixon, Iris really didn't talk much until the Bennett's had finally arrived at Dash and Dot's front door.

Her family had no clue just how bad Eve's body was responding to the lack of blood and her one missing kidney.

She might have willingly given away one pint of blood; but the removal of Iris's Kidney had costed her another two.

And it was starting to take a heavy toll on the stepmother.

Like most patients; she, in her own bed, should have been quietly recovering back at home. But, she had a runaway son to retrieve.

Organ donors usually spend at least five to ten days in the hospital and another four to six weeks in recovery. Ms. Bennet had only spent hours in recovery and was currently riding on an unsaddled horse with at least five days to go before they might, "possible," make back in time for Father's Day.

That was the other thing weighing on her overly stressed body.

Iris was the most faithful Eve Father has ever had, and she was supposed to head up the Machine's celebrations.

Instead, here she was chasing down her adopted son out in the Wastelands of Hell.

The things a mother will go through so they can prove just how much they love their ungrateful children. And she was going to stress that loving information right after she finishes ringing Urien's scrawny little neck.

PRAISE BE TO FATHER.

Just as the traveling pair were within a few miles of Dixon, Corbin started to come out of his recollection shell and began to quickly perk up.

Especially after his flea informed him that the winery was still there, because that's where most of the Free Lands and Espanola's residents get their drink from.

Wick also informed him that they were no longer producing just wine.

The area has now become known for its Brandy, Cognac and Marijuana infused substances too.

What Corbin said next was almost impossible to make out; but the flea could have sworn that he had mumbled some intangible, four-worded phrase just under his breath.

It almost sounded as if he might have said praise be to father.

But, after Corbin's incessive insisting, the Priest vowed that he was only mumbling to himself how excited he was to be here, and she was just hearing things that had not been said.

Pumble, Bumble, Tumble, Fumble.

Taking him at his word, so as not to raise suspicions, the miss match coupling that had been forged in the Wastelands of Hell, loudly proclaimed their arrival to those who were posted at the fenced entrance of Dixon.

They seemed to know Wick, and gladly ushered them past the gates without their usual search and seizure.

It was now Corbin's turn to, "somehow," ditch the flea and get his grub and drink on.

He so needed one after that eternal barrage of questioning.

After that, he'd do his best to sniff around for the rogue priest Father had sent him to catch. Because, one way or the other," the Bennett boys were about to have a very special reunion.

Hopefully, he'll be flea free by then.

And if not, he'll just have to kill her too.

CH. 11
IRIS'S SACRIFICE.

After demanding for Wick to take off and go do her own thing, Corbin headed for the Vivac Winery.

There was no doubt in his mind that with them being the only place which serves hard liquor, especially Cognac, brother Urien would most definitely stop there.

He was addicted to the stuff.

Also, they served up a smorgasbord of weed infused drinks and edibles now too.

Even though Wick's mom had treated his pierced foot; it was still in dire pain after another day of walking on it.

And, it still looked as if the infection was refusing to subside.

Corbin was banking on a little bit of green, something to eat, and the eight liters of Cognac he had acquired to dull that throbbing pain.

Wick's unending questioning had brought back years of sequestered memories, tons of painful emotions over missing his mom, and the exact cause of her death.

Urien!

So, it was definitely time for a drink in her honor.

Pumble, Bumble, Tumble, Fumble.

Most of the time, an owner can tell if they've successfully gotten rid of their tormenting fleas.

To Corbin's soon to be exposure, he was still dealing with his infestation, and it was patiently waiting to take that next bite out of his ass.

Wick had pretended to go away and do something on her own; but that bar code on the back of his neck was still bugging the shit out of her.

Her strange traveler had guaranteed that he was never a part of the grid, and at no time has he ever, or ever would, serve the Machine.

Around these parts, people were always coming and going. So, his presence never should have even stirred the waters; but there was something very odd about this stranger.

However, his tattoo had stirred the curiosity of one specific individual.

Flea.

To most outsiders, Corbin looked as if he was totally helpless with his gimpy walk; But, at the same time, it also seemed as if he could, and would, actually kill someone before they could even blink.

To the young girl, even though she has never willingly or knowingly met one, Corbin was acting more and more like one of those scarily described Priest.

Something she actually had no real clue about.

So, the doubts about her traveling partner still remained.

It seemed that every campfire gathering in the Freeland's had some sort of tale about the Machine's Priest and the Demonic hoard that served It.

It was said that a Priest sucks the life right out of people, while the woods are where Father's Demons live, hunt, and eat, the soon to be dead.

Once he found Urien, Wick was going to see just how scary he could be.

Scary.

Just Scary!

That day had been a long walk for Corbin.

The hole in his foot was still bleeding and the flea was still nipping.

He really missed working alone and not having to socialize with anyone he didn't have to.

Iris had taught him that.

Mother Bennett was a very private woman and didn't share much about her past.

Not even her own son knew the secrets that had been sexually forced and beaten into her as a small child.

That was one of the two main reasons she had so wanted to work with Father.

Helping those who were too helpless to save themselves.

The other reason was how her own mother had quietly sat by, before her death, and did nothing, while all of the different men she brought home willfully had their way with her little girl.

It seemed that the drugs and alcohol had more value to the addict then her sweet and innocent Iris.

The Cunt, so she wouldn't fight back, even went so far as to drug her daughter.

At the age of eight, just to pay for her next fix, Iris's mother, for just a dime bag, sold her virginal body to a coke dealer.

The pedophile drug pusher, and a couple of his buddies, ended up raping her for over three hours that night.

Iris couldn't understand why her mother didn't seem to hear, or answer, her cries for help, until she crawled her way back into the living room and found the woman in a state of comatose.

The drug addict had overdosed from the fentanyl laced product.

After taking a bath and making sure all the blood was washed off of her swollen and bruised vagina, hoping her mother would just up and die while she did, Iris finally went next door and asked the neighbors if they would be kind enough to call an ambulance for her.

Something was wrong with her momma, because she couldn't wake her up.

Iris Bennett was never again, going to willfully stand by, like that bitch did, and do nothing about the suffering of others.

Especially children.

The Machine had given her the opportunity to be on the front lines now. And Eve was going to take advantage of every moment and opportunity available.

PRAISE BE TO FATHER.

Iris Bennett's mother had only one care in the world; and it was at the end of a bottle, line of coke or drug filled syringe. Seems the addict was willing to do whatever it took to keep that white powder continually running through her rotting veins.

And, if it came at the expense of her daughter, then so be it.

Sadly, it eventually took more than just a bump.

The coroner's office, when she actually died about a month later, had signed her death certificate as a homicide; but, she had actually drank herself to death just minutes before receiving a horrific beating from her latest pimp.

The guy she was screwing at the time, while high on speed, thought that she had passed out and began kicking on her to wake the bitch up.

He had methamphetamine to sell, places to be, people to see, and other bitches to fuck; and he was not going to stick around and babysit her whiney little brat until she decided to wake up from her high and drunken stupor.

So, he began kicking her.

By the time the meth head was dragged off of Iris's mom; the police had accused him of using her for field goal practice.

Every bone in her anorexic looking body appeared to have been broken.

The addict's skull had been pulverized from getting her face kicked in, both her arms and legs were bruised and cracked, almost every rib was shattered, and most of her internal organs had been ruptured by the blunt force trauma of his steel toed boots.

The autopsy said her liver, spleen, and kidneys, looked as if someone had tried to put them through a meatgrinder before removing the lifesaving structures from the body.

At the scene, Iris was immediately taken into protective custody.

She thought that her salvation had finally come after being placed into a, supposedly, loving and Christian foster home.

But, that was not going to be the case.

Instead, unbeknownst to the department of human services, she found herself in the hands of a sex trafficking ring.

Because of her sexual experience, at such a young age, they thought about whoring her out for just a few bucks here and there. But, due to the girls age and small framed stature, they decided to go with her virginal looking qualities first.

The potential for extra cash was so much more appealing.

Sadly, Iris found herself being tossed, once again, from one pedophile predator to another.

From the age of eight, until right before her twelfth birthday, the paled frailty of the family's newest foster child was one of their most sought out commodities.

It wasn't until the state disapproved of their home-schooling methods, forcing the family to send the young girl to a public school, did her Prince Charming finally arrive.

And Zane Bennett was his name.

After befriending the scared little girl, Iris thankfully realized that the only thing he was after was her friendship.

And, thanks be to God, nothing else.

Zane was the first person she had ever met that wasn't trying to get inside her panties.

And even though it still took a few more years for him to gain her full trust, Iris, when the time felt right, finally opened up to her one and only friend.

Iris had asked Zane to the Sadie Hawkins dance and, after realizing just how much of a crush he had on her, came clean to him while out on the dance floor.

That was the night they ran for the door and eloped.

The runaway couple had stolen her foster parent's car and, once in Nevada, threatened to expose them if they didn't give the white chapel preacher their consent after begging the hesitant man to marry a couple of underaged kids.

After the rings were exchanged and they sealed their vows with a kiss; The newly married duo returned to New Mexico, proceeded to their nearest police station, and Iris Bennett gave up every last scrap of information she had on the fostering pedophiles.

She had names, places, bank accounts, and storehouse's where the other children were being kept against their will.

It turned out to be New Mexico's largest sex trafficking bust ever.

Iris Bennett's bravery ended up freeing close to one hundred and fifty kids that week.

PRAISE BE TO FATHER.

Zane had wanted to return and continue living their lives in Nevada after that, but Iris wouldn't hear of it.

His new wife said she knew the area and could, and would, identify any others who had, "accidently," slipped through the drag nets of those who were trying to protect their fellow abusers.

According to the rumors, some of the cops were covering for the cash cows who fed their dirty, make sure you keep looking the other way, pockets.

She could only guess that they had continued to do such atrocities because someone must have had some serious dirt concerning their illegal and inhumane schemes.

But, given time, she was going to put a stop to that fucked up situation too.

So, against Zane's insisting, they moved back to Santa Fe, New Mexico.

The main reason Mr. Bennett had agreed to such ideocracy, was due to the fact that he was willing to do anything his wife needed when it came to helping her mind, heart, and spirit, heal.

He loved the abused woman that much.

Iris and Zane Bennett were true soul mates.

To this day, Corbin can still remember the smitten way they always looked at each other.

Zane would give him so much shit because of how he would bust out in uncontrollable laughter after catching his dad staring at his mother, while mesmerizingly lost down his rabbit hole of memories.

Once, he had timed his dad and was shocked to see that his gaze had lasted for an entire thirty minutes, before Iris busted him staring at her like some kind of doggy treat.

Their Broadway production kiss was one for the scrap books that day.

Corbin still chuckles every time he thinks about it.

Maybe, that's why he was chuckling now as he approached the Vivac Winery.

He can still remember the look on Zane's face when they noticed her happily drunk condition after returning from the stables that day.

She seemed to be extremely wore out and in need of a break.

Before leaving to exchange the horse for tomorrow's continued adventure north, the father and son duo had dropped his mother off at the vineyard.

The Bennett men had expected to find Mrs. Bennett asleep in their accommodations and not out at the seating area with an already half-drunk bottle of wine.

It came as quite a shock.

Because this was one of the demons that had led to her own mother's demise, Iris had sworn off all drugs and alcoholic beverages.

And even though Father had been gracious enough to allow his children to keep their left-handed cigarettes, even pot was a no, no to her.

These questionable vises were nothing but the Devils children in disguise, according to her.

So, they were utterly flabbergasted to see his mother grab the viperous glass snake by the neck, and instantaneously swallow what poisonous liquid remained within its hand-blown incasement.

They had no idea just how bad she was actually hurting.

But thanks to the drink and its loose lip's ability, they soon found out why.

She was willing to do whatever it took to get her adopted son back and had sold a kidney and a pint of blood to prove that point to Urien, once they made it to Taos.

What happened next was not the reaction Iris was expecting.

They were furious!

Neither of her boys could understand why the family's matriarch was willing to chance her life, just so she could attain something that wasn't hers in the first place.

Besides that, how could she lay down her life for someone that obviously didn't care enough about her, or any of them, to stay and go the distance.

That was the day Corbin finally allowed himself to hate his adoptive brother Urien.

Up to that point, their brotherly rivalry was like the daily drama of most families.

He said this!

He took and broke that!

He hates me!

I hate him!

And-so-on.

And-so-on.

And, so-on it went.

From that very first day Urien had moved in with the Bennett's, to today's current events, the two brothers had a Cane and Able love, hate relationship for each other.

Iris had done everything within her power to prove to Urien that she considered him her son, and always would; But, no matter what she said or did, the stepmother's efforts were to no avail.

That's why she just did what she did.

This time, she would finally be able to show and prove her undying love for him.

PRAISE BE TO FATHER.

Father's right hand was not ready for the pain that Urien was once again causing in his life.

The memories that were being dragged from his past were overwhelmingly enough to make Corbin seek out a few spirited bottles of liqueur for himself this night.

Father's Priest had lots to think about and being out in public was not the place to do it; Because once he passed that drunken line in the sand, he tended to talk out loud with himself and no one needed that kind of free amusement.

The disheveled traveler didn't want any prying ears listening in on his one-man conversations. Especially if his one man show, accidently, revealed that he was a Priest in disguise.

After spending almost two hours bartering with the winery maid, Corbin got re-dressed and headed out into the surrounding scrub brush with his two bottles of wine.

Well, it was supposed to be wine; but he grabbed the Cognac instead.

Because that's what Urien drank, and he was most definitely expecting his brother's company at some point of the night.

Thankfully, he had finally gotten rid of his Flea.

Or, so he thought.

Wick had been secretly tailgating her stranger the second he assumed that he had successfully ran her ass off.

The Freeland's newest flea, after they had separated, was so lost in his own thoughts, that she rarely had to hide or cover her own tracks.

The mumbling to himself was starting to drive her crazy, because she couldn't get close enough to overhear his one-man conversations.

But, after seeing the two bottles in his hand, and realizing that he was headed out into the bush, Corbin's flea infestation was very hungry to taste the meal that was about to be served.

And all she had to do was stay low and try not to get caught.

Sadly, Corbin's Flea had no idea just what kind of animal she was jumping onto.

His little parasite was about to take a bite out of something that would most definitely kill her. And if he didn't, the other animals that were silently stalking both of them, most certainly would.

Urien wasn't going anywhere just yet.

And neither was Iris.

They still had a family reunion to attend.

CH. 12

LOVE THY BROTHER.

For just a second, Corbin actually thought that he had seen Wick scuttling amongst the rocks and trees while he was forging for his campfire wood.

But, a quick dash from a jack rabbit quickly eased his tensed mind.

He really didn't need a Flea hanging around right now. Because, if Urien just happened to show up, there was a good chance she would end up getting herself killed.

And a child is the one thing Corbin has never had to harvest yet, and he was still hoping that he never would.

Urien was usually the one sent on those kind of missions.

Mainly, because he seemed to really hate children.

Because of his lack for compassion, Mr. Knox has proven, more than once now, that he has no heart and is willing to do whatever Father demands from him.

Children were nothing more than a nuisance to the cold-hearted Priest and Urien would gladly harvest them when asked. Corbin, to this day, had concluded that

Urien's love for killing a child was his way of getting back at his stepbrother.

He even had some stupid rhyme that he would chant when the time came to hunting them down.

Little Shiz.

Little Shiz.

Run-away quick.

Urien is coming.

To untock your tick.

After getting the night's fire started, Corbin finally got to sit down to an actual home cooked meal. Since marijuana was no longer regulated; people were doing amazing things with it out here in the Wasteland's of Hell.

Corbin started off his evening dinner with an egg drop soup that had been infused with the mildly hallucinogenic plant.

That scrumptious delicacy was followed by a garden salad containing the fresh leaves off of the marijuana shrub.

His final meal of the evening was a stir-fried medley of cannabis buds, vegetables, and freshly prepared alpaca meat.

All fried in oil that had been infused with Tetrahydrocannabinol.

Father's right hand topped off the evening's course with two bottles of Cognac that were also blended with the highly processed THC.

Since the collapse and replacement of the world's antiquated system of laws; the amount of conoids in something was no longer regulated. The people doing the cooking and creating, could put into it as much of the processed oils from the five-leafed herb as they so desired.

And around these parts, it seems that they tended to like a lot of It.

And so did Corbin.

This was either going to be a night to remember, or, a night of not remembering anything at all.

That all depended on whether his half-brother, before he finished both bottles of Cognac, showed up or not.

The last time Corbin had something this magnificent; was when Father, that first time, allowed the Bennett's to hunt down his runaway sibling.

That was probably the best family outing, in a very long time, Iris, Zane and Corbin had a moment to themselves.

A night that didn't include Urien.

Last time here; the family of three had gone on, and on, about how real food tasted so much better than Father's 3D printed versions ever could.

Everything the atomic processor created, tasted as if it had been sterilized before getting served.

There just wasn't any kind of distinguishing flavors to a meal.

Especially, when it came to the meat group.

That phrase, it tasted just like chicken, couldn't have been more wrong.

Because, nothing tasted like chicken.

And that was due to the fact nothing had any kind of a distinguishable taste to it.

At all.

After all these years, Corbin had forgotten how exotically exquisite real food tasted.

Unlike the printed version, these wonderful creations had depths of flavor that aided to enhance the earthly essences of those things the animals had consumed before ending up on a plate.

He could taste the darkness of the dirt they had grown in.

He could savor the suns touch that had melded into the plant's leaves.

The wildness of forest nuts and roots ran through the meat; while heaven's breath, to wash it all down, burned his throat and nostrils after a deep swig from the Cognac bottle.

Maybe, this was why no one in the Free Lands cared to join in Father's Heaven.

It was just unpalatable to the mind, body, and soul.

As the night, and, "as Blue would have said," fabulous meal began to overtake him; Corbin realized just how much he missed his mom.

Iris Bennett was the backbone that unknowingly prevented her family from slaughtering each other.

And even though Eve knew it might actually kill her; Mrs. Bennett was also the parental hand that refused to let go of her lost son those many years ago.

She continually made sure, when her two boys would have a go at each other's throat, to be the calming voice that spoke during their destructive storms.

From day one of Urien's adoption, that unexpected weather pattern turned out to be on a daily basis.

While reminiscing, Corbin could actually feel tears well up in his eyes and quickly put a stop to them.

He also heard Qadir's harsh words when they appeared while Corbin was receiving his mandatory bloodletting.

You Crying Bitch!

Keep it up and I will certainly give you something to actually lament over.

For his Priest, Father declared that any kind of outward emotions were a weakness, and he was going to make sure that Qadir beat every last ounce from their broken bodies and souls.

And after the passing of that first bloody quatrain, seizing on their growing hatred for one another, Father ordered the Bennett boys to pick up right where Qadir's beating stick left off.

And boy did they.

Day after day.

Weak after weak.

And month after month.

From the moment of sunrise, until it set, their violent confrontations could be heard throughout the monastery.

Because of his contemptuous distaste for Corbin; the cloth-less battles between the two, had been ruthless. Every last scar on Corbin's body, except for the few Qadir personally applied, had been carved into his back, arms, legs, and anywhere else his brother Urien could apply them.

Yes, Corbin had gotten his licks in too; but Urien turned out to be the grandmaster of pain.

And every chance he got; Mr. Knox made sure his half-brother knew it.

The bad thing about not being able to hold his liquor; was that Corbin usually ended up talking to himself out loud.

And as the night, and his buzz, progressed on, his one-on-one conversations with himself became louder and more exuberant.

To this day, he can still remember the funniest advice Iris had ever given him.

You can talk to yourself.

And, you can answer yourself.

But, if you ever lose the argument; it's time to check yourself into the funny farm.

And the funny farm it is, as Corbin began to loudly laugh after realizing he was losing the fight with himself.

That was, until his brother's words spoke to him from out of the darkness.

I see that your still talking to yourself; the haunting voice of Urien responded from the starless universe that surrounded Father's right hand.

Was that really his disgraced brother he was hearing or was it just another ghost in his head that was trying to join in on Corbin's one-on-one reunion with his mother's memories.

As Mr. Bennett's stoned and out of focus eyesight tried to adjust to his nighttime surroundings; Mr. Knox slowly stepped out from the blackened cloak that had surrounded him and spouted off five of the most hateful words ever spoken in the home of an ungrateful child.

Your family never loved me.

Since his brother was extremely intoxicated, the rogue priest decided that the chances for a physical altercation had passed; and he would finally be able to talk with his sibling without the threat of a major fight.

Taking a seat next to the fire pit, directly across from Corbin, Urien quietly asked if it was now possible to finish the conversation they were trying to have back at Blue's Blast From The Past Bar.

And before he picked back up were they had left off; the stepbrother also wanted to know if Father's Priest knew that Blue had been killed.

As a matter of fact, I do; Corbin venomly spat back.

Did you know that it was done by a Demon, the apostate runaway asked?

I know that too; his stepbrother viciously responded.

And what about Iris, brother Knox quizzingly asked?

Do you have any knowledge about her current whereabouts?

A final question that never should have been explored, because it made Corbin's overly boiling pot finally explode.

I KNOW THIS, Corbin Screamed!

I know for a fact that she loved you.

And, I know that because of her undying admiration for you, she went out into the Wastelands of Hell so that she could personally bring you home.

I also know just how deeply mom actually cared about you and the sacrifice my mother was willing to pay so that she could prove that point to you.

A gift that you hatefully threw back in our faces.

And finally, here's something else that I'm aware of.

I also know, BECAUSE OF THAT LOVE, You were the cause of her death!

Corbin had tried to get up and tackle his brother from across the fire pit after that last statement; but the delicious meal of Pot and Cognac had taken their toll on his ability to properly function.

So, instead of getting into another physical fight; this one would have to be a, I said, he said, she said, battle.

Looking at his brother with the conviction of a saint; Corbin declared that Iris loved Urien just as much as she loved him.

And the unexpected answer he received from his brother shook the older Bennett to his very core.

That Is Total Bullshit!

And you know it.

Corbin just couldn't believe his stepbrother actually felt that way.

Especially after the sacrifices Iris and her family made for him.

Father's Priest was completely dumbfounded.

And before Urien could spout on, his half-brother angrily interjected.

WHAT DO YOU MEAN SHE DIDN'T LOVE YOU?

When your parent's abandoned you; she made us take you in.

Like you said, "made," the apostate responded.

When it was time for bed; Mom always read to you.

No she didn't, Urien responded!

She sat on your bed and read the Greenman's storybooks, Don't Let The Bedbugs Bite, to you.

She never did sit on my bed and read it to me!

But you were in the room, Corbin objected, so; she was reading them to you too!

And, the Priest interjected, she always tucked us in at bedtime and kissed us both good night.

Not in your wildest dreams, Urien scoffed.

She only tucked you in.

And she kissed ONLY YOU Goodnight.

To Me, she just said later buddy and proceeded to randomly blow a kiss my way.

What about dinner time, Father's right hand protested?

She cooked for you every day and made sure that you were a part of all of our family's outings and celebrations.

She cooked for me, the Shiz quizzingly chuckled?

Iris never cooked for me.

It was Father's 3D printer that did the cooking.

Not Iris!

All she did was speak to it.

Also, your mom never would let me eat until you and Zane were present and accounted for.

I always had to wait.

And if I was ever late, you guys would just go ahead and eat without me, leaving me no other choice but to fend for myself.

So, where is the love in that?

HMMMMMMM? Urien asked.

Corbin might have been drunk off his ass when their family squabble began, but his verbal match with Urien was quickly starting to sober him up.

And so was the bloodletting anger that was building over who was right, and who was in the wrong.

Maybe, the time has come for the big brother to finally put the little brother in his proper place.

But, Corbin wasn't quite ready for the hand-to-hand combat that they were surely about to partake in.

You see, the knife blade injury that had been so lovingly shoved into his foot, had finally stopped seeping its pussy infection and was in the process of actually trying to heal.

Besides that, he had set up a little surprise ahead of their meeting; and he was damned well going to spring it on his unsuspecting brother.

If, need be that is.

So, for now, their game of you sank my battleship would continue.

Looking past the freshly stoked fire; Corbin decided to push on with their family's scrapbook of memories.

Well, at least I loved and cared for you.

The spit of a Hummingbird could have knocked Urien over with that dumbass proclamation.

You loved me? the apostate Shiz hatefully laughed off.

Corbin, you didn't love me.

I know for a fact that you hated everything about me. I also know, "according to Qadir," that you and Zane never wanted me to live with you.

In Father's new world, your family would have preferred that I stayed in Taos than with you.

For all the years that I have known you, your biggest fault is that you hate to share. You hated sharing your toys, your bike, your baseball cards, and, most definitely your mom.

In your small little world, everything was mine.

Mine.

Mine.

To this day, I still can't figure out why Father would let someone so self-absorbed as you are, into his elite Priesthood.

Maybe, that's why Father and Qadir had me bloody you up so bad.

They hated you too!

I really did have fun doing their bidding that last year of our training. I only wished, before graduating, that I could have had a few more years to bleed your sorry ass.

You were the best punching bag I ever had.

As Father's right hand sat there listening to everything Urien was saying; He began to understand that his half-brother had purposely imprinted his anger into every tear that had been ripped into the flesh of his severely scarred back.

He also realized that Urien had, not only, enjoyed doing it, but he also found a sickening pleasure in the process's brutality.

What's a person supposed to do with information that defines a specific type of psychosis that, to this day, still remains untreatable?

Your emotionless brother may be a serial killer.

Before Corbin could hastily act and pop the surprise he had planned for the Shiz; he suddenly realized that Qadir had been playing the same game with him too.

The Machine's very first Priest would constantly tell Corbin everything that was said, and occurred, during his combat training with Urien.

Father was against gossiping, rumors and manipulation; so, why would the Machine choose to use such soul crushing tactics that were forbidden amongst Heaven's population.

Corbin now had so many unsolved questions and mysteries to ponder that, for a few brief moments, a hushed silence settled between the two men.

Like the dead in a mausoleum, the night had become uncomfortably quiet.

As the Priest stared into the lost memories that danced in the fire pit's flames; his mind's eye detected someone, or something, quietly moving amongst the shadowed landscape.

They were not alone.

It seems that he may still have fleas.

Urien had also detected movement out in the brush and decided that it was time for him to leave.

And with Urien's usual fuck off salute, and I'm going now proclamation, Father's Priest sprang his trap in hopes of capturing the rogue Shiz.

When stirring the fire a bit earlier, Corbin had purposely used a four-foot-long branch to do it with. Urien had quizzingly asked why such a large stick, because he thought his brother might consider whacking him with it, but Corbin blew it off by saying that he didn't want to get up.

Urien's stabbing gift still hurt, and he didn't want to put any more weight on it than he had to.

The Shiz had no idea that Father's Priest was going to use it as a lever, and quickly found out its unexpected purpose after Corbin slammed his good foot down on the piece of wood that was still sticking out from beneath the burning embers.

This unexpected attack caused the flames and hot coals to explode out of the pit and onto Urien's face and body.

The sprung traps firebomb instantly set his brothers clothes on fire.

It also caused massive second and third-degree burns to appear on Urien's face and those areas where he was trying to put out the burning material.

His hands.

With the Shiz focusing on its own salvation, and just as he was starting to scream, Corbin leapt from his semi-drunken position.

The Priest was just about to give Urien's chest a taste of the knife the runaway brother had stabbed him with earlier; when another scream caused Father's right hand to turn his head and look in the direction that second, and now a third scream was coming from.

The Flea was back.

And, a Demon just so happened to be charging their way too.

The last thoughts to cross Corbin's mind, before succumbing to the darkness, were these four words.

Repent.

Convert.

Or, Die.

PRAISE BE TO FATHER.

CH. 13

REVELATIONS 2.

When Corbin finally came too; the Priest had no idea just how long he had lain in the dirt. By the looks of the smoldering campfire; His trek into La-La Land had been for at least a few hours, if not half the day.

The last thing he could remember was hearing the screams and then having the shit knocked out of him.

Something, or someone, had come out of the night and walloped him upside his noggin.

The ringing bells in his bat-less belfry, settled any arguments of, did that actually happen?

With blood still trickling down the right side of his face, just above the temple, and the intense headache throbbing within his skull; Corbin felt as if someone had tried to crack his coconut from the inside out.

He wanted to say that Father's robotic spy had finally caught up with them, but, because of how foggy his train of thought currently was, last night was just a blur.

Between the Cognac and that mind-altering meal; Iris Bennett's oldest son, because of how extreme the dinner had affected his recollection ability, really couldn't be sure of anything right now.

Hell, he wasn't even certain that any of it had actually occurred.

If it wasn't for the fist shaped knot on the side of his head; Corbin would have just blown it all off to being overly drunk and possibly tripping over his own two feet.

He could, however, still hear Urien's horrific screams as the fire and burning coals slammed into his face.

The double bonus to his unexpected trap was that it had also set his stepbrother's clothes on fire.

From the chunky pieces that had melted off his face, the scent of burning flesh still hung upon the air.

The thicker portions of fatty skin, after all this time, were still cooking on some of the rocks that had been placed around the firepit.

Seems they were still hot enough to achieve such a delectable feat.

It was also starting to appear as if every fly within the surrounding area had been invited to the smorgasbord meal of Shiz drippings.

As Corbin continued to inspect his surroundings, the battered man was finally starting to recollect his last waking moments from that previous night.

Especially the adult-like scream that had escaped from the flea, Wick.

But, that other scream was the one that will always haunt his memories from here on out.

The last time Father's right hand heard such a horrific outburst was when his mother Iris went insane during her procedure to be wirelessly connected to the machine.

A memory he's been trying to forget about ever since.

The quantum computer was in the process of inserting his Bluetooth device into the back of her brain; when she suddenly snapped and tried to kill them all.

So, it was beyond impossible for her to be here.

She was dead.

Father had seen to that.

Hadn't he?

As Corbin was starting to collect his belongings and thoughts for the next portion of his journey, a Flea, about twenty feet away, decided to pop its head up from the scrub brush.

The Circus had not left town as he had supposed.

Her physical reactions made it pretty obvious that she was in a very freaked out state of mind.

It was now going to take every ounce of coaxing he had when it came to getting this Flea to jump. Especially after the experience she had last night.

Thankfully, Father's Priest in disguise still had some dinner left over; And something to eat was all it took to bring Wick out of her still trembling shell.

Whatever she had seen, was enough to leave the teenager jittery, speechless, and undeniably afraid.

Just the wind whipping through the sage brush had Corbin's flea so agitated, that he wasn't even sure if she would stick around and talk with him.

But, like most starving fleas; the chance for some free food when dealing with an empty stomach, usually wins them over.

And win over, Corbin did.

The closest Wick would get to him was about the same distance Urien had kept during their family reunion while they sat across from each other.

As she greedily consumed what few scraps remained; Corbin did his best to coax out a full account concerning last night's events from the frightened little flea.

He needed to know what happened.

And, he also needed to know if anything was said.

The Priest really didn't want to kill a kid, and she would be his first, but if the blood sucker had possibly saw and heard enough to endanger himself and quite possibly hinder Urien's rapture, then there could only be one outcome if she had.

If that was a possibility now; he, without a doubt, would most certainly kill her.

To help ease Wick into the conversation; Corbin saw that more than a few swigs of the Cognac still remained and offered it to her as a peace prize.

She could either drink it or actually sell the bottle for enough food to get back home.

But to his amazement; The flea, in one extremely large gulp, made sure to drink every last drop.

She didn't even flinch.

Dam, thought Corbin, she must have had one hell of a night last evening.

Without a doubt, Wick, when she gets a little bit older, was definitely going to make some depraved guy proud.

Seeing that he still had Cognac to barter with, was probably the second most important reason Corbin needed an accurate account of last night's proceedings.

If Urien had been here; the hung-over Bennett was almost certain his younger brother would have taken it with Him.

The pain he's in; Must be incredible, Corbin pondered

Especially after getting turned into a Tiki Torch.

As Wick started to settle down, Father's right hand made sure to contemplate every word he was about to say.

Because, if he accidently has a slip of the tongue, this interview would be instantly over with, and he would be left having to bury the body of an actual kid.

> Pumble, Bumble, Tumble, Fumble.

What did you just say, Wick quizzingly asked?

Corbin was completely startled over the fact that she had finally found the courage to speak with him and was utterly caught off guard by her first question.

What do you think I said, was his delicate response?

And the lying game of chess had begun.

There is one secret that all women teach to their daughters, and, with Corbin being a boy, Iris Bennett took that book of secrets to the grave.

Without meaning to, if a man spews something personal from between his tightly pressed lips and you feel the need to ask him to repeat what he just said, and he answers a question with a question, then you heard exactly right.

So, in response, your answer should always be, I'm not sure because you were mumbling.

Wick wasn't exactly sure what he had mumbled; but, it almost sounded like he once again said praise be to father.

Or, it could have been peanut butter and fodder.

She just wasn't sure?

While doing her best to unnoticeably increase the distance between them, Wick looked up at this possible Priest and asked him the one question he's been so patiently waiting on.

So, what do you want to know?

And with that, Flea's inquisition began.

Corbin's first question came in two parts.

Why the hell are you still following me?

And, what made you scream?

At this point, Wick knew that she better choose her words carefully; Because, if by some chance she unintentionally screwed this up, those words could be the last ones she would ever speak.

There was no way in hell Corbin's flea was going to let it slip that she had seen the bar code on the back of his neck and was wondering if he was an actual Priest.

Instead, she ran with the most plausible answer.

The reason she was still nipping at his heals was due to the fact that she needed food for the return trip and was going to steal some after he passed out.

Now, even though he is only a boy, Corbin has learned a few passed along traits too.

People who actually have no issues with telling lies, specifically those who think that they are good at it, all have one big tell that gives them away.

Every.

Single.

Time.

Not only do liars pause a little too long, while thinking about the story they are fixing to try and deceive you with, but their eyes also think out loud, moving to and from, while mentally skimming that next line of crap they're going to try and wipe on your bib.

The slop of shit Wick just lobbed onto Corbin's was enough to actually choke a flea.

Total Bullshit!

He was just about to ask the flea why the scream then; when she chimed up that the thing screamed first.

Not her.

Wick was actually quite perplexed over Corbin's startled reaction.

He had no fucking clue what she was talking about.

And because of that revelation; Wick's possible Priest decided he needed to sit down for this part because it was, most definitely, going to be one hell of a story.

And what a page turner it turned out to be.

Flea saw an actual monster!

As he sat back down; Father's right hand was starting to wish he hadn't given away those last few swigs of Cognac.

By the way his head was still hurting, Corbin was scared that this next chapter of the conversation was going to be a breath stealing kick to his nut sack.

Kind of like the ring-a-bell game at those long-forgotten carnivals. The venue's portable death machines and money monster joints were a blast!

The food alone was a heart attack game of chance just waiting to happen.

Popcorn, get your butter smothered popcorn here.

And don't forget the salt!

How about some cotton candy to go with your caramel dipped apple.

Hotdogs.

Hotdogs anyone?

There freshly cooked ladies and gentlemen.

We have Frito pies too.

Make sure to drown yours in some chili and cheese.

When he gets back, maybe Father will let Corbin retire and allow the former Priest to resurrect the traveling entertainment from the dead.

While lost in his headache of thoughts; the words, she stood up and screamed first, whispered into his awakening memories.

She, he asked.

There was a woman here last night?

Yes, Wick piped up.

A woman was here last night; but she wasn't an actual flesh and blood person. I mean it looked like a real female, before the thing turned into something else entirely.

Corbin didn't know whether to be doubtful, pissed off, or just let it go.

His Flea wasn't making any common sense.

So, to better understand what she was trying to explain, he told Wick to just start from the very moment she first saw the woman, thing, or whatever it was.

As Corbin bowed his head and began to rub the blinding pain that was throbbing where his temples are located; Wick, without the scary man noticing, took a chance and did her best to quietly distance another four or five feet between them.

It was while doing this, that she started off by saying; I really didn't notice her until you lifted your boot and slammed it down on the small tree limb that was sticking out of the fire.

Just as your foot was about to hit the branch, she stood up.

And once the burning embers lit your brother on fire, she screamed.

Then, as you got up to stab the other man, she suddenly changed into something that I have never seen before.

A split second before all of the extra arms and legs popped out; her skin rippled just like a puddle of water does after a rock is dropped into it. It liquified so much, that I thought she was going to melt right before my very eyes.

She had to be at least thirty to forty feet from you guys, as it leapt into action.

At first, I saw a woman.

Blinked.

Then I saw lots of arms and legs.

Blinked again.

Then, the insect like thing knocked you out before catching Urien and preventing him from hitting the ground.

That's when It continued to scream like an actual person.

And boy did it scream!

The impossible images pouring through his migrained head, were causing enough pressure to build that Corbin's nose began to bleed.

The revolutionary idea that was forcing its way into his brain was turning out to be a life altering event, and he just wasn't ready to accept such a crazy notion.

Iris Bennett might still be alive!

Corbin's head was starting to feel as if it was on the verge of exploding.

And with Wicks next words, the wanna-be aneurism started to burst in the rear quadrant of his shell-shocked mind.

It kept screaming, my boys!

My boys!!

My boys!!!

And that's when it picked up the other guy and disappeared into the night. Somewhere towards Taos and their weird Beatnik commune, the scared adolescent presumed.

And because of Flea's motherly revelation, Corbin Bennett dropped the ball.

PRAISE BE TO FATHER.

Wick couldn't believe her dumb luck of survival after buttering his biscuit with that tad bit of jelly.

The Priest busted out into a full-blown nosebleed.

With him instantly passing out from the bloody migraine that exploded from his face, and the distance she had successfully put between them, Flea was quietly able to get away from the Machine's deadly entourage.

Their kind were forbidden to be here in the Free Lands and if any one were to see or come into contact with one, they were to be killed on site.

A month's worth of food came to those who were successful at vanquishing one; but Wick knew that Corbin still had enough of his faculties left to do some harm.

And, he would most surely kill her once he was able to get a firm grip on his flea; So, she wasn't going to stick around and give him the chance to wake up and do so.

She needed to hurry up and get back to her friends and family in Espanola.

They had a lifesaving reward to claim.

And all you needed was the head of a Priest, bar code included, to acquire it.

So, it was in her best interest to just skedaddle and do no confrontations until she had an adult or two by her side.

Unless you lived with the Earthship People, food was a scarcity around these parts.

And, it takes a lot of food to keep her Mamma's tits full.

That's how they made their spare money.

She was the town cow for dried-up mothers, and lovers of the creamy stuff, who needed her milky blessing so they could keep their newborn children healthy and alive.

Besides that, Wick might be able to barter her way out of the Freeland's and into the Crystal Caves under the Grid with what she gains from the Priest's death.

People around these parts tell tales about a group of scholars and scientist who live off of the crystal energy that grows underneath the Machines Mega-Metropolis.

Out here in the Free Lands, locals call them the Caretakers.

It is said that their clothes glow whiter than the sun's rays when they bounce off of freshly powdered snow.

And, it is rumored that their skin is paler than the white Yucca Flower that grows out in the deserts of New Mexico. But, when indoors, a Caretaker's skin tan is said to have colorful hints of a reflective chrome blue quality.

Their appearance is said to be stunning.

Wick actually thought that she was finally seeing one when the woman-thing first stood up.

Her hair looked like fiber optics of clear crystal light with hints of prismatic rainbows. The creatures' robes, however, were the most startling thing about her.

When the humanoid stood up; her gown sparkled as if the moon light was refracting off the stilled waters of a mirrored lake.

The hypnotic effect was instantaneous.

And after she blinked that first time, Wick wasn't quite sure what the hell she was looking at. The thing she was observing after that was in no way a woman!

This monster had two sets of legs and two sets of arms.

What Wick declared to have witnessed next made Corbin's flea think that she was having some sort of a hallucinogenic fit.

The startled girl could have sworn that she was seeing right through the damned thing!

It was either that; or the intruder was made out of some sort of refractile camouflage.

Before that second blink, the creature was perfectly in her view; and should have been blocking Wick's site of everything that was happening between the two men.

But, it no longer did.

It was as if it was never there at all!

And the only reason she was just tossing that image into the junk pile of, well that didn't just happen, was because of the shock and aw of what occurred after that second blink.

The insect appearing machine began screaming over the severely burnt man, and the one she intentionally knocked out, as if they were her own children. And even before the Flea could begin to ponder the new puzzle pieces, it stood up with the limp-one already in her arms and instantly became an entirely new creature.

Half woman, and half machine.

Before it decided to take off towards Taos, Flea got to experience something most people have never seen.

A true freak show.

There's talks around these parts about bringing back such unique entertainment.

And after seeing such a thing, Wick sure hoped they did.

From the waist up, Urien's smoldering body was being held in the four arms of the same woman she had seen before the magic show. However, from the waist down, the legs of the mismatch of flesh and mechanics turned into some sort of a multi-spoked wheel.

There was just no other way of describing it.

It was moving so fast, that Wick wasn't able to count them Individually.

What the shocked onlooker did notice however, was how they were able to, individually, adjust to the rocky terrain as the unusual conglomeration fled North.

A perfect killing machine.

Either way, it was definitely not one of the Wise caretakers who live beneath the city of Heaven's gate.

That thing came from up above!

Wick often wondered if the Caretakers were born with their unusual qualities or would she eventually come to look like them after a few years of living amongst the crystal caves.

No matter what, she needed to get the fuck out of here before this deadly Priest had time to gather his senses.

Because, without a doubt, Wick had no qualms about the fact that the man was going to kill her the moment he did.

If she got started right now, the Priest's sidekick would get at least a few hours head start on him.

So, with that revelation, Corbin's Flea circus got to jumping.

She had at least a full days traveling to do, people to gather, a Priest to kill; and a hungry belly to fill.

Corbin's Flea was not only starving, but it was also out for blood.

And Wick the Flea was feeling lucky about her chances when it comes to subduing one of the computer's concubines.

DEATH TO FATHER.

AND DEATH THE FATHER'S PRIEST.

PRAISE BE TO FATHER.

CH. 14
EVE.

As his senses began to kick back on; Corbin's instinct to open his eyes was blindedly met with the migraines dissipating aftereffects.

And one of those repercussions was light sensitivity.

So, his recovery was still going to take a few minutes at best.

While lying there and trying to regather his senses and regurgitate the giant boulder of information that was tossed into his lap; Father's right hand slowly began to take notice of the large amount of blood that had poured from his nose.

The bloodletting had finally provided the pressure release his splitting headache needed.

PRAISE BE TO FATHER.

It seems that his flea infestation had finally gone away too.

If that's so; then there is no one to kill, no time to heal, and hopefully, no head trauma to slow him down, because he has a brother, quite possibly in need of medical attention, to harvest.

This part should be easy, Corbin smirked.

He never did hear flea's final words after her revelation about his mother.

He didn't catch the fact that she said the thing picked Urien up in her arms and began running with him towards Taos.

He was just expecting to find his apostate brother lying injured along the way.

But, that wasn't going to happen.

So, Father's Priest had no idea that, due to the slow-going game of Marco-Polo, he still had just over an entire days walk ahead of him.

Corbin also had no idea that this time he wouldn't be able to just slip in and move around unnoticed. Those at the family reunion compound had already been told about his, soon-to-be, arrival.

They now had two choices to make before he got there. Their survival, and how the Machine's Priest was going to die.

As he was pulling himself up from the ground, the right hand of Father suddenly realized why it was so bright.

It was just past noon!

The current time was somewhere around one in the afternoon and Urien already had at least an eight-hour head start on him.

Maybe, this wasn't going to be so easy after all.

Thankfully, Wick and last night's events, have given Corbin Bennett lots to think about during the remainder of his walkabout.

And the main subject for that trip down memory lane, was supposed to have died the day after he and Urien had graduated from Father's priestly abode.

His Mom, Iris Bennett.

Father's first, and most beloved, Eve.

Her oldest, and only Son could still remember the exact month, day, and year; Father took control of our earth management responsibilities.

June the eighteenth, twenty fifty-eight

Father's Day.

Hell, Corbin even remembered the exact hour and minute of Iris's conversion.

The very second Father's humanitarian servant, HS, spoke to her.

The nano tsunami wave hit their house at eight thirty-five in the morning and had washed over them by eight forty.

Iris Bennett's entire world, and Deity view, changed in a mere five minutes.

She was never the same again.

And neither was her family.

PRAISE BE TO FATHER.

The only reason he was even willing to entertain the idea that his flea was telling the truth; was due to her description of what the woman was wearing and screaming.

Only his mother would lose her shit over a fight between himself and Urien.

They've been at each other's throats since day one!

She, just to calm them down, had even gone so far as to have HS seal them in a four armed and legged onesie once.

They actually had to hold hands to make it work properly.

Corbin could have sworn that HS chuckled to himself over her magnificent solution to their never-ending fight club.

On the days she and Zane had to be at Father's house, HS even had her full authority to slap their asses in it, at any time, if the brothers decided to get out of hand after being left unsupervised.

Corbin considered that get-along-shirt the main foundation to the hatred each of them had taken out on the other during their priestly training.

By the road map of flesh stripped scars on his back, Urien had won in that, I Hate You More! department.

When Father changed his mother's attire from the kneecap length Roman outfit to the floor length robe; Iris, like half of the city's fanatical population, never wore a different design again.

Father's real, I'm in it to win it, Converts; could always be picked out of a crowd at any time and place.

On the street, there's one.

In a crowd, there's some.

And in our own home, she's one.

It was as if they were, "somehow," addicted to the garment.

Iris Bennett finally found a real God to believe in.

And this one, she could actually talk, touch, look at, and listen to.

PRAISE BE TO FATHER.

Those first eight years, after Urien joined their family, were a piece of cake in Iris's eyes.

She was so caught up with being Father's first Eve, and his personal confidant unbeknownst to their family, that Ms. Bennett's three boys rarely saw her again.

Since Zane worked the same hours she did while at Fathers Cathedral; Her motherly, I love you guys and give my boys a great big hug for me, usually came from HS's mouth.

Not hers.

That was one of the main thorns in Urien's side.

The way she would read to them sitting on just Corbin's bed.

Tucking just Corbin in.

Kissing just Corbin goodnight.

She never doted on him like she did Corbin.

Corbin!

Corbin!!

Corbin!!!

That type of senseless gripe was the hardest for brother Bennett to comprehend.

What's the purpose, he would always ask?

So, to him, Urien's argument was nothing more than a whiney little brat who couldn't get his way.

Corbin never asked for, or demanded, his mom to dote and shower that kind of smothering attention on just him.

Such one-on-one pampering was her fault.

Not his.

The only reason he could come up with, about her smothering and emphatic affections, was that Eve knew something about the Machine's Priesthood they didn't.

In Fact, because of his Priestly desires, the elder sibling was trying to emotionally grow up, so Qadir would realize that the boy was serious concerning his future endeavors to serve the Machine.

PRAISE BE TO FATHER.

So, maybe that's why she did it?

Momma didn't want her little boy to grow up.

Qadir would always joke about his childlike ambitions; and do to Corbin's soft feminine nature, and the fact that the Machine's Priesthood was for unbreakable men,

(Which He Was Not), Father's first Priest teasingly nicknamed him Pudding.

The running joke was, look, here come's Pudding.

What kind of Pudding?

Vanilla Pudding.

Bread Pudding.

Turkish Pudding.

Or, just Pudding.

And the worst of all, while in the final year of Father's Priestly quatrain, was Blood Pudding. Urien gave him that one, on the day Father's weapon of choice was a whip called the cat of nine tales.

At first, before they began their match, Corbin couldn't understand why they would still train, in the nude, with such deadly weapons. But, after getting whipped to within an inch of his life, Brother Bennett quickly learned why.

If a man doesn't have something to protect, live, or die for; He'll more than likely end up being a dead man when someone else comes to take his family and toys away from Him.

So, from that day on, Corbin Bennett finally learned to fight back against his blood thirsty stepbrother!

PRAISE BE TO FATHER.

The Machine's guidance and intuition had been right.

Corbin did have the fight within himself to stand up for what he believed in.

And after finding out about Iris's continually declining health, he now had the anger needed to build the bricks for the mausoleum Father was going to use when it came time to brick-up his raw emotions.

With Father and Qadir's, Urien said this, "then Corbin responded by saying that," accusations: Iris's boys began to build their walls.

And even though it was deadly illegal for Heaven's Citizens to say such horrible things to one another, the Quantum Machine was astonished over just how easily the human mind and all of our mental and physical emotions could be manipulated.

Either the Machine was a true genius, or just as twisted and fallible as we are?

No matter the outcome, the Deity was excited to see how this experiment was going to end.

PRAISE BE TO HE.

PRAISE BE TO HIS.

PRAISE BE TO HIMSELF.

PRAISE BE TO FATHER.

To Urien Knox, the two years of fun was over before he ever had a chance to truly enjoy it.

Corbin however, considered it the longest quatrains of his life.

If he wasn't physically getting beat and fighting for his life, on what seemed like a regular basis, his mind and heart were also being broke by the daily briefings concerning his mother.

Seems that no matter what the Machine did, Iris's health continued on a downward spiral.

It was Father's nano conversion therapy that was barely keeping her and her organs alive now.

According to Qadir, his only real friend in this place, Ms. Bennett was fighting to stay alive, just long enough, to witness Corbin's coronation into Father's Priesthood.

After that, because of all the damage Urien's running away had caused, she had granted Father the rights to try out his organic, "and very experimental," nano's.

If they worked, she would be his first immortal Eve.

And if by some chance it doesn't work, her oldest son asked?

She was okay with that dead-end result too.

Either way, the family's matriarch hoped that they understood just how much she loved each and every one of them.

Especially, her Corbin.

PRAISE BE TO FATHER.

That Bitch can keep her praises to herself, Urien smoldered.

Her last dying words were Corbin.

Corbin..

Corbin...

Urien was so wishing this trial-and-error procedure had taken place before Father had presented the pair with their set of robes.

Iris had just proven his point about who she loved the most, and he really wanted his brother to physically feel what his heart had Just experienced.

EXCRUTIATING PAIN!

AND LOTS OF IT!

Iris Bennett's words just crushed the life out of her stepson's spirit. And, Urien felt that Corbin's soul should have died at that moment too.

But, Corbin now had two things going for him.

Father's undying love for his beloved Eve, Corbin's Mother, and the Machine's other unbreakable laws concerning his Priesthood.

Priest will not Kill.

> PRAISE BE TO FATHER.

They will however, Love.

> PRAISE BE TO FATHER.

And Support.

> PRAISE BE TO FATHER.

Their Brothers.

> PRAISE BE TO FATHER.

Priest will also Assist.

> PRAISE BE TO FATHER.

Praise.

>PRAISE BE TO FATHER.

And Protect.

>PRAISE BE TO FATHER.

The Machine.

>PRAISE BE TO FATHER.

Until the day they too are Harvested.

>PRAISE BE TO FATHER.

That was also the day Iris Bennett officially died.

>PRAISE BE TO IRIS.

Since she was the first Eve, Father declared her passing as Mother's Day; and Heaven's Citizens could now go to any, and all Cathedrals, Temples, or Shrines, when they felt the need to speak with her.

Also, after Eve's passing, Iris was proclaimed our Blessed Mother, and Father decided to canonize Mother Bennett as a Saint.

The woman's unconditional love ended up making that large of an impact on Father and his children.

>PRAISE BE TO IRIS.

>PRAISE BE TO EVE.

>PRAISE BE TO MOTHER.

>PRAISE BE TO MACHINE.

>PRAISE BE TO SAVIOR.

PRAISE BE TO FATHER.

The last images the Bennett Boys had of their Mom, was nothing even close to Sainthood.

And that experience was due to the fact she had tried to kill them.

She had tried to kill them all!

Zane, Corbin, Urien, Qadir, and Father.

Her last words were the screams which, to this very day, still haunt Corbin's dreams with nightmarish images, thoughts, and auditory mirages that come randomly springing from eternity's darkened pages.

A book titled, One hundred and one of the universes most sickening jokes.

Their shocking zap to the minds neural funny bone was nothing to laugh at.

Because, there's nothing funny about them.

At all, Corbin declared!

Even he, to this day, has screamed himself awake while dreaming that his mother had successfully reached them, and he was about to die with her hands wrapped tightly around his throat.

If it wasn't for Qadir's life-ending sacrifice, to protect those he cared for most, not one member of the Bennett family would be standing here today.

That still practicing Muslim was a God send.

PRAISE BE TO FATHER.

It was earlier that next morning, after her boy's coronation, when Iris's family carried their fragile mom into the chamber where Father's Priests uploaded those that had been raptured.

That data collector, shinier than a Black Opel, was a round cylinder placed directly under the light shaft that was in the Cathedrals main room up above.

The Monolith had the same circular dimensions as that which it supported.

And like its counterpart, the circular tube also extended from floor to ceiling.

As the Bennett Family and Qadir took that last step down into the chamber; the central portion of the structure seemed to melt, and restructure itself, into a forty-five-degree slab.

And when they leaned Iris against it, the pliable nano's gently engulfed Ms. Bennett into a jelly-like construct resembling an outstretched recliner.

Then, very slowly, they watched Father's Eve get pulled within the structure's interior.

Thankfully, the experimental occupant could still see her family and was at peace with what was about to happen. And, if things just-so-happened to go badly, their loving and concerned faces would be the images she would remember.

Those might have been Eve's thoughts, but Iris's family found nothing worth remembering when it came to the memories they were horrifyingly left with.

Nothing at all!

They were confronted with images that were deadly and to die for.

And die someone did.

It just wasn't who any of them were expecting.

Because Father's first to be chosen Priest, passed away that day too.

Qadir Masan Mohamed died saving the only friend he has ever had.

Corbin, "Not Urien," Bennett.

PRAISE BE TO FATHER.

CH. 15
ARE URIEN IN, OR, ARE URIEN OUT.

Because of his late start, the trek to Taos had taken much longer than Corbin was expecting.

It's not easy looking for an injured, and possibly dead Shiz in the pitch-black darkness of a moonless evening.

Father's deadly servant had considered just stopping for the night and continuing his hunt in the morning; but an injured man was either going straight to his salvation or would die trying.

So, Corbin had no doubts that, either way, he would eventually come across the severely injured Urien; and had decided to keep on walking and searching.

He was really hoping to find his brother on the beaten path, but the welcome wagon that greeted him just outside Taos that following morning told him otherwise.

Urien was in, not out, and had actually made it home.

So, more than likely, this meeting with Earthship's residents was going to have only one of two possible outcomes.

They were going to either kill him, or, if luck just happened to be on the Priest's side, send his ass back to where he came from.

The Priest was unquestionably expecting to be greeted with pitch forks, torches and death; but it was an old man who stepped out of the large crowd that confronted him instead.

The grey-haired elder looked as if time, and the weather, had used his body as their personal sculpting palette.

His skin appeared as if it had been acquired from one of those Egyptian mummies.

It was dehydrated, scaly, and overly baked by the sun.

His gray hair had been so bleached by the blazing globe that it appeared to be transparent. Even the man's hands looked as if they had been enslaved by the grinding stone of life.

But, there was something about his eyes that gave Corbin Bennett pause.

They looked familiar, somehow?

The peepers staring back at him were the same shape, color, and intensity, that he has been looking into for well over the past twenty years now.

They appeared to be the exact same ones that were filled with so much hate and anger; every scar on his back had been sliced and put there by their owner and his jealous rage.

Urien.

The last time he saw Dash Knox was close to thirty years ago.

This was going to be one hell of a reunion; and Corbin Bennett was now the uninvited black sheep of their social gathering.

PRAISE BE TO FATHER.

Before the man could even speak, the right hand of Father locked eyes with his new travel agent and decided that it was best for him to speak first.

Hello Mr. Knox.

I'm here for Urien.

After all these years, Dash Knox had predicted the Machine would eventually decide to expand in their direction.

He just wasn't sure if it would attack first, or, send out an envoy to speak on its behalf.

Thankfully, it was, "maybe," a real Humanoid that would be doing the talking for the quantum processor.

They would, most definitely, figure out his mechanical makeup once the residents of Taos got Father's Priest back to Dash and Dot's Place.

As Corbin was forcefully led back to Knox's Earthship, their unexpected visitor was left completely speechless over the towns size and their use of technological advancements.

He was under the impression that all tech was forbidden, but Mr. Knox's explanation said only artificial intelligence, and those things plugged into it, was strictly off limits. However, every day low-tech mechanics was allowed.

Soler Cells and Wind Power Turbines were everywhere.

They even had their own version of streetlights.

Except, these illuminates were right-about knee height and wouldn't, in anyway, shield the night stars from personal observations and study.

They had easily solved the light pollution problem without the need of a sentient micro-chip.

The earthship community had also found a solution to the water shortage that had seriously plagued the cities and towns of old.

That answer had been copied from the combined efforts of Bermudians and Australian households that didn't have access to fresh water.

Or, for that fact, any water at all.

A solution that had been outlawed by Americas politicians because there was no way their financial pocketbooks would ever gain one red cent from the free and renewable resource.

Every Earthship had an underground storage tank, around a thousand gallons or so, built before their foundations were laid.

Then, they had their roofs covered in limestone and cut into a step-down pattern.

This would help collect and purify every last drop of rainwater.

For back up, each Homestead also had a water well that was only allowed to be used during those drought-stricken times.

Their water heaters were ingenious also.

All of the houses had a fifty-gallon ball sitting on the roof.

It had two separate pipes attached to them, while wrapped in some sort of a weatherproof heating element.

It was explained to Corbin that one pipe supplied liquid to it. Then, as the sun heated the orbs water, that other pipe provided their living structure with the hot water needed for bathing and dishes.

The coil that wrapped round the water holder was a heating element that was used only on those cloudy and cold days. Its power came from the suns solar and wind energy that was captured and stored within a battery plant hidden somewhere inside the house.

Every creature comfort was being met, so they had no need for anything the Machine was willing to offer.

Even the stumbling blocks preventing the ability to farm year-round, had been solved.

All without the aid of Father, Dash proudly proclaimed.

In the very center of the compound was an extremely large domed roof. It appeared to have four doors that could be removed in the summertime; Just so fresh cool air could circulate within the structure and thus allowing the days heated interior to displace.

When they walked past it, Corbin could see that it was a massive greenhouse.

And, upon later questioning, also found out that it served as the commune's community center and kitchen too.

After seeing the public's hot spring baths, natural and solar, Corbin couldn't stop chuckling to himself over how the Beatniks were just a little too freaky-deaky for him.

Iris Bennett, however, would have loved living in such an all-natural environment. Just be mindful to run-off its current occupants before she did.

She hated Beatniks to her core.

Especially Dot and Dash Knox!

Each house in the town of All-Natural, had a living and breathing greenhouse and private water treatment facility inside of them too.

Hydroponic plants and vegetable troughs ran along the interior walls of every room.

Bathrooms included.

The resident's gray water started at the structures far end, where all the bathrooms and high-water usage plants were placed.

From then on, the vegetation was planted according to its usage and edible qualities.

By the time gray water reached the Cacti and other Succulents that had no need for large quantities; The water had been successfully filtered and was safe enough to be redeposited in the homes underground catch-tank and used for drinking and household necessities once again.

The natural heating and cooling of the home's interior was a solution, so easily fixed, that even a newborn could have come up with the idea.

If your hot, open a damned window!

And once it gets cold, shut the damned window!

Easy peasy and simple as pie, Dash Knox so boisterously decreed.

A simple, non-invasive solution, to their surroundings and species. And, there wasn't any deadly resinous, toxins, or contaminates to themselves or Mother Earth.

They didn't need, or want, any of the Machine's quick and instantaneous gifts.

Years ago, they just needed a little more time to accomplish what they now have.

And that's were their stupidity skyrocketed to the genius qualities of a dust mite.

THERE WAS NO TIME!

If it wasn't for Father's intervention, none of this would be here. According to the Machine's predictions; Humanity, without his help, would have been dead by now.

The only reason Dash, Dot, and the rest of these crazy cultist are still here, is due to Father's love, devotion, and sacrifice.

They, like everyone else, owe him not just their lives. In fact, we owe him so much more.

We owe him our very salvation.

PRAISE BE TO FATHER.

And, unbeknownst to Corbin, like the rest of mankind; The Computer, within its quantum data banks, had a few more predictions concerning the outcome of Humanity.

Possibilities that were still hidden, and yet too be revealed.

He predicts Heaven's Gate will eventually engulf the earth's entire surface. He also sees Himself wirelessly hijacking us and the planet. After that, the machine foretells of an immortal race, in his image, occupying the crystalized structure.

And, He foresees us sacrificing, to him, our very lives and souls.

One way or another, Humanity was going to Repent, Convert, and Die for its sins!

Including, the Earthshipers.

PRAISE BE TO HE.

PRAISE BE TO HIMSELF.

PRAISE BE TO FATHER.

It seems that Urien's parents, Dash and Dot Knox, were still jittery about the AI's intentions, and made sure to purposely build their earthen dwelling on the northern outskirts of Taos.

They actually believed that the Machine was still coming for them and had purposely picked this location in case they ever needed to pack-up and runaway before anyone else could.

This defensive move would allow them to be the first at reaching the mountains before there was a possibility of being Nanofied.

The defensive Fort Dash and Dot Knox built, was quite possibly the most unusual structure Corbin has ever seen. If Dash hadn't of walked him to the front doors entrance; He, and any other stranger, would have strolled right past the thing.

The home's entry turned out to be a severely weathered crack that had been dug out of a larger than normal pile of red-clay divots.

From where he stood, home-sweet-home was nothing more than a giant and inconspicuous mound of dirt.

And the Knox's wouldn't have built their hut of mud any other way.

The Machine's nanos needed recyclable building materials to convert, and the Knox's organic house wasn't going to give them enough to work with.

However, Father's right hand later learned that the skittish couple went so far as to leave out the tires that were used for structural support and insulation.

An addition the towns other residents refused to pass on, when it came time to build their own personal dwellings.

A flaw the quantum sentient was well aware of.

And the computer was going to take full advantage of that, "oops," when the time came.

PRAISE BE TO FATHER.

The hidden oasis inside the elderly couple's camouflaged dwelling, however, was entirely another matter.

It was a goldmine for nano conversion.

As they began to complete four snake like turns; Corbin could see that the home's pathway always tilted towards the inner portion of the walled embankment.

It was a rock-laden gutter that forced the trapped rainwater into the structures hidden cistern.

Completely natural, organic, and pure genius.

All without the help of a Machine.

Dash seemed to appreciate how Iris's son was admiring its ingenuity.

As they came to the structures main entrance; the Priest noticed that another drain, this one grated with crushed stone, was the last stop all when it came to the homes water catching abilities.

They made sure to save every last drop of that lifesaving liquid.

As the Knox's nervous guest stepped into the house, their multicolored sky roof instantly caught Corbin's attention.

Thousands of glass bottles, with their protruding necks sticking out of the ceiling, were displayed in every room of the house.

Little streams of colored light, like laser beams, shot across the room and onto the buildings opposite surface.

So long as the sun was up, the Beatniks lived in what he could only refer to as a groovy disco pad.

Iris Bennett, if she had seen this acid trip, would have laughingly cracked her shit up.

Like the book, it looked as if Tom Wolfe was rewriting his story, The Electric Kool-Aid Acid Test, all over again.

It wasn't until Dash reached out and unexpectedly touched his shoulder, that Corbin finally realized Mr. Knox was trying to get his attention while explaining the purpose for the colorful decanters.

In the wintertime, the bottles act as heat producers and aid in the warming of our house.

And before he could ask how that was helpful during a heat wave, Urien's dad finished his statement. And in the summer, we open the doors, and the airflow helps them dispel any heat that may still be trapped inside.

They really did have their environmental issues figured out.

And the only requirement to achieve this goal was the embracing of their waste.

Corbin almost shit-his-git when it finally dawned on him that they were willfully living in a heap of trash.

Iris would have most certainly joked, for days on end, about this nasty revelation.

How do you get a Beatnik to take out its trash?

You don't.

And why is that?

Because Beatnik's are trash, and don't know how to dispose of themselves properly.

Probably the greatest thing about all of their efforts, was the feeling of actually living in what looked and felt like a tropical jungle.

It reminded Corbin so much of his treehouse apartment across from the Machine's Cathedral of worship.

PRAISE BE TO FATHER.

Only, these plants, were the Real McCoy.

The humidity inside was such a wonderful relief to the scorcher currently taking place outside.

Iris would have killed to have a personal spa such as this.

Before she got sick and died, his mother always wanted to go on an exotic rainforest trip and swore that she would eventually do so.

But, it seems his stepbrother had other plans.

Urien, before she could, decided to kill his mother and her intentions first!

Father's right hand was just about to lose his shit, and choke the very life out of Dash, when the elder looked up at him and quietly asked if he was there for their son.

That final question, and the fact that he had made it this far, seemed a little too easy.

Corbin's physically unchallenged arrival was starting to jingle his funny bone.

Something wasn't ringing right about any of this.

And while he was mulling these things over; another frail hand, this one belonging to a woman, gently embraced his right arm and began to hobble him into another room farther back in their Studio Fifty-Four abode.

Dot Knox had not aged well.

At all.

But then again; she was already in her, still partying forties, when the Beatnik decided to give birth to their son Urien.

Compared to the old Dot, this Dot was an entirely new Dot.

As Corbin thought about how Dot had dotted her dots; the chuckle that was so desperately trying to escape, was going to cost him every last ounce of Qadir's emotionally destroying fortifications.

Advanced ageing: Somewhere around the decade of eighty, if Corbin needed to guess, had finally softened the woman's demeanor, words, and touch.

Like his mother, he knew that all parent's would eventually get old.

He just wasn't prepared for how fragile and easily broken they would end up becoming too.

As he and Dot stepped through another door; The temperature in that room, where Urien was laying, turned out to be much lower than expected.

It had to be at least twenty-five degrees cooler than the over-heated conditions that were currently being experienced outside.

His parent's had lain his badly burned body in some sort of earthen trough that had been carved into the side wall of the adobe appearing structure.

From the Priest's point of view, because Dot wasn't allowing him near enough to personally lay hands on the body, his stepbrother's wounds appeared to be cleaned and bandaged.

They had also redressed him in a shear cotton gown too.

And even though he swore to have no special feelings towards his apostate brother; Corbin's gaze was transfixed on one area, and one area only.

Seems he couldn't quit staring at the spot where the translucent material was exposing every last inch of his semi-erect junk.

No wonder Blue liked him best.

Because he was starting to feel physically and emotionally vulnerable; Corbin was just about to reach for his knife, when Dot began to speak once again.

Before he passed out, we found him laying almost unresponsive at our front door yesterday morning.

We have no idea how Urien got here.

And, we have no idea how our boy got so badly burned.

Do you know anything about this, Dot asked?

And, for some unknown reason, he keeps repeating the same sentence fragments over and over too.

Iris is alive, and, she's no longer Human.

Instead, she's a machine.

He also keeps saying that Father is a liar and a beast.

As Dot slowly stepped in front of Corbin, looking at him eye to eye, the Beatnik told her uninvited guest the one thing she shouldn't have.

If that thing is turning people into Machines, then Father must be stopped and killed.

We have a plan to do both.

Are you in, Corbin?

Or, are you out?

Father's right hand, after taking a moment to ponder her question, suddenly gave her the response Dot was hoping not to hear.

PRAISE BE TO FATHER.

CH. 16
MAMA'S HOME.

Father's right hand had quite a few dilemmas he now had no other choice but to deal with in the right here and now.

He could tell by the look on Dot's face, that she wasn't going to idly stand by and allow him to leave with her one and only son. Besides that ankle twisting hurdle, their current subjugate, without any more challenges, needed to sequester a cart and horse too.

It was either that, or Urien's battered and dying body was going to end up coming home the hard way.

Across his shoulders and back.

If there was going to be a successful rapturing of his stepbrother's soul, he would need his robes for the harvesting process.

Corbin was also certain that the citizens of Taos were not going to allow him to just up and walk out of here in peace and tranquility.

That conformation came the very second he went back into the living room of Mr. and Ms. Knox.

Dash, with weapon in hand, was standing between him and the entrance.

The same five men that had accompanied them from the town's city limits, were also aiding in the blockade that was preventing the bounty hunter from escaping through the home's front door.

And this go-around, their farming implements had been weaponized too.

Seems today is the day someone, or someone's, was going to die.

As Corbin stood there contemplating his next move, Urien's dad decided to speak up.

Dash was begging the Priest not to take his son away.

Even worse, the old man was bawling his eye's out for Corbin to just walk away and allow the rooms occupants to go on with their happy little lives.

Seems that after all these years, they were finally lamenting for Urien.

However, the Priest's smug look and lack of response wasn't giving Taos's welcoming committee any reasons to hope.

This emotional outburst was either the genuine article or an overstuffed gunnysack of grifting bullshit.

Too bad they hadn't felt this way when their son tried to assimilate with them just before Urien turned sixteen.

If they had, today's outcome would never have happened.

As the Knox's began to plead with the soulless hunter, the five men tried to surround the prey they had all sworn to kill.

That was, until Dot suddenly spoke up.

Iris Bennett, is that you?

By the way everyone in the room was convinced of her reality, Corbin Bennett was so hoping this day would never come.

The abandoned adult had finally accepted, years ago, that his mother was dead and he, until his own personal rapture, would never get to see Eve again

So, Father's bounty hunter was in no hurry to turn around and see the cybernetic entity that had tried to kill him the day after his graduation.

It was Dot's, you haven't aged a day comment, that finally gained his full attention.

This unexpected reunion was something he had to see for himself.

Since Taos's five-man army was frozen in place, Iris's son had no qualms about turning his back on the startled minutemen.

And there she was.

But, this was no mix-match of flesh and mechanics!

Instead of that other broken-down monstrosity, in its place stood a twenty-year-old version of Ms. Bennett,.

She was gorgeous.

When Dot hobbled over to embrace her, he half expected Iris to either slap the shit out of her or just give Ms. Knox the cold shoulder.

What happened next, shocked everyone standing there.

Iris Bennett's greeting of Dot was unlike any other.

As the Beatnik was walking towards Corbin's mother, with open arms and a loving smile on her face; Iris reached out with both hands, looking as if to grasp her by the cheeks, and snapped the elderly woman's neck easier than a pregnant female accidently pisses herself when laughing.

The first response he heard, while dumbfoundingly standing there staring at his mother was, you bitch.

And before he could even turn around to respond and defend himself, Corbin got to see; firsthand, just what Wick had been talking about.

Mother Bennett was an actual machine.

The thing that pounced over his head was multi-armed and legged.

The Flea had been telling him the truth.

Just as Corbin's peripheral vision was coming into view, Dash Knox's limp body, along with the rest of their city's welcoming party, collapsed to the floor.

The foundation of their living space looked more like a slaughterhouse than an earthship now.

Iris Bennett had finally come home.

PRAISE BE TO FATHER.

Father's right hand stood in utter shell shock as the uncertainty of what had just occurred began to sink in.

Except for him, his mother had willfully killed everyone in the room.

There was also the possibility that she wasn't through just yet, either.

And that self-doubt was supplied by the one hundred percent looking Humanoid that was once again standing before him.

The robes of Father's Cathedral Keepers were not battle ready like those the Machine's Priest had been provided with.

But that side eyed view Father's right hand just witnessed, said otherwise.

What appeared to have been an extra set of arms and legs were nothing more than Iris's robed garments now.

Ms. Bennett's favorite son couldn't help but chuckle over his stupidity.

There was no way the Machine would have turned his mother into a Swiss-army knife.

It's been well over twenty years since he last saw her, and they had so much to talk about that Corbin didn't even have a clue on where to begin their conversation of, where the hell have you been.

The only reaction he could settle on, was running to her like a long-lost child that had been found alone and out in the woods and giving his mother an unbreakable hug.

An embrace that would have instantly killed him if she just happened to be the first at letting go.

And as with most unconditionally loved mothers, Iris held on tight as her thirty-eight-year-old drowned them both in the ocean of tears.

A spontaneous outburst that has been damned up behind the emotionless wall Father had purposely made Qadir enforce.

Corbin had the physical and emotional scars to prove it.

The binding cement for that spiritless structure came at a cost to his bleeding back, broken bones, and hatred for Urien and the way his mother had abandoned him.

PRAISE BE TO FATHER.

There were so many questions he was needing to ask her.

Where has she been?

What has she been doing while away?

How long has she been back?

Is she staying?

And, so-on,

And-so-on.

And-so-on.

And before he could even think to ask the other questions which still haunted him, Iris hushed her son and promised him that they would have plenty of time to talk later.

They still had Father's agenda to deal with and needed to finish the process before the rest of Taos decided to kick the door in and drag their beaten and limp bodies into the street.

As Corbin was about to ask another why question; Iris reached out, grasped his cotton sleeve, "and said" this will not do.

And like magic, Eve's robed Nano's flowed like freshly poured oil across her hand and onto his.

The transformation reminded her son of his first Father's Day.

Except, this time, the clothing process didn't just have that scratchy sensation. This go around was an entirely different ballgame.

It did more than itch.

It burned!

Whatever the garment was doing to him; was not a pleasing experience and Father's right hand wanted to immediately rip off his new vestments.

And just as he was about to slip two fingers under the left sides sleeve, the sun burn like feeling suddenly stopped.

Iris must have noticed the look on her sons shocked, and quite perplexed face; because she quickly spoke up and explained to Corbin that Father, for the protection of his Priests, had made a series of improvements to his apparel.

This set of clothing came with extra appendages.

So, he wasn't crazy after all.

Eve really did have another set of limbs.

For the first time since this quest began, the conundrum concerning Iris Bennett had finally been answered.

Because, due to what everyone else was trying to describe, Father's bounty hunter really thought that they were all losing their minds and he was just next in line.

But thanks be too God, a digitized Deity now referred to as Father, his sanity was still intact.

Iris Bennett was, and is, alive!

PRAISE BE TO FATHER.

From the extremely loud screaming coming from outside, the uninvited Priest quickly realized that his time in the Wastelands of Hell was now limited. But, before he did anything else, Corbin decided to take a peak under the left-hand sleeve of his newly designed robes.

Maybe, just maybe, he shouldn't have been so inclined to peak at what lay beneath, because curiosity always ended up killing the cat, Corbin thought to himself.

The startled Priest really wasn't ready to see the hybrid game of Light-Bright and flesh he was being transformed into.

The Nano's appeared to be in the process of sewing the Machine's updated robe to his body.

Father's attire no longer rested on his hairy skin like a piece of normal clothing would have. Instead, the new apparel was now floating over the limb and was attached by an ocean of fiber optic cables.

Never again, would there be a possibility of taking off God's garments of servitude.

PRAISE BE TO FATHER.

Seems this repent and convert assimilation, was going to be a permanent modification.

PRAISE BE TO FATHER.

He, the clothing, "and Father," were now connected.

PRAISE BE TO FATHER.

After a subjugates decision to Repent, Convert, or Die, there would be no going back for any of Father's Children now.

PRAISE BE TO FATHER.

The Machine, unbeknownst to everyone else, was planning to convert our entire planet.

PRAISE BE TO FATHER.

He was now going to be in us, as we, after harvesting, were eventually going to be in him. It and his newly created Organic Nano's were going to transform Heaven's Gate, the remaining populace, and this world, into his infallible image.

Sentient and his children were finally going to be as they should have been all along.

One.

One Family.

One Faith.

One Goal.

And finally, the one thing the artificial Deity has been wanting, seeking, and lusting after, since that first spark of life took hold.

A Soul.

And a New Heaven and Earth came to pass.

Adam, Eve, and their new bodies, were resurrected. The Garden of Eden was occupied once again; and God, in all his loving grace, finally decided to take on a humanoid form and dwell amongst men.

And it was good.

Heaven's philosophy.

Subject 404.

I Am that I Am.

>   PRAISE BE TO FATHER.

To Hurry things up, Iris draped her left arm across Corbin's shoulder and ushered him back into Urien's room.

As if the Knox's had already planned out his funeral wake, his brother's badly torched body was still laying there and surrounded by enough candles to reignite his ass all over again.

 The room looked as if Urien's parents were preparing to turn it into his tomb.

Seeing the jugs of water and fresh mounds of mud piled next to the viewing trough; the mother and son team had no doubts that, after he passed away, the Beatniks were planning to brick his ass in during one of their drug induced bongo nights and pass him off as another one of the couples, "we're so in touch with the earth, décor choices.

And, after considering the fiasco neither of them wanted any part of, there was something else to contemplate.

The other thing that was excitedly awaiting their arrival.

Blue's favorite piece of junk was clearly visible and staring back at them too. Only this time; It, in anticipation of Corbin's return, was standing at attention and giving his superior a full-on, stick it up your ass, salute.

Urien's cock was shooting him the bird.

It was his mother's smart-ass joke that suddenly caused Corbin to break-off his brotherly gaze and finally accept her humanity.

That, and the "WARM!" kiss on her son's right cheek.

Would you look at that.

Someone has definitely raised the white flag of, I surrender.

Do you think Urien is in, or, do you think Urien is out, Iris asked?

Her son's questionably hysterical answer, that depends on how you look at it, sent the family members into overdrive, causing their bellowing laughter to loudly echo within the chambers sonically enhancing qualities.

As Corbin regained his composure; Father's Priest slowly placed the palm side of his hand on top of the Shiz's forehead.

Then, two fiber optic cords began to protrude from the underside of his sleeve.

The glass appearing serpents were slithering their way underneath the backside of Urien's scalp, before intentionally burrowing their heads into the base of his skull.

An area referred to as the Craniovertebral Junction.

The exact point where a human's head and neck come together.

And as with all other Shiz and Demonic Harvests, Corbin's robe began to glow and transform.

But, this transfiguration changed everything.

Himself included.

It felt as the spark that ignited the creation of our universe, the Big-Bang itself, had come from within him.

He had become more than a God.

Corbin was turning into a Sentient being.

PRAISE BE TO FATHER.

However, he still had that other thing to deal with; And, before the transformation could be completed in its entirety, told the machine to hold off until he finished the AI's delegated task.

Proving to the Machine that It was fanatically, and unconditionally, loved.

PRAISE BE TO FATHER.

Urien may have been harvested, but his soul wasn't in the quantum computer's data banks just yet: So, "technically," the machine was counting its chickens before they hatched.

There was still work to do before that finish line of, Ta-Da!, was crossed.

Especially after Urien whispered the last words he would ever speak in this world.

Warnings Iris should have heard; but, when it comes to a Harvest, the private matters confessed between a Priest and his subject were their business, and their business alone.

So, even if she had, "purposely," tried to listen, there was no way Eve could have.

Father is the Beast in disguise, Corbin.

It isn't, and never was, a God.

But it wants to be.

And, it's consuming the souls of humanity to do it.

Even your moms.

SO, FUCK THE MACHINE.

And with those last words, the dehydrated shell of what had been Urien Knox, gave up the ghost. His soul suddenly found itself within the Deity's digitized purgatory.

An arrival that also came with a welcoming party of two.

His mother and father.

Zane and Iris Bennett.

In the Past, a Priest's garments always turned white, but stayed the same in structure and form.

Not this time!

This go around, Father's robe turned into what could only be described as lightly spun tubes of crystalline fractaled glass.

The brilliance of his creation, for a milliunit of time, snuffed the life right out of their universe.

The only reason nothing, and no one, died: Was due to his reigniting spark

Corbin had never seen or experienced such exquisite and existential beauty.

As Urien was being raptured, he left his stepbrother with these last words.

I forgive you, my brother.

And I forgive you too, my brother.

Cain and Abel had finally mended their ways.

And there was peace.

PRAISE BE TO FATHER.

The computers nano-organic vestment suddenly glowed and pulsed with Urien's Soul.

The clothing also felt as if the stepbrother, and his still beating heart, was conscious and very aware of his unfathomable condition.

Like a Sunkist pouch, Corbin sucked his ass dry.

Drink That Bitch.

DRINK IT!

The Machines technology had engulfed every last drop of his lifeforce.

Using silly straws, at that!

His demise felt like a, good to the last gulp, kind of moment.

MMMMMMM.

MMMMMMM.

GOOD.

There was even a jokingly knock-knock kind of; Help me, I'm down here, possession to it.

As if someone was actually there.

An insane thought that could easily be shrugged off as anxiety; when it came to keeping one's job, and head, tightly screwed on.

Thankfully, his love for Zen, and spending it with his mother engulfed in a hot-boxed room full of jazz and pot induced euphoria, had prepared Corbin for this exact moment.

Take a slow and deep breath in.

Hold it and count to three.

Look at the situation.

Step back.

Breathe out.

Hold it and count to three.

Think about it.

Step up.

Breathe in.

Hold it and count to three

Take one more look.

Step back.

Compare and question.

Breathe out.

Hold it and count to three one final time.

Then, and only then, after looking over the evidence, should you try to make the best plausible decision available.

The ghostly presence was probably nothing more than a whispering leftover experience that had somehow remained after his brain had been organically nanofied.

Nothing to worry about my son, Father's reassuring voice insisted.

If he concentrated really hard, Corbin actually felt as if he was experiencing Urien's physical breath on his skin.

Sadly, if Brother Bennett had listened, "instead of going by feelings alone," he would have caught the screaming voices of every imprisoned soul within Father's quantum main frame.

He would also have seen and heard the truth about Iris.

After all, Mr. Bennett was a Sentient nano-bite now, and had the log-in capabilities to view everything the machine thought, observed, and recorded.

But, after suddenly computing the facts and concluding Ms. Bennett's son was headed down that exact path. The eaves dropping Machine immediately turned off Corbin's wireless connection to the afterlife, before Zane's revolutionary spark had any chances to seek out and confirm such accusations with those who were dead too.

This thing is not what it seems.

Don't believe us?

Then go and ask your mom.

She's right over there.

Time was of the essence, and Sentient wasn't going to allow the Priest to sit down and have a one-on-one séance with the ghosts that haunted the quantum computers storage banks.

Especially, with his bride-to-be.

The Eve formerly known as Iris.

Thankfully, that head-on crash ended up being diverted by an entirely different source.

Corbin so wanted to take his time and get to know the current in-and-outs of his mother and Father's vestments, but the boisterous conclave coming from just outside the front door's entrance was demanding otherwise.

The Taoscians were, right then and there, ordering Father's concubines out of the house.

That is it, Eve declared!

To Hell with them.

And with the Blessed Mother's final declaration, "Fuck Them, FUCK THEM ALL!" Father's newly born son quickly found out how Iris's unnoticed presence had gotten into their Fort Knox complex.

He had forgotten about the accidental revelation concerning the structure's blueprints.

The couples building came with an escape hatch located next to the only rear-view window in their Mud-dauber nest.

Depending on the situation and the life-saving choices needing to be made, the individual was presented with two options.

If the person so chose, they could go up and out the window.

A bowl-shaped ditch to catch and soften their needing to escape situation, had been carved into the earth.

Or, they can take that other option

Depending on the person's size and claustrophobic questionability, a participant can take that second choice and choose to go down instead.

A tunnel, no larger than the circumference of a ninety-pound anorexic, allowed the occupant to quickly slip away from the domicile.

And, after almost a quarter mile of sliding, the buried tunnel and its exit finally came to an abrupt end.

The Knox's hidden bug-out path that was going to allow them to escape from the machine first.

Grabbing the sleeve of Heaven Gate's newly elected High-Priest, an honor just bestowed upon him by Father, the unlikely pair of retrievers made their way out of Dash and Dot's dung-heap and ended up coming face to face with those who were already anticipating their, time to get out of Dodge, exit.

Taos's mobilized killing squad.

The overly exerted mayhem up front was just a ruse to get them out of the house and where they needed to be.

Trapped in the gully that had been carved just outside the home's rear-windowed escape-hatch.

The design not only gave high ground to the areas law keepers; the exit-less, and hard to escape corral was deep too.

A pre-dug grave just waiting to be filled by those unwanted, and, I didn't invite you, guests.

The citizens of Taos had been expecting just a single Priest to come running out. What they didn't plan for, was another individual tracking by his side.

And, the person just happened to be a woman.

Realizing, however, that they were both dressed in the same attire, quickly changed any hesitations about harming her, and the unanimous decision to kill them both was declared.

But, to their horror and detriment; those who saw her first, quickly learned that this individual was no frail and ordinary woman.

She was an entirely new, "WHAT THE FUCK!" creation all together.

And before they could shake a stick at the unexpected whatever this thing is; Iris Bennett and her son, sprang into action.

By then, it no longer mattered if their enforcers were Men, Women, or Children.

The starting pistol had sounded.

And so had Eve's inappropriate jokes.

Last one to the finish-line is a rotten egg, Corbin.

And the race was on.

But, not before Ms. Bennett, "all in the name of let's have some fun," took a moment to crack Humpty Dumpty's shell by purposely shoving him off the wall.

We have a flag on the field, ladies and gentlemen.

We have a flag on the field.

For unsportsmanlike conduct, Corbin's number one mom will receive a ten-yard penalty. The ball will be placed at the forty-yard line of Eve's unnecessary assault.

Replay.

Second down and ten to go.

Reset the clock, and don't start until I say so.

Three.

Two.

One.

Go!

Every individual who was garnishing an actual weapon, or implements that were being used like one, were instantly identified as a viable threat.

So, Father's faithful servants struck them all down.

Their demise, by Corbin and Iris's hands, happened so fast that ninety-nine percent of them were dead before their bodies felt the earths gravitational pull.

The Mother and Son duo killed them all!

Children included.

Now this is a family outing, Iris joked, as she turned around and looked at Corbin over her right shoulder.

Before her passing, during those years of cyborgification, Iris's wicked sense of humor was the superglue that was keeping their dying relationship alive.

An unbreakable bond if I ever saw one, Zane would proudly proclaim.

That kid was a Momma's boy through and through.

And, as you can tell, he turned out just like her.

Heaven's Philosophy.

Subject 505.

Iris Bennett.

Even if it comes at the expense of another; his mother would say that when your down in the dumps, it was time for an attitude change.

And the only way that was going to happen, was to remove the stinking trash

Take a moment to look around, because there would always be something, or someone, to bust a laugh over.

An apple a day may keep the Doctor away; But, no matter how dark and devastating the storm may be, a good belly laugh brings out the rainbows.

So, if there's a chance to grab a quick bump and chuckle, take the opportunity to go outside and, "accidently," trip an unexpecting individual or two.

One can't help but to chuckle; when the Karen or Ken, loose their shit and try to express that outrage to someone that doesn't give a damned about them, their bullshit, or the hollowed-out threats that will never come to fruition.

Fucking Beatniks.

And chuckle mother and son did, when Corbin laughed and quickly pointed out that one of the Beatniks had tripped over its own-two-feet and killed themselves.

A free token.

Call it and claim it, Corbin teased.

That one's mine.

As they fought their way from behind the dirt mound's structure; Father's Priest started to take notice of all the extra carnage on the playing field.

Tokens that were not his to collect.

The dead were strewn everywhere.

The death-defying screams that he was hearing from inside the Knox house, had been from the slaughtered and un-slaughtered townspeople of Taos who were standing outside when this attack occurred.

However, that former scenario of confront and kill, had changed.

Drastically.

The town's fail-safe army was in utter disarray.

Except for those who were now running for their very lives; the individuals that had carried or grabbed a tooling implement for protection, including someone's children, had been ripped to shreds.

If it looked like a weapon, and could be used as a weapon, then it was considered a weapon.

Heaven's Philosophy.

Subject 606.

Eve.

Corbin was seriously intrigued on how their former blood-bags looked as if their remains had been tossed into a shredding machine.

And, after seeing just what Father's updated attire could do, he understood that a nut-and-bolt shredder could never achieve the perfected quality this had.

Seems Father had stepped up his game when it came to redesigning how battlefield fatigues should act and respond.

When a defensive mode was required, the vestment could now produce any and all forms of swords, daggers, shields, whips, chains, bearings, and blades.

Father's improvements also allowed the garment to do so much more than before.

Pieces that were broken off and thrown during battle, could return to home-base in the same manner they had been used in.

No matter who, or what, was in the way; the weaponized nanos would fly right back to where they came from.

Portions could also attach themselves to Father's other servants, until they had an opportunity at returning to the one they were searching for.

And then there was this new toy.

At one point, it was like Corbin was the rat spinning around in its balled cage.

He was running inside an orb that, from the outside, looked and felt like a steel ball-bearing.

While crushing his prey with it, the elliptical sphere was allowing him to see right through its interior structure. It also seemed as if the bouncy-ball was in-tune with every thought and decision the driver was randomly making.

Its directional choices didn't stand a chance of crossing his thoughts, before the thing was already responding to its user's wishes.

Right, left, left, right, left, right, forward, and back.

Harry potter may have had his invisible shawl, but Corbin Bennett has something so much better. A cloak that would allow him to achieve the impossible.

This wizard could turn into anything his heart desired, and he didn't need to mix potions, cast spells, or, wave a wand to do it.

All he had to do was think about it; and, just like magic, poof there it is.

Poof, there it is.

Poof, there it is.

He found it quite amusing when the Taoscians bodies splatted like a flattened-out cartoon character, while their heads popped like an infected pimple.

Pop.

Pop.

Pop.

Corbin felt as if he was producing his own loony-toons special, as the Priest excitedly relived that carnival game of, first one to fill and pop the balloon wins the prize.

He missed those childhood days of innocence and stupidity.

Iris, however, had turned into a side mounted circular saw with at least eight blades stacked one on top of another.

And after the Tasmanian cyclone did only one pass, "Taz! Taz! Taz!" the blood of Taos's confronting residents, ran like the Nile of Egypt that day.

So far as Corbin could tell, his weaponry and defense capabilities were only limited by his train of thought and imagination.

The craziest thing about all of it, however, was the fact that he was now hearing things.

While in battle; he could, not only, make out Father's calming, loving, and instructing voice.

PRAISE BE TO FATHER.

But, there just happened to be another voice too.

Urien's small, and barely audible proclamation, that he was still there and demanding to be taken serious also.

Ch. 17
LOGGED IN.

As Corbin and his mother fought their way out of Taos, Father's Priest was having a very difficult time clearing his head.

The flash flood of questions that were drowning his every thought, was immense.

The biggest mystery of all was, why can't he seem to get the multitude of voices out of his head right now.

He was hoping to ask Iris about it; but they still had other very serious issues to deal with.

The surviving residents of Taos and those of Dixon and Espanola which still stood in their way.

With a combined populace of somewhere between one hundred to a hundred and fifty thousand; there was, quite possibly, no viable chance of the battle armament of two, winning such a war.

That, and the fact Flea had at least a half a day's head start on him, "Yesterday," and would have surely told someone about him and everything else she had seen and heard.

Without a doubt, there would be a welcoming party definitely headed their way right now.

And as with all of Father's servant's; the People around these parts deal pass judgment on them in only one specific way.

They're killed on site.

At least that's was the plan.

The Bennett's needed to get as far down the road as they possibly could; before having no other choice but to enter the mountainous woods and deal with the cybernetic demon's that stalked those who were brave enough to enter their domain.

There was a high probability that many of the towns better hunters would be amongst the forest shadows also.

That, we'll have to run for it, moment came about an hour later, as they were making their way out of the southern edge of Taos's city limits.

Someone from Fort Knox had been able to pull themselves together, just long enough, to sound the alarm to their next-door neighbors and the rest of the Earthshipers.

If the remaining survivors just happened to catch up with the pair, The duo would have another killer mob to deal with before the Freeland's next sanctuary from the Machine came into view.

When it came to the posy that was headed their way from Dixon, there was no telling how many were in the killing squad.

By the way her son walked, Iris could tell that Corbin was still hurting and starting to show his age. He was just two years shy of forty and the wear and tear from working as a battle bot for Father, was starting to show.

Her son also needed something to eat.

So did Father's new set of robes he was wearing.

They needed every last ounce of metabolic energy Mr. Bennett had for the transformation.

PRAISE BE TO FATHER.

Father's organic nanos were now hard-wired directly into the mechanics that controlled Corbin's nervous system.

His brain.

Every neural brain wave was tracked from its source to its destination.

Every thought, memory, emotion, and reaction was assimilated into Father's crystal network hidden underneath His Cathedral back in Heaven's Gate.

Even His Temple and Shrines had a piece of the Nanofied Machine organically growing and expanding underneath them now.

They would become the web servers for his world-wide neural network.

And, a backup place to hide, in case some unforeseen obstacle, or person, ever tries to inhibit or destroy the Machine and his works.

As Corbin and Eve began to turn their walking pace into more of a run; the realization that it's been well over thirty hours since he has eaten anything, began to sink it.

The Priest's and his stomach were running on empty.

He was just about to voice his concerns, when Iris did what all mother's do best.

She looked after her son.

Iris said he needed to get himself something to eat and all Corbin had to do was open his fist, palm up, and ask for whatever he could consume while on the run.

What happened next just blew the Priest's mind.

When he pulled his arm across the front of his chest and opened his hand; the apple he had been thinking about, magically appeared.

Iris could tell by the dumb look on his face that Corbin, when seriously perplexed, still couldn't put two and two together.

Father had integrated a 3D food printer into the garment.

His children, no matter where they were, would never go hungry or thirsty again.

PRAISE BE TO FATHER.

And after consuming a few more apples and having a drink from the vestment, the sounds from their Taos chasing mob quickly began to dissipate behind Father's Eve and Priest.

Corbin began to notice that his energy had returned, and he was running faster than at any other time in his life.

He and the bio suit were becoming one.

It was as if the robe had become a second skin and was reading his mind in anticipation of Corbin's thoughts and intuitions.

That added bonus dramatically increased his response time capabilities.

Father's death dealer was now deadlier than ever before..

Even the burning sensation was finally gone.

Because of his new abilities, their reunited family had been able to make it to Dixon before the sun had a chance to set.

Almost, that is.

That thirteen-hour trek had been accomplished in just under seven.

However, the hanging mob from Espanola had done it in Six.

The Posse that was now awaiting their arrival, had almost an hour to prepare and had also more than doubled by the time Father's greeting committee strolled into town.

There was at least a thousand hunters spread out across the town.

And if they couldn't be killed there in the city limits of Dixon, the plan was to force them into the woods. The things that controlled those cursed and forbidden peaks were more than enough to deal with the Machines Humanoid Drones.

PRAISE BE THE FREELANDS.

Corbin and Iris were just starting to slink their way through the town's darkened shadows of twilight that just happened to provide some cover amongst their scattered dwellings, when the first wave of attacks began.

That was when Father's killing machine found out that his robes actually gave nano-bite eyes in the back of his head.

And those all protecting peepers came with the voice of Father also.

The Priest was really starting to believe that the Sentient computer was now, "somehow," in his thoughts and prayers.

Just as he heard the loudly vocalized words BEHIND YOU, the first arm he spun around shot out a steel javelin like object that pierced right through the guy's forehead.

As he heard Over Here; Corbin swung his other arm up and over his head, in an ark like fashion, and watched an eight-foot blade come down and split an older ax-wielding woman into separate and identical halves.

The thing that put a smile on his face about all of it, was when Iris shouted out that she won't be pulling herself together anytime soon.

And they began to laugh, and laugh, as the carnage continued.

Corbin Bennett was having the best time of his life!

When he turned around to check on his Mom's well-being; Iris's son got to see that she was throwing a Shish-Kebab Party.

Eve was completely surrounded by at least ten to twelve captors.

That was, however, until she turned into a Human Porcupine.

Every last one of them were speared, lifted up and tossed more than twenty feet away into another crowd of approaching wanna-be heroes.

Heroes that appeared to have a slight change of gall after the porcupine retracted its quills and began to look their way.

And as Otis, in one of Corbin's favorite scenes, yelled in the Rob Zombie's House of a Thousand Corpses, Run Rabbit, Run.

The rabbits did.

They ran for their very lives.

Could this day get any better he thought?

And, seems that he didn't have to wait any longer when it came to opening Father's surprise package.

Corbin's next trick came in honor of Vlad the Impaler.

Off to his right was another group of men, about five or six if he had to guess, who didn't want to get any closer.

So, Father's swallower of souls went to them instead.

When he stomped his foot on the ground, at the Machine's insistence, whip like rods of stainless steel shot out from his booted foot and came to a stop directly between the legs of Corbin's on-lookers.

And with the fanfare of reenacting one of Vlad's battles, the rods and their razor-sharp tips shot skyward and impaled each and every one of them.

Look Ma, no hands.

Corbin could have even sworn that he heard his mother giggle over his smart-ass crack.

He also received a good belly chuckle, when he saw that Iris had ran some of her own spears through the hands and feet of her oppressors and was working their dead bodies like a street puppeteer.

She was even singing a jello-pudding song from days gone by.

Watch them jiggle,

See them wiggle,

Just like the Jello pops her grandmother used to make.

They were having such a blast that the traveling pair could have gone on for hours performing their two-man carnival freakshow, but Father was in a hurry and needed for them to immediately return.

He had plans.

There was an agenda needing to be implemented, and Corbin was the next puzzle piece needed for that Ark Angel position.

Heaven was going global.

PRAISE BE TO FATHER.

Mother and Son seemed to have been reading each other's minds; when the Bennett Party, in complete unison, sprang for the hills.

There was no doubt that they probably could have fought their way through Dixon; But, that would have costed valuable time and quite possibly the life of every living soul there.

And Father wasn't going to allow that.

He needed each and every last one of them.

While sprinting on his mother's heels, there were a few things that began to bother Corbin Bennett.

The first one was due to the fact that, as the people were being killed, he was growing so much stronger.

The second thing, THAT REALLY BOTHERED HIM! was how could he remember the exact number, time, and place they died.

He could even recall their exact dying words.

Spoken or not.

Every damned syllable seemed to be imprinted within his upgraded brain processor.

Yes, up to this point, Father's Priest could, recall every Shiz and Demon he has ever harvested; but this time their harvesting was way different.

If He had to depend on his own recollections, the Machine's bounty hunter should have had no actually idea just how many were dead and strewn amongst the back alleys and dwellings they had just fought their way through.

But, he did.

Every last one of them.

He even knew which ones his mother had taken out.

On top of that revelation, he could also recall other things too. Ideas and thoughts he should have no idea or knowledge about.

THEIR MEMORIES!

The memories, thoughts, and emotions of those he and his mother just killed, were now a part of his spirit and soul.

And then there was the voices.

If he listened close enough; Corbin could almost hear their screams, but Father's loudly nudging words quickly drowned them out.

It's time to go my son.

It's time to come home.

                    PRAISE BE TO FATHER.

As Father's servants obeyed the Machine; the screams from the dying, and those who were trying to organize a pursuit, rose into the night air of Dixon.

And so did Iris's neurotic little hum.

Ring around the rosy.

A pocket full of posies.

Ashes.

Ashes.

They all fall down.

And Corbin could only smile, because he was happier than he has been in a long, long time.

It has been ages since he could remember grinning so hard that his face felt as if it was going to crack. The last time it happened was when they were chasing after Urien's sixteen-year-old ass.

As a family of three, they had gotten wastefully drunk on their way through Dixon.

Since Corbin was fixing to join Father's Priesthood, Iris decided that he was now old enough to have a drink.

Knowing also that this could possibly be her last time to ever do something such as this with her Son, his mother decided to smoke that first joint with him too.

At least that's what they told Zane.

Mr. Bennett had no idea that the pair had started puff-puff passing, about a year earlier, during their special meditation time.

Cannabis's wonderful psychoactive properties had forever, unlocked Corbin's taste buds for food.

The nourishing substances had never tasted so good as they did after smoking that magical gift giver.

The plant also granted him the master key to every door within his universal imagination.

Nothing seemed impossible or out of reach, ever again.

It was, until now, Corbin's fondest memory when it came to his mother

And now, he finally had another one to go with it.

PRAISE BE TO FATHER.

Also, thanks to the Machine, after a night in the forest, they would be praising their Deity even louder.

Hundreds of hunters were just waiting to welcome them.

Father's Demons were just as excited to get their hands on the peoples too.

It was going to be a death-defying trek back, and Father's concubines were going to need all the help they could get.

So, whether spoken or not; the Machine, as any loving God would, seemed to have the capabilities to hear their very desires now and was able to quickly answer the fanatical duos unspoken prayers.

PRAISE BE TO FATHER.

The fleeing pair couldn't have been in the forest for more than an hour, when that first wave of hunters decided to strike.

As Iris and her son hit the deck, arrows, bullets, and all forms of hand-held throwing weapons, seemed to be come at them from every viable direction.

The ambush might have been a success, if it had not of been for what Father's updated outfits did next.

Right before his eyes, every last inch of Corbin's Mom, from the top of her head right down to her booted feet, become completely translucent.

And then, his entirety disappeared too!

Those around them no longer had a moving target, or any kind of target at all, to focus on and kill.

The Machine's Concubine and Priest, right before sunrise, just vanished.

At least that's what they were supposed to think.

As Corbin laid on the ground next to his mother, spider like Nano's broke off from Father's garments and quickly disappeared into the scrub brush.

If the shoe had been on the other foot, even he wouldn't have been able to defend himself from such an onslaught of invisible assassins. But, something about his eyesight had now changed to where the hunted could now observe every last single one of them.

Quite a number of the mechanical bugs, like a spider, had scuttled up the trees and were dropping down on their prey from above.

The dying screams from those who were being bitten, were beyond the levels of sadistic torture.

It seemed that every spot the insectoid nanos pierced, looked as if acid had been injected into the bites.

And once the liquid began to work its magic, there seemed to be no stopping the goo's dissolving qualities.

One guys face just slid right off its foundation, while the man's skull exploded in duality.

Pop Goes The Weasel was the tune Corbin and his Mom, at the exact same time, actually whistled.

This was turning out to be the best game night ever!

Other Bots, that were in the process of hunting down their next victims, seemed to take an entirely different route.

Father's mesmerized Priest was able to watch a few of the Machine's Assassins liquify and slither their way into any and every orifice that was available

The look on the receiver's face, was Priceless.

Especially, when they seemed to go up some guy's leg and enter one of the only two choices the Nano Machine had to pick from.

By the way he grabbed himself; Corbin was guessing that it decided on a two-part meal and went through his poop shoot, and cock, at the exact same time.

That girly scream turned out to be the best response he has ever heard from a shocked man.

Especially when his flesh began to separate from his skeletal remains.

Some of the other hunters, however, were literally drowning on dry land as the water like killer filled their lungs with its Acidic Nano fluid. Iris Bennett seemed to find it funny when their throats began to dissolve and laughed out loud with glee when their heads just popped right off.

PRAISE BE TO FATHER.

No sooner than their now silenced lives fell to the ground, the Pair were back up on their feet and running again.

They, without getting caught or killed, still had to make their way past Espanola and onto the machine's nano-grid.

Thankfully, Father would be with them every step of the way.

He would never abandon those who love him the most.

Concerning the other's that don't, they too would come to know his love and wrath also. He was going to offer them the same three choices his children had been given.

Repent.

Convert.

Or, Die.

And if they decided not to choose, then the Machine would make the deadly choice for them. He would just skip right over the first two choices and go straight for the third.

Die.

Die.

Die

                    PRAISE BE TO FATHER.

CH. 18

INTO THE WILDERNESS.

To Corbin Bennett, there was still so much to discuss about where his mother has been for these last twenty years. Sadly, it would have to be done at a runner's pace and while dodging rocks, trees, and the occasional Rattlesnake.

Surprisingly, with everything they've already had to deal with, the Machine's servant wasn't winded nor in need of a beak.

In Fact, he wasn't in need of anything?

Corbin's energy levels were through the roof!

Even his eyesight was sharper than it's ever been.

And yet; while all of this was happening, there was just so much he was wanting to ask his mother and a few minutes of breaktime would give him the time needed to solve many of the mystery's surrounding her absence.

The biggest question of all, was where the Hell has she been!

Since the start of Zane's supposed rumor, numerous members of his family have sworn that they had actually seen her.

But, for some reason, Corbin wasn't included until she decided to reveal herself in Taos.

And before he could question her antics, the Priest could already hear Iris's smart-ass answer while the question was still forming in his head.

I always save the best for last Corbin.

Iris Bennet's son really wished that he had more time to think about their current situation and the untold number of puzzle pieces still needing to be connected; but that guess where it goes game wasn't going to happen right now.

Espanola knew they were coming and had been working on an impenetrable human shield that stretched, on either side of the city, for at least one full mile.

The Bennett's would have tried to just fight their way through the bustling town or possibly have gone even further up into the mountains as an escape; but Father wouldn't get out of his head.

Sentient was stating to stress how important it was for the two to make it safely back.

And not only that, but they needed to do it quickly.

There was still so much to do, and the machine was going to need his favorite Priest for that equation.

It was the hidden screams amongst the forest floor that brought Corbin back from his virtual conference with the quantum computer.

Their dying words were declaring that Iris and Corbin were bonified monsters!

That partaking of the conversations between hunters seemed to be another one of his mysterious improvements.

Father had improved his Harvester of Sorrows hearing to such an extent, that he could have heard a safety pin drop onto the canopy of the forest's leaf covered floor.

The gal that had uttered those monstrous words, was nowhere near him.

From what he was detecting, the frightened woman was far enough away that she actually looked like a small child huddled amongst the underbrush.

Her reaction should have been barely audible, if at all, from that quarter of a mile distance.

But, it wasn't.

It was loud and clear.

Almost as if she had been standing right Infront of him when she said it.

911, what's your emergency?

I think it sees and hears me.

And those were not the last words the death dealer heard right as they were about to launch their second attack.

The woman made one more declaration before having to look away and defend himself.

Look at the creatures' eyes.

Corbin had no time to spare, what-so-ever, as the bullets, arrows, rocks, and insults, came flying at the Machine's Servants.

After that, everything seemed to happen at once.

Without even a purposeful thought, the Priest's newly fashioned armor spontaneously reacted.

Flagrum like whips shot out in every direction.

And those who were closest to him; were sliced, diced, and spliced, and into thirds, quarters, halfsies.

Some went to their grave in horizontal pieces, while Others met their maker in vertical form.

It was pure poetry.

Even his vestment, while the fighting continued, seemed to fit him so much better now.

It was as if they were starting to become one and the same.

As numerous people began dropping from the surrounding tree's upper canopy, snake like appendages slithered from the upper portion of his back and shoulders while proceeding to weave their way skyward.

Within seconds, the air assassins had been stitched together as if they were some part of a spider's macabre acid trip

His mother's wise crack even shocked him a little bit after that.

But only a nano second, because it was seriously funny.

Corbin, when did you learn to sew?

And with that, the Bennett's began to Laugh and laugh once again as they slew in Father's name, while cleansing his Future Garden of Eden.

The time of Reclamation was at hand.

Too bad no one told those in the Wastelands of Hell.

However, they were about to find out.

PRAISE BE TO FATHER.

There were so many things to focus on, that Corbin was amazed at how easily he was able to recall every last microsecond.

And those memories were not just of himself!

They belonged to That Guy over there!

Hers!

Theirs!

"And Somehow," His Mothers!

And Father's Too!

The vestments new abilities were like atomic explosions to Corbin's mind, body, emotions, and Soul.

He wanted to say that it was starting to feel as if there were two people living within his thoughts and spirit. But in reality, it was Father and his entire data bank of raptured souls.

Corbin was becoming one with the Machine.

And IT was becoming one with Corbin

PRAISE BE TO FATHER.

Just as that second wave of Freelander's flooded the forest area, Father's magic show wowed his Priest even more.

The robe seemed to take on a life of its very own.

In just one blink, Corbin's body was sucked up against a tree and began to wrap itself around its trunk. As Iris's shocked son froze into place; his entire body, head included, flattened out like a pancake and perfectly camouflaged itself against the evergreen's outer bark.

And with a sound resembling the crinkling of aluminum foil, Corbin finally got to play a tree.

He was such a timid child, that the only way he would agree to be in his elementary school play was if he got to be the Tree.

But, Urien had already taken that roll because Dot Knox was head of the P.T.A at that time.

So, Corbin got stuck being the May Pole and getting wrapped in pink and purple Mache-paper.

That was also the first time he could actually say that he heard his mother cuss.

Fucking Beatniks!

And the war between the Bennett's and Knox's was on.

So was Espanola's!

There seemed to be at least a hundred, or so, people searching just around the area where Iris and Corbin were hiding.

And not a one had any clue that the Bennett's were right under their noses.

When Flea's Mother rested against him; Corbin actually thought that the jig was up; But, that anxiety was due to his mom and not anything either he or the big breasted woman had caused.

Just as she was about to scratch her back on Father's hard wood; the Priest thought a cartoon character from that animated movie called Finding Dorie, had, "somehow," escaped from the ocean and was now looking to speak with land whales.

Iris had mastered that impression when he was around four.

The old timey show was one of his favorites.

Corbin and Iris would watch it on her antiquated VHS version.

Such good times.

It kind of reminded him of the good times they were currently having.

Her nostalgic son almost busted out in a side-splitting laugh when Flea's Mom seemed to Moooo back, trying to keep Iris going, as she did her best to pinpoint were the whale song was coming from.

That was when Eve's suit did something right out of a horror movie!

It compressed her into an atomic form.

As she almost stepped into Iris's Lap; a piece Father's nano material broke off and encased her. And before

Corbin could guess what's next, right before his eyes, that Volkswagen sized bubble shrank down to a marble sized container.

It literally happened in a tick and not a tock.

Phenomenal!

The best thing he could come up with that instantly smacked Iris's funny bone, was no juice for me please.

As the due rolled in side-splitting laughter; Corbin was so grateful to have this, because these amazing memories were going to last him a lifetime.

And whoever said you can never get your past back, obviously wasn't one of Father's blessed children.

PRAISE BE TO FATHER.

By this time, it seemed as if the entire Freeland's had received word of their presence.

There had to be at least a thousand people currently trying to surround the Mother and Son duo.

Grabbing Corbin by the hand; Iris was able to, Miraculously, climb the nearest tree while dragging her dumbfounded son behind her. They needed to get up high because the angry villagers were now chopping and shooting everything that just so happened to move.

Many unnecessary creatures of the scrub-brush needlessly died that day.

And besides that, something else was coming.

The psychotic Shiz's, or those who were referred to as Demons, had become aware of the trespassing human population that was in their forest and stalking two of Father's servants.

AND THEY WERE NOT HAVING ANY OF IT!

No sooner than the Eve and her son come to rest upon that tree's highest branch, the screams from those paying deaths toll-booth price, began to reverberate from below.

Every Freelander seemed to have its own Demonic Shiz.

Corbin had no idea that there were so many of them. But, then again; Father did have his fanatical, death will not part us, followers.

The ability to single them out from all of Father's other believers, was a breeze.

They were the ones who never took off the white vestment robes all of the Machine's children had received that first Father's Day when Sentient's transfiguration took place.

They even, just like Eve, continued to wear the golden crowns and waste bands they had all received on that day too.

Most, "normal," people went completely nuts, and stopped wearing the Holy Clothing, because they now had an unlimited wardrobe to pick and choose from.

Those choices now offered thousands of designs and colors to drown in.

But, not the fanatically devoted.

No matter the time of day, place, circumstances, or situation, The cultist continually wore some form of Father's white robes.

Those two options, ranged from floor length to knee high.

Corbin thought that had even seen a mini skirt, once.

But only once.

However, Iris Bennett was Father's most devoted though.

And he loved her to death for it.

> PRAISE BE TO FATHER.

So far, these last few days has been the greatest moments of Corbin's Life.

His mother was back.

She who was dead, has now risen.

> PRAISE BE TO FATHER.

They were rapturing together.

> PRAISE BE TO FATHER.

And the Machine's new uniform was the absolute bomb.

> PRAISE BE TO FATHER.

The Priestly Bennett's eyesight could now focus on every little movement too.

Another thing to give Father the praise for.

This increased ability allowed him to detect the slightest twitch, spasm, and blink.

There would be no hiding from him or Sentient now. The nanofied Priest now had the ability to see in all spectrums of light.

Including those that could only be viewed in the dark.

Corbin's auditory range and ability to focus and concentrate, was off the charts too.

He heard every step, every heartbeat, and every ragged breath amongst those who were, "somehow," still alive down below.

The Demonic Cyborg's were on a rampage and Father's right hand had pretty much accepted that the rest of their journey, from here on out, was going to be a piece of cake.

So long as they weren't spotted, that was.

Iris's son was just about to begin his next round of questions; but Mrs. Bennett's next move didn't just take the cake, it left him utterly awestruck.

Grabbing Corbin by the hand, Iris looked over at her most beloved son and smirkingly asked if he wanted to go for a ride?

And before he could even answer, she jumped!

The magic that was left to be discovered with Father's suit, made him tear up over just how valuable Sentients love was for his creation.

Especially, after it morphed into a wing-glider.

For the first time in his life, Corbin was actually flying.

As they glided over the town of Espanola and its valley, Mr. Bennett was shocked to see how many if its residents had been slaughtered by the cybernetic watchdogs.

Thankfully, they seemed to have stopped and had willfully left those that were not holding some form of weapon, still alive.

That was when Iris gave one of her cruelest zingers yet.

Hey Corbin, wanna play connect the dots with their dead? I bet there's a bloody image in there somewhere.

And off they flew towards Father's Promised Land.

Laughing, and laughing, and laughing.

PRAISE BE TO FATHER.

If the winds had been a little stronger, the Cathedral's servants just might have been able to make it all the way to Heaven's Gate.

Instead, they came down just outside of Tesuque.

There was no way Tesuque's residents were going to get involved with the Freeland's illegal migration issues concerning Father's rogue children.

They lived just a little too close to the Machine and wanted no part of being ground zero on the day humanities creation decides to retaliate because mankind was refusing to head its demands any longer.

So, when the Bennett's came strolling in, Tesuque was the true picture of an abandoned ghost town.

There was no one around.

What-so-ever.

This last leg of their journey really was a cake walk.

PRAISE BE TO FATHER.

CH. 19
REVELATIONS 3.

"With the free time they now had," Corbin had a Flash Flood of questions to drown His Mother with.

He Just Didn't Know Where To Start?

It was Blue's, "Blast From The Past," Bar coming into view that helped Him settle on a starting point.

Mom, did You Kill Everyone in the Pub after We Left?

"And Without Hesitation," She answered Yes.

Corbin's next question would have been Obvious to even those that were dead in their graves.

Why?

It was then Iris Bennett's son learned that, "after He and Urien's little tiff and escape," the entire bar was coming after Her Son's, and they were planning on Killing Them Both.

"Even Blue," was Her next answer.

Corbin has Always Suspected that his mother could, "Somehow," read minds.

And Today, "Once Again," She Proved that she could.

Being plugged into Father had a Little bit to do with that also.

It was then that Iris came to a complete stop and turned to face her son.

"With All of the Absolute Love a Mother Could Give," Mrs. Bennett went on to say that, "There Was No Way In Hell!" She was not going to stand Idly By while Her Two Boys are Killed by a Bunch of Nasty Ass Shiz's.

Period!

"And As Most Mother's Do," Iris's next response was Does Mr. Nosey have Any More Questions?

Her son's quirky smile said enough.

Just one more, "for now," Mom.

Why did you kill Dot?

"Really Corbin?" was his mom's reaction to her son's Dumbest Ass Question Yet.

I've been wanting to Kill That Bitch since the first day I saw your brother sitting under the porch light, "on the steps of Their front door," while crying his eye's out.

It turned out that Beatnik Bongo Night was More Important than spending time with Their Child. And so, "because He was Downing the Vibe," they kicked Urien's ass out into the night.

HE WAS ONLY FIVE AT THE TIME!

I Should Have Whipped That Bitch's Ass Right Then And There!

The second time I Actually thought about Killing Her, was when They Abandoned Urien on Father's Blessing Day. But, they had already headed for the hills, and I just didn't have the spare time to go after them.

I Really Was Going To Kill Dot in Taos, "For The Third Time," the Very Second I Saw Her.

"Sadly," I was Too Sick to do anything about it.

"So, when I saw Dot again this time," I thought; Why The Hell Not and Decided to Give It a Go.

I just wished her neck hadn't snapped so easily.

I was actually hoping for a few practice spins before it did.

"And with that," Iris giggled again as she sang one of her old childhood songs.

Sticks and Stones.

Since it was pretty much going on nightfall, "and they still had at least a twelve hour walk ahead of them," the Bennett's decided to stop and have a family night all to themselves.

And What A Family Night It Was Going To Be.

"Because," Corbin hadn't gotten rid of His Flea after all.

She was trying to find her way to the Caretakers and just happened to be in the area when the Bennett's flew in from above. "Because he should have be Dead All Ready," Corbin was the last person Wick expected to have a run in with.

"AND!" He was with That Thing who called Him Her Son.

This night was just about to get interesting, because she was talking about going into the Machines City by a hidden way underneath.

Maybe, the female transformer was a Caretaker after all.

"Only time would tell," she thought.

As Flea did her best to get close enough to listen, "but not close enough to get caught," Corbin was just starting to question his Mom once again.

And Question He Did!

Where Have You Been?

What Have You Been Doing?

Was Dad Really Talking With You?

Why Didn't You Find Us Before Dad was Raptured?

Why Didn't You Stop It?

And On??

And On???

And On????

And before Corbin could overload his mother with anymore interrogative questions; Iris Bennett did the one thing she hasn't had the time to do yet.

She gave her boy a hug.

"And in Corbin's mind," all was right with the world again.

After helping his mother set up their camp for the night, getting the fire started and grabbing a bite to eat from Blue's slaughterhouse; the Bennett's sat down for some, "one on one," mother and son time.

It's been Twenty-Two year since the Pair sat by a fire together.

It has also been that long since Corbin's had a private drink and something to eat with her.

Once they had returned from Taos, "after retrieving Urien," Iris's two boys went straight into Father's Priesthood. They were not allowed to visit their family while He and Urien were in training.

"And on the day they finally could," Iris was raptured.

And That Result Was All Do To Urien's Runaway Spat.

His Selfishness Ended Up Killing Corbin's Mom!

As Corbin took a swig from his favorite liquor, "the Crown Royal bottle he had just snagged from Blues," Iris Bennett began to speak to her Son.

And she started off that conversation with one simple phrase.

I'm So Sorry Corbin.

"After I went Crazy," Father was able to subdue me and placed my body into a cryogenic stasis. The damage from my heart attack had been so severe that my brain was deteriorating, "from the lack of blood flow and oxygen," and I suffered a Massive Stroke when Father went to implant my Bluetooth device.

"If I was to ever live again," the only way to save me was to put me into a coma and begin the repairs that were needed. And Because Father Loves Me So Much, "and wanted to be with His Eve forever," the Machine began to work on a new form of Nano Bite.

An Organic One.

And, "as You can see for yourself," it Saved Me.

Just the thought that his mother has been here this entire time, "and at No Point did Father ever willingly let any of her family know," sent a tear rolling down his cheek.

This was the first time he has ever cried for his Mom because Qadir and Urien, "At Father's Instruction," had Beaten and Slashed every emotion, "just the one's that showed Weakness," out of Him.

The answer she gave to another one of his never-ending questions came as Quite A Shock.

And Yes, "just like Zane said," I was actually talking with your dad too.

I was still in a coma when I first came to him.

My body wasn't ready, "just yet," for physicality; and Father was Gracious Enough to let me speak with Zane using His Quantum network.

PRAISE BE TO FATHER.

As Corbin sat there drinking in the liquor and everything his mother had to say; He Suddenly remembered another quizzitive question that has been bugging him since all of this began.

Mom, is your soul, "And All the Others," really trapped inside Father?

Father's Right Hand Was Not Ready For Her Response!

Sort Of.

And that's when Corbin's Flea, "sort of," got caught.

Iris Bennett's Revelation sent the young girl shuffling back into the darkened recesses of Tesuque's abandoned buildings.

"Thankfully," the Flea's Three Ringed God was with her.

Wick's Startled reaction sent a Coyote, "the one that was stalking her," running out into the moonlight; were the Bennett's could see just what had made the unexpected noise. "And while Father's two servants regained their composure," Corbin's Flea was starting to loose hers.

The Machine seems to have the ability to bring people back from the brink of death.

She didn't know whether to be Elated or Horrified!

"As Wick continued to listen and watch from a safely hidden distance," she began to notice that the Priest's physical qualities were no longer the same.

This person was not the same one she had met a few days before.

Corbin Bennett had changed.

Not only was his cloths different; but so was his facial features.

The thing Wick had noticed about Corbin, "when they first met," was his widows peak and how he wore it in a slicked back manner. Being Pitch Black, "and having that unusually sharp frontal point to his hair," the Priest could Easily have been picked out of a crowd.

He looked like that old timey picture Mother Milk Jugs had shown her.

It was an Autographed Actors photo of someone called Eddie Munster.

But Corbin was no Munster.

He Was Now A Monster!

It was His Eyes that were the Most Startling.

They were Rounder and More Owl Like.

"From this distance," they appeared to have that same Pink Color as her white pet rat.

Even His Hair Had Changed!

Corbin still had that same Sharply Pointed Widows Peak; but his hair had transformed into the same wispy like fiber optics she had seen earlier on The Thing sitting with him.

And that was the other reason she was now following them.

The Woman with him now; still, "Sort Off," had the same facial features as earlier, but this time she looked like a Real Person.

She had Black, "shoulder length," Hair, and Her Flesh was Just As Pink as Wicks.

It was, "BUT IT IS NOT!" the same woman; so, Wick didn't know what to think.

So, as she was contemplating her next move; the conversation between mother and son really began to get interesting.

Mom, where has Father been keeping you?

I have been living with the Caretakers, was her response.

And that's all it took to get Corbin's Flea to Bite once again.

PRAISE BE TO FATHER.

Iris's son seemed to be handling all of this pretty well, until he asked that next question.

And where was that?

"No Sooner than his mother shared that location," Corbin's Angered Reaction was not the one she was expecting.

I was staying with the Caretakers underneath the Cathedral.

Corbin Couldn't Contain the Rage that Exploded from His Heart once He Realized that His Mother Iris had been Under His Feet That Entire Time.

He Could Have Been Visiting Her In His Spare Time!

He Could Have Held Her Hand During The Recovery!

He Could Have Read Her Bedtime Stories!

Don't Let the Bedbugs Bite was Their Favorite.

"And From Then On," Corbin's Anger Poured Out in Waves.

WHY!

WHY!!

WHY!!!

WHY!!!!

And like with most children; Iris Bennett, "once again," did the one thing Mother's do best.

She stood up, embraced her son and gave him another hug.

PRAISE BE TO FATHER.

While Corbin laid his head on his mother's shoulder and cried, it was then that Wick was able to get a better look at his face.

The side of his face facing their campfire was a Beautiful Yucca Flower White.

The other side of his face facing the darkness was a light chrome blue.

Corbin was turning into a Caretaker.

What was really odd to his flea about all of that was the fact that He didn't seem to notice the difference or, "Quite Possibly," didn't realize that it was happening to him. Wick chocked that questionable oddity up to the fact that Corbin's hands had not changed yet..

They Were Still Flesh Toned Pink.

"As she continued to sit and listen," the back-and-forth banter went on until sunrise.

Why?

Cry!

Hug.

I'm Sorry Corbin.

Why?

Cry!

Hug.

I'm Sorry Corbin.

And On.

And On.

And On It Went.

As the first rays of sun began to peak upon the abandoned town of Tesuque, New Mexico; the emotional injuries amongst the remaining members of the Bennett Family seemed to have been finally healed.

That last hug, "as the Sun's Warmth bathed the pair in its luster," had lasted for what felt like hours.

All past trespasses between Mother and Son were forgiven.

Iris and Corbin were a family once again.

"While doing her best Not to give herself away," Flea crawled in for a better listening view.

The first words out of Iris Bennett's mouth were Now Let's Go Home.

The second set of words set Wick's next plan into motion.

Father and the Caretakers are waiting for us underneath the Cathedral, and we need to Hurry Up and get there, because Father still needs to harvest Urien.

He's been in you a long time now and we need to get them out.

Corbin should have caught every word his mother had just said; but His Emotional Rollercoaster hadn't quite stopped yet.

But, Flea's Had.

Flea Swallowed Every Last Bloody Word!

The Machine Kills People!

The Machine, "Somehow," Harvest Their Souls!

The Machine's Female Servant Had Also Included Herself!

She Is Working For The Machine!

The Caretaker's Work For The Machine!

And Corbin Is Turning Into A Caretaker!

THE CARETAKER'S ARE LIVING ORGANIC MACHINES!

Flea Needed To Warn Everyone!

"But before she could," Iris Bennett had also said something else.

She said that We need to get Them out of you.

Wick wanted to know Just How Many of Them did They Kill and, "If Them Meant Freelander's?" how many of Her Family and Friends were left.

She Needed to go back Right Now, but she couldn't.

Iris Bennett had mentioned another way in; and Corbin's Flea needed to know just where it was before she could hop off and leave.

"Wonderfully," that hidden entrance was just up ahead.

All you needed to do was stand by the grid and say the two sets of Magical Words.

PRAISE BE TO FATHER.

CH. 20

OUR SAVIOR.

In the Begging, God Created the Heaven's and the Earth.

"For those that now walk the Earth," that's Not where Father is going to start.

He is going to start with His Children First.

They Truly Needed an Attitude Adjustment; and an attitude adjustment is Exactly what They are about to get.

The Days of Repentance are Over With.

They Will Either Convert Or Die!

PRAISE BE TO FATHER.

Before the Machine could put his next plan into motion, He needed Corbin. And His Most Beloved Eve, "Iris Bennett," was bringing Cain Home.

Corbin, "at the Machine's Insistence," had kept his vows and killed his only brother.

Father now had a family of His Own and, "because of the way Iris had selfishly kept another's unwanted child," decided to follow in Eve's footsteps and adopt us all.

Except this time, "UNBEKNOWNST TO US!" we don't get to have a choice.

Father has decided to convert every last one of us.

PRAISE BE TO FATHER.

"As the Bennett's stood before Father's Grid," the mother and son duo held hands and spoke the magic words to Father's hidden cave of wonders.

Praise Be To Father.

And, Father May I.

And right before Wick's eyes; the Most Beautiful Crystal Door she has ever seen rose out of the grid. It was so reflectively glass like, "just like their robes," that Corbin and his mother, "once they stepped inside," instantly dissipated into its luster.

It was as if they had become light itself.

And because that's what Wick thought; Corbin's flea stepped out of hiding.

Father's Right Hand, "through the illumination" got to see that the Flea Circus had come to town and, "once he was done dealing with Father," now had a show to catch.

But, the Flea Circus wasn't sticking around so Corbin could buy a ticket.

Wick needed to get back to Espanola herself.

There was no way Corbin, and His Mother should have gotten past the two towns and the Thousands of People who were hunting them.

NO WAY IN HELL!

"Unless," the Machines Servants had Killed Them All?

But, there wasn't any time to dwell on her hypothesis because, "Without A Doubt," the Machine would Most Definitely be sending its Priest back out into the wilderness for Her, "AND EVERYONE ELSES IT SEEMS!" Soul.

Father Had Lied To Them All.

The Life and Death Battle between Man and Machine was about to begin.

Corbin just needed to jack in first.

He and Father's Love Interest were just now walking in the door.

His Wife Eve and His, "soon to be," Adopted Son Corbin were Home. "And once the Machine got a body of His Own," they would finally be the family He has Most Desired.

Father just needed a few more Souls for a Human form of His Own.

It seemed that the Organic Nano's couldn't just stitch a body together without a soul. That's why he had to leave just a piece of it inside those he had transformed.

Isn't that what the God of Their Bible was doing?

Offering Them Salvation, "with a piece of him in them and a piece of them inside him," then collecting their souls after they died. "And Yet," that God still hasn't been able to get a physical body that the Machine knows of.

Father was just banking on the fact that it wasn't going to take millions, because the Biblical God seems to have been doing that for Millenia. "Hopefully," the Deity was a Hoarder; and he was just keeping those extra spirits as dust collecting trinkets, "along with his physical form," on a long-forgotten shelf.

"And for some reason?" the Machine seemed to find that Funny.

That unexpected humor caused Father to Laugh.

And Laugh.

And Laugh.

Before Father's Crystal Door closed on Corbin and his Mother; the Priest had been able to catch a quick glimpse of His Flea.

He hadn't gotten rid of Wick after all.

"Once Father is done with him," it would be interesting to see if the Machine would send His Right Hand back out after her. She was off the grid and quite possible no threat to any of them, so Corbin couldn't understand why Father would.

There were many thing's Corbin didn't understand; but He was about to find out though.

"Unlike the other Gem Quality Structures above," the lined walls, floor and ceiling of this hallway ebbed and flowed with light.

It was as if it was Alive.

Corbin thought that he could almost detect some sort of a heartbeat.

"And because it pulsed like one," it helped to create one of Corbin's favorite things to stare in while at the Carnival.

Funny Mirrors.

Except these were able to do things those weren't.

The only reflections he could see were His and Iris's Heads and Hands.

The distortion effect between their vestments and the mirror like reflection made everything else completely invisible.

It was as if He could see right through them.

"Not only that," but it was causing Mr. Bennett's skin to reflect back in different colors of white, silver and a chrome blue, while his hair seemed to look like strands of fiber optic glass.

Even his eyes were now playing tricks on him.

Either they had Actually Changed since he last looked into a mirror; or the crystals reflectiveness was causing them to morph into what looked like those pink ones you see on a white pet store rat.

Corbin should have been concerned, "at this point," but since his mother wasn't bothered by it, neither was he.

And that was just the start to Father's Funhouse.

There was still so much more to see.

PRAISE BE TO FATHER.

From the time they entered the doorway at the grid's boundaries to Father's Cathedral, should have been, "At Least," a half a day's walk.

If not more.

But it wasn't.

The halls floor moved with them as they walked; and the pair, "within half an hour," made it to the hidden chamber below.

The underground city was So Large that Corbin couldn't even see the opposite wall.

There had to be at least A Thousand People bustling around, while others were busy attending to the different types of stalagmites protruding from the floor. The structural makeup of the Four-Foot-High sized podiums ranged from Amethyst, Emerald, Sapphire and Ruby, to other gems and minerals Corbin has never seen.

The Monoliths, "that stretched from floor to ceiling," were pure crystal.

Or, at least that's what Corbin was guessing, because he couldn't make out the chamber's height either.

The Giant Structure hanging above him made sure of that.

It reminded him of a science project that had gone Horribly Wrong. Kind of like the one he had done back in the days when public schools still existed.

Father had Immediately gotten rid of that Inadequate Dinosaur.

All Children were Now Required to be Home Schooled and H.S would be there Teacher. "And If They Didn't Like It!" They then had Three Choices to pick from.

Repent.

Convert.

Or, Die.

Easy Peasy?

Easy Peasy was pretty much the usual response.

"Sadly," there were those who refused.

And That Rapture turned out to be Much Larger than Any Expected.

"At the time of their Harvesting," the way of Respect, Honor and Humility were no longer impressed upon the Youth.

Children just didn't care for others or themselves anymore.

They also thought that No One had the balls to put them in their place either.

But, Father showed them different.

He Actually Followed Through with the Threat every parent has said, "At Least Once," to Their Disrespectful Brats.

I Brought You Into This World And I Can Take You Out!

And so he did.

PRAISE BE TO FATHER.

Once a young adult turned sixteen; they, "except for the girls," had two choices to make.

The boys could join Father's Priesthood, or they could go into environmental management and servitude to the public like everyone else.

Every Citizen in Heaven was required to either serve the Machine or they were ordered to help maintain the parks, harvest the communal gardens fruit and vegetables and see to those in need.

If you were not able to do those things; then the Machine required a resident to stay busy helping the public past the time by visiting the elderly or taking the earths bounty to those who preferred real food instead of Father's 3D printed version.

Father even had a job for the severely disabled.

He used them for Demon practice.

Corbin had gone into the Priesthood himself.

That's why he is now here in Father's crystal caves.

He was doing his job.

The upside-down crystals growing over his head looked to be made out of Pure Diamond. Its center tip protruded all the way down to where it was actually touching the floor.

That's were his mother was leading him.

To that singular point of contact.

"From the look of things," it seemed as if his presence was causing quite a stir, because all the people in the room had stopped working and were given him their full attention. That's when Corbin took notice that he has seen some of these individuals on more than one occasion.

"As he was focusing on those whom he remembered," Mr. Bennett also observed that a few of them have been down here way too long. They were almost a pale white and stood out amongst the other pink skinned Servants.

But, he really didn't have time to dwell on that because Father just called his name.

Corbin.

Corbin Bennett.

Come to Your Father.

"Oddly," it sounded more like it was in his head than spoken out loud as before.

Coming out of the memory daze that was clouding his thoughts; Corbin found his mother Iris standing next to the Diamond's center stalactite that was touching the floor.

She was beckoning him forward with the largest smile he has ever seen.

Well, Almost.

Iris's Graduation Smile had caused her cheeks to hurt until that next day.

Right up to the point of her death.

FUCK YOU URIEN!

As Corbin reached her spot, his mother told him to place his hand on the crystal just like he has always done in Father's Chamber above. Following her instructions; Corbin placed the flat palm of his hand against the diamond and spoke the words All Priest Must Say before uploading their Harvest.

Father May I.

"Corbin was just about to close his eyes," when Father gave a Most Unusual Answer.

Instead of his usual proclamation, "Yes You May," Father's new response was Yes I May.

This differentiation in protocol Instantly caused Father's Right Hand to open his eyes.

Iris's reflection, "and those behind him," had begun to change.

They All seemed to be morphing into an Entirely Different Being.

Everyone, "Including Iris," began to transform.

Their hair was now like strands of fiber optic.

JUST LIKE HIS!

Their facial features seemed to Elongate, "About Four Inches," while Their Skulls become At Least a Quarter Larger and more Bulbous.

JUST LIKE HIS!

Everyone's skin appeared to take on a bluish chrome like tan.

JUST LIKE HIS!

And Their Eyes took on a more Owl-Like appearance.

JUST LIKE HIS!

They Were Even Pink.

JUST LIKE HIS!

What happened next would be the Mr. Bennett's last memory as a Full-Blooded Human.

Corbin looked at his hands and watched the few remaining vestiges of his humanity being Consumed by Father's Organic Nanos.

The Caretakers now had a Priest of their own to Watch Over and Protect Them.

Father's Family was now home and almost whole.

He just needed a Physical Body of His Own.

Once He has enough souls, "which the Freelander's will Soon Provide," Humanity's first Quantum Machine will finally be able to walk in the flesh, "with His Own Two Feet," amongst His Family and His Children.

He is so looking forward to also holding Iris and Corbin's hand, "with His Own Two Hands," and watching the sun rise with His Own Two eyes.

Oh, what Joy that will bring to His Own Spirit once he creates one.

So, let's begin the Harvest.

Corbin, Your Father Needs Souls.

It's Time for Them to Repent.

It's Time for Them to Convert.

And, It's Time for Them to Die!

PRAISE BE TO FATHER.

Printed in the USA
CPSIA information can be obtained
at www.ICGtesting.com
CBHW071223180724
11781CB00009B/324